PRAISE FOR *DON'T MAKE A SOUND*

"Those who like to see evil men get their just desserts will look forward to Sawyer's further exploits."

—*Publishers Weekly*

"Overall, a great crime read."

—*Manhattan Book Review*

"[A] dizzying flurry of twists and turns in a plot as intricate as a Swiss watch . . . Ragan's warrior women are on fire, fueled by howling levels of personal pain."

—*Sactown Magazine*

"A heart-stopping read. Ragan's compelling blend of strained family ties and small-town secrets will keep you racing to the end!"

—Lisa Gardner, *New York Times* bestselling author of *When You See Me*

"An exciting start to a new series with a feisty and unforgettable heroine in Sawyer Brooks. Just when you think you've figured out the dark secrets of River Rock, T.R. Ragan hits you with another sucker punch."

—Lisa Gray, bestselling author of *Thin Air*

"Fans of Lizzy Gardner, Faith McMann, and Jessie Cole are in for a real treat with T.R. Ragan's *Don't Make a Sound*, the start of a brand-new series that features tenacious crime reporter Sawyer Brooks, whose own past could be her biggest story yet. Ragan once more delivers on her trademark action, pacing, and twists."

—Loreth Anne White, bestselling author of *In the Dark*

"T.R. Ragan takes the revenge thriller to the next level in the gritty and chillingly realistic *Don't Make a Sound.* Ragan masterfully crafts one unexpected twist after another until the shocking finale."

—Steven Konkoly, bestselling author of *The Rescue*

"T.R. Ragan delivers in her new thrilling series. *Don't Make a Sound* introduces crime reporter Sawyer Brooks, a complex and compelling heroine determined to stop a killer as murders in her past and present collide."

—Melinda Leigh, #1 *Wall Street Journal* bestselling author

NO GOING BACK

Other Titles by T.R. Ragan

Sawyer Brooks Series

Don't Make a Sound

Out of Her Mind

Jessie Cole Series

Her Last Day

Deadly Recall

Deranged

Buried Deep

Faith McMann Trilogy

Furious

Outrage

Wrath

Lizzy Gardner Series

Abducted

Dead Weight

A Dark Mind

Obsessed

Almost Dead

Evil Never Dies

Writing as Theresa Ragan

Return of the Rose

A Knight in Central Park

Taming Mad Max

Finding Kate Huntley

Having My Baby
An Offer He Can't Refuse
Here Comes the Bride
I Will Wait for You: A Novella
Dead Man Running

NO GOING BACK

A
SAWYER BROOKS
THRILLER

T.R. RAGAN

THOMAS & MERCER

This is a work of fiction. Names, characters, organizations, places, events, and incidents are either products of the author's imagination or are used fictitiously. Any resemblance to actual persons, living or dead, or actual events is purely coincidental.

Published by Thomas & Mercer, Seattle

www.apub.com

ISBN-13: 9781542093927
ISBN-10: 1542093929

Cover design by Damon Freeman

Printed in the United States of America

Jesse, Joey, Morgan, and Brittany
Thanks for bringing so much joy to my life!

Chapter One

The first thing Nick Calderon noticed as he walked up the stone path leading to the front door of his house was that the entry light wasn't on. He glanced at his watch: 7:10 p.m. The light should have automatically gone on an hour before he arrived home. He slipped his key into the lock, opened the door, and stepped inside.

The air-conditioning was on full blast, and his dog was nowhere to be seen. "Rocky! Come here, boy!"

Feeling uptight after another shitty day at work, Nick headed for the kitchen, dropping his coat and briefcase on one of the dining room chairs along the way. That's when it dawned on him that something was very wrong. It was too quiet. Where was the dog?

"Linda? Are you here?"

Linda was his ex-wife. He had a restraining order against her. Obviously that hadn't stopped her from sneaking into his house uninvited. He'd filed for divorce three years ago. She'd fought him tooth and nail for everything they'd owned. In the end, even though he'd moved out, he'd been court-ordered to continue paying the mortgage and utilities on the house where they had lived together for ten years. His ex-wife would leave all the lights on and crank up the air-conditioning with the windows open so that the utility bills would skyrocket. Three months ago, Linda had finally met someone else and sold the house.

He'd thought the whole dirty mess was behind him, but apparently he'd been wrong.

He heard a dog whimper. "Rocky?"

A thought struck him. What if it wasn't Linda? His gun was upstairs, locked away in a safe in his closet.

A lot of good that did him.

He figured he had two options: sneak upstairs and get his gun, or head back the way he came and let the police handle whoever might be hiding inside. Opting for the latter, he took slow, careful steps back toward the front door.

"Leaving already? Aren't you worried about Rocky?"

At the sound of an unfamiliar voice, he whipped around. Someone was standing in the shadows near the pantry. Too tall to be his ex-wife. "Who are you?" he asked, not liking the squeaky sound of fear clogging his throat. "What are you doing in my home?"

"Don't worry. I'll be leaving soon. I just want to ask you a few questions."

The voice was muffled. The black, shoulder-length hair told him it was a woman. She was slender. Nick hadn't worked out in a while, but he had at least fifty pounds on her. He figured he could overtake her if it came to that.

Her arms hung loose at her sides, her hands visible. She didn't appear to have a weapon. That gave Nick a boost of confidence. If she came closer, he could take her down. "How did you get inside?" Nick asked.

"I'm the one who's going to be asking the questions, so why don't you take a seat."

She gestured to the chair where Nick had left his coat and briefcase.

Nick thought about making a move, lunging for her and taking her to the ground, but decided against it. She was too far away. He needed her to move toward him before he made any rash decisions. He took a seat. "Okay. So what do you want to know?"

"I have a couple of questions, but there are rules."

This was ridiculous. Nick didn't need this shit. He had problems of his own. "I've had a really bad day, and—"

"Shut up!"

Nick's eyes narrowed. "Did my wife send you?"

The intruder folded her arms across her chest. "I didn't realize you were married. Where is she?"

"At work. She should be home any minute now."

"Liar."

In three long strides she was next to him. Hand in her pocket.

Before Nick had time to blink, she pulled out what looked like a gun. Without much time to react, Nick raised an arm in a defensive move to stop her, but it was too late. He felt a sting as an electric current whizzed through his chest. His muscles contracted. Gritting his teeth, he fell sideways from the chair to the floor. She had zapped him with one of those high-tech Tasers used by law enforcement.

The lights came on then, bright and blinding, right before a heavy foot landed on his chest, pressing down. "No lying. And no talking unless you're answering my questions."

Unable to think clearly, Nick concentrated on breathing. His vision blurred. His arms and legs were stiff. He couldn't move.

The intruder's movements were jerky. She worked fast, removing one of his shoes and his sock, tossing them aside. He tried to pull his foot away, but his leg wouldn't budge.

Nick had read about people who'd been tased. If he recalled correctly, the effects didn't last long. He needed to wait this thing out. As soon as he regained his strength, he would get control of the situation. The bitch wouldn't stand a chance.

She held up a syringe.

Something wet dripped down Nick's thigh. He'd peed himself. "What are you doing?" His question came out sounding like one long squeal as the needle was inserted into his big toe. A burning sensation swept through his body.

He'd been injected.

With what?

His limbs tingled as the effects of the Taser began to wear off. He waited, glad she turned and walked off. When she returned, he had regained enough strength to lift both legs and slam his feet into her knees.

She stumbled backward, overturning a chair and crashing into the nearest wall.

Nick struggled to get to his feet. His adrenaline was off the charts as he lunged for her and took her to the ground. They rolled across the floor. His head hit the wall. Another chair toppled over. He reached blindly for the woman, grabbing a fistful of her hair and pulling hard, surprised when the silky locks slid off her head.

Beneath the wig, she wore a skintight cap.

She pushed him away, jumped to her feet, and reached for the Taser lying on the table.

Nick's heart pounded against his ribs as he staggered to his feet. He needed to get outside and shout for help. He felt dizzy and nauseous.

What is happening?

He reached out for something to grab hold of, but it was no use. He toppled over like a newly felled tree. His head crashed into the floor. He was on his back, once again unable to move. Whatever had been injected into his system was taking effect. "What do you want?"

She hovered over him, her face inches from his. Her wig was crooked now, her red lipstick smeared and looking like blood. "I want to know if you ever once regretted what you did to me when you were sixteen and I was only ten."

Sixteen? Twenty years ago? Do I know this person? His erratic breathing slowed until he found himself gasping for breath. His chest drenched in sweat, his throat constricted.

"You and your friends treated me as if I were inhuman," the intruder said. "You threw bottles and trash at me and kicked me every chance you got. You called me Cockroach. I begged you to leave me alone. Your friends laughed when you tied me to a tree and raped me. And now you're being punished."

Nick struggled to breathe. He needed air. His mouth was dry. What had she given him? "Thirsty" was the only word he managed to push out of his mouth.

"Yes," she said. "You must be thirsty. That's one of the side effects." She squinted at him as she leaned closer. "Your pupils look like tiny pinpoints."

Nick's hand came to his throat. He tried to beg for help but choked instead.

"There it is," she said. "That gurgling noise is what they call the death rattle. Your lips are turning blue, just as I read about."

"What—you—give me?"

"Karma. I gave you karma. Oftentimes karma simply happens, but in your case I decided to give it a nudge." Her brow furrowed. "You ruined my life. I did all I could to 'let it go,' but every single day, I think about what you and your friends did to me. I can't let you get away with it. You must be held accountable for your actions."

Nick's mind was muddled. All energy had drained from his body.

He was dying.

As he struggled for each breath, he heard her walk away. There was no mistaking the sound of a bedroom door being opened, followed by the pitter-patter of dog feet against the tile floor.

Maybe Rocky would save him—alert the neighbors or bite the intruder.

The refrigerator door came open. The woman was in the kitchen. "What's this, Rocky? Looks like leftover steak from last night's dinner."

Rocky barked with excitement.

"Let's cut this up for you. And how about some nice fresh water? I bet you're thirsty."

Rocky whined.

"Such a good dog. Maybe I'll bring you home with me. Would you like that?"

Nick's mind traveled back in time to when he was sixteen. He'd done a lot of bad things during his teen years. Too many bad things to count. He'd taken a bat to hundreds of mailboxes. He'd stolen cars, taken whiskey from a bum and money from an old lady.

The sounds of slurping and chewing, and of Rocky's tail thumping happily against a lower cupboard as he ate, drew Nick back to the present. "Rocky," he tried to say, hoping the dog would come to him. Man's best friend. Rocky was all he had. He wanted to feel the dog's wet tongue on his face. He attempted to tap his hand against the floor to get Rocky to come, but his finger merely twitched.

It didn't matter. Rocky would never help him.

Nick had kicked the dog in the ribs, whipped him with a belt, and left him out in the cold too many times.

Nobody would come to his aid. His mother had made sure of that the day she'd given birth to him and then tossed him into a public trash bin. No basket or warm blanket. Just tossed away like garbage.

The anger he'd felt growing up had consumed him. Nick couldn't remember a time when he wasn't causing others pain. He'd always been a bully. Which was why the intruder could be anyone. *Tied to a tree? Why can't I remember?*

Nick's eyelids grew heavy. He could no longer keep them open.

I was sixteen and she was ten.

Nick gasped for air as a crystal-clear image of the ten-year-old kid popped into his mind.

Did she say he'd called her Cockroach? It couldn't be.

He remembered it all—every horrifying second.

As he struggled to fill his lungs with air, a tear slid down the side of his face.

Chapter Two

Investigative journalist Sawyer Brooks pulled up behind a police cruiser and parked. She then shut off her engine and climbed out of the car. The time was 9:43 a.m. It had taken her about twenty minutes to get to Elk Grove, a city just south of the state capital of Sacramento. Although she didn't own a police scanner, she had the next best thing—Geezer, the crime scene photographer for the *Sacramento Independent*. Minutes after he texted her about a homicide that was being linked to the Black Wigs, a group of female vigilantes getting revenge on the men who brutalized them, Sawyer had rushed out of her cubicle at work and made her way to Elk Grove in record time.

Farther up the block, she saw Geezer talking to an officer outside a pale-yellow, well-landscaped house with brick accents. The warmth from the morning sun felt good on her back as she headed their way. By the time she reached Geezer's side, the uniformed officer had walked away.

"Thanks for the heads-up," she said to Geezer.

He looked surprised to see her. "That was quick."

"Not much traffic. So what's the deal?"

"Dead guy's name is Nick Calderon. You'll have to wait for the police report for all the details, but apparently the neighbor's security camera caught a slender person of about five foot nine walking toward the house around two p.m. yesterday. Six hours later, about an hour after Nick Calderon returned home, the same person was seen leaving through the front entrance followed by a dog."

Sawyer took notes on her cell. "Was the dog on a leash?"

"Not that I know of." He lifted the camera hanging around his neck and began adjusting the lens. "A bystander, Tim Moore, he lives over there"—Geezer pointed to a blue house on the corner—"told me that the dead guy had a dog named Rocky."

Sawyer made note of the dog's name, then waited for Geezer to finish fiddling with his camera before she asked, "I wonder if the killer took the dog?"

Geezer shrugged. "My guess is the dog followed the intruder right out the door and then ran off."

"Anything else?" Sawyer asked.

"The intruder appeared to be wearing a black wig that fell to their shoulders and dark lipstick."

"How could you tell it was a wig?"

"It didn't sit right—it looked as if it had been put on haphazardly."

"You got a peek inside, didn't you?" She knew how Geezer worked. His scanner usually garnered him early access. He kept disposable gloves and shoe covers in his car just in case.

"I might have."

"Come on," she said. "Tell me. What did you see?"

"The usual—toppled furniture, a jacket tossed over a chair, and a dead guy."

Sawyer nodded.

"Not so usual," Geezer added, "I didn't see any blood, and the dead guy was wearing one shoe."

"Weird."

"Yeah. The shoe and sock had been tossed beneath the dining room table."

"Was there blood on his foot?"

"None that I could see. I was ushered out of there pretty quickly." He scratched his neck. "They won't let me inside, so I'm going to take a few more shots and head off."

"Thanks for the call. I appreciate your help."

"You're going to need it," Geezer said. "The newspaper business is a dog-eat-dog world, and without Sean Palmer there to watch over you, you're going to need eyes in the back of your head."

Sean Palmer was her boss and mentor who was on sick leave, recovering at home after a recent injury. "A little dramatic, don't you think?"

"Let's hope so for your sake."

Sawyer wasn't worried about Geezer's comment. She already knew that she had to work longer and harder than most if she wanted to get anywhere at the newspaper. After Geezer walked away, she headed up the stone path leading to the porch and leaned into the yellow crime scene tape.

There was an officer standing guard. He looked bored. She flashed him her badge. "Any chance I can take a peek inside?"

Arms crossed over his chest, he shook his head. "You need to move back to the street."

She did as he said. Standing beneath the shade of a giant red maple tree, she used her phone to do a quick search on Nick Calderon.

"Oh, my God, it's true."

The high-pitched voice came from behind Sawyer, prompting her to spin around. The woman looked harried, as if she'd jumped straight out of bed before coming. She wore denim jeans. Her cotton shirt was wrinkled and had a stain on the collar. Her face was pale, and sweat glistened across her forehead.

"Was Nick really murdered?" the woman asked. "I mean, is he really dead?"

Sawyer nodded. "I was told it happened last night." Before Sawyer could say more, two attendants rolled a body bag atop a gurney out of the house. The officer standing guard lifted the tape so they could get through. After they passed by, Sawyer looked at the woman and offered a hand. "I'm Sawyer Brooks, crime reporter with the *Sacramento Independent*."

They shook hands.

"Linda," she said. "Nick Calderon's ex-wife." She shook her head and said, "Nick could be an ass, but I never wished him dead."

"Are you okay?" Sawyer asked.

"Surprised . . . shocked," she said. "But I'll be fine." The woman looked closely at Sawyer. "Are you doing a story about Nick?"

"Sort of," Sawyer said. "Do you have time to talk?"

"There's a coffee shop not too far from here." Linda gestured at a black Toyota Camry parked down the road. "If you want to follow me there, I'll let you buy me an iced latte and ask all the questions you want."

Caught off guard by her ready agreement, Sawyer said, "Maybe you should talk to the investigator first."

"To hell with them. After hearing from a friend that something happened to Nick, I made half a dozen calls. They wouldn't tell me anything. Every one of them took my name and number, but nobody bothered to call me back. They know where to find me. Let's go."

Ten minutes later, they were sitting at a square, wobbly table on the sidewalk outside the coffee shop. Linda dropped at least ten cubes of sugar into her latte and stirred while Sawyer took a sip of her iced mocha. It hit the spot.

"So tell me what you know," Linda said.

Sawyer related what she'd heard about the person seen coming and going.

Linda's eyes grew round. "A wig? Really?"

"Have you read about the Black Wigs?"

Linda sucked her latte through a straw, then said, "Is that the same group of women who cut off that guy's one-eyed rattlesnake?"

Sawyer nodded as she struggled not to laugh at the woman's phrasing.

Linda smiled. "Yes. I've heard of them. You think they went after Nick?"

"I don't know enough yet to come to any conclusions, but it might be helpful if you could tell me a little bit about him."

"Like his childhood and stuff?"

"Yes," Sawyer said. "That would be a great place to start."

"Well, jeez. It's a sad story, and it all began when a newborn baby was found in a dumpster."

Sawyer's chest tightened. Every state had a safe haven law, which meant any person could safely relinquish their baby without risk of prosecution.

"Nick only talked about his past when he was drunk, which was often enough, I guess. I always got the feeling that he regretted being a bully. He said it was the only way he knew how to survive. I didn't really understand why he felt such anger until later when I caught him having an affair."

"Is that why you divorced?"

"That's part of it," Linda said. "I never should have married him. He beat me, gave me so many black eyes it's a miracle I can still see."

"That's horrible."

"I always thought his anger was due to his traumatic upbringing, being abandoned and all that, but that wasn't the whole story."

Sawyer waited.

"Our marriage ended after I returned home early from work and found two naked, sweaty bodies in my bed! That's when everything started to make sense. My husband, a proud and outspoken homophobe, was gay. The hypocrisy." She shook her head. "If only he had told me. Maybe I could have helped him."

"You had no idea?"

"No."

"How do you think you could have helped him?" Sawyer asked.

"I think his anger stemmed from his own inner conflict with same-sex attraction. Nick and I hadn't been intimate in years. If he'd tried to talk to me, maybe I could have helped him see that the world was changing and that it wasn't too late for him to live his best life by being who he wanted to be."

"Any ideas on who might have wanted your ex-husband dead?"

Linda appeared to ponder the question before shaking her head. "Sorry. No."

"What about family and friends?" Sawyer asked.

"No family, of course." Linda sighed. "No friends either. I never even learned the name of the man I found in my bed."

"Where did your ex-husband grow up?"

"In Sacramento. At a home for troubled children. He despised almost everyone—the other kids, the staff—and yet . . ." Her eyes widened, and she wagged a finger at Sawyer. "He did stay in contact with a couple of the boys from the home."

"Do you remember their names?"

"No," she said with a shake of her head. "I've never been good with names."

"You said Nick was a bully. Any idea who he might have bullied?"

"Sorry. No idea. I'm not any help at all." She glanced at her watch. "I should go."

They exchanged phone numbers in case Sawyer had more questions or Linda thought of anything else she might have forgotten.

As Sawyer watched Linda Calderon walk off, her intuition sounded an alarm, telling her that the Black Wigs had nothing to do with his death.

Chapter Three

Sixteen-year-old Tara Alcozar and three of her closest friends—Rachel, Laura, and Mandy—sat cross-legged on the white shag rug in her bedroom. In the center of their human circle was a plastic bin filled with black wigs and eye masks.

"I don't know if I can do this," Rachel said.

Laura rolled her eyes. "Don't be a weasel. We're not going to hurt him. We're just going to scare him, show him what it feels like to be powerless."

Tara nodded. "He deserves it after what he did to Pamela."

"Pamela has had a crush on Kyle since the beginning of time," Rachel said. "I saw her coming on to him at the party. She wanted him as much as he wanted her."

The party had taken place two months ago at Trey Matthews's house, the most popular guy at Rocklin High School. All five of them had told their parents they were sleeping at Pamela's house. Since she was their designated driver, Mandy had stayed away from the spiked punch while Tara, Rachel, Pamela, and Laura had gotten wasted and spent most of the night dancing and flirting with the upperclassmen.

"Pamela just wanted to make out with Kyle, not screw him," Tara explained to Rachel. "But he took her upstairs into an empty room and locked the door. They kissed. When he slipped his hand under her shirt, she told him to stop. But that only made him more aggressive, and he wouldn't let her go. He held her down while he pulled up her skirt. She said she became numb and it was horrible, and that when he was finished, he zipped up his pants and walked away."

Everyone was quiet while they finished putting on their wigs and masks. When they were done, Tara made a few adjustments. She tucked in loose strands of hair peeking out of Rachel's wig, then handed the red lipstick to Mandy and told her to put some on.

Although Tara was nervous about tonight, she was glad Kyle was going to be taught a lesson. The moment Pamela said she wanted to make Kyle pay for what he did to her, Tara had gotten an idea. They'd started brainstorming and come up with a plan. Tara's parents would be staying overnight in San Francisco. When the time came, Pamela would tell Kyle that she'd decided to forgive him and even had a surprise for him. If everything went well, they would be arriving here at Tara's house in the next ten minutes.

Tara pushed herself to her feet and went to the computer sitting on her built-in desk. She clicked on the tab and opened the YouTube video she'd saved that showed a group of girls, mostly in their twenties, who called themselves The Slayers. They mimicked the Black Wigs by getting revenge against college men accused of date rape. Every few weeks The Slayers uploaded a new video. The room they used looked like a dark cave with a bed in it. Once their target was tied to the wooden slatted headboard, they would make a show of sharpening their knives while explaining to their viewers what was going to happen. The guy would either beg to be let go, curse them out, or scream until his voice gave out. The Slayers never hurt anyone physically. All their targets were released, but not one guy had come forward.

Tara readied the camera on the tripod and then looked through the lens. She could see her full-size white canopy bed with its fluffy pink duvet and matching shams perfectly. "Where are the zip ties?" she asked.

"Right here." Mandy held up a fistful of plastic ties that Tara had found in the garage.

Tara checked the battery in the camera. It was full. The bin had one more mask and wig for Pamela, but for now the bin would have to go into the walk-in closet, way in the back, so they would have room to hide.

"Here they come," Laura said from the window. "Everybody grab a zip tie and hide!"

Tara had left the main door to the house unlocked. Pamela would ring the bell and then make her way inside. Once Pamela brought Kyle upstairs to the bedroom, she would tell him that they had the house to themselves.

When the doorbell rang, they all giggled like ten-year-olds at a pajama party and ran into the closet. Tara quietly shut the door. Her heart was racing. It wasn't long before they heard the front door open and close and then the sound of Pamela's and Kyle's voices as they walked up the stairs.

This was really happening.

"Where's Tara?" Kyle asked when they entered the bedroom.

"Tomorrow is a Staff Development Day. No school. She's spending the night at Laura's."

"What about her parents?"

"Gone for the night."

"So it's just me and you?"

"Surprised?"

"Yeah, I am. I thought you were mad at me after what happened between us."

"I was, but I've had a change of heart. I thought maybe we could start over."

"Seriously?"

"Yes," she said. "But this time I want to be in charge. Take your shirt off and lie on the bed."

"Whoa. What's the hurry?"

"What do you mean?" Pamela asked. "I thought you liked it fast and furious."

"Yeah, sure, I guess. But hold on. What's the camera for?"

"Tara makes videos to post on social media. You've seen her videos."

"I saw one. It was stupid."

"Well, if you're not going to do what I ask, then you might as well take me home."

"Okay. Okay."

Tara could hear him climbing onto the bed.

"Now what?" he asked.

"Now I get to tie your hands to the bedposts."

"Getting kinky, huh?"

"You could say that again," Pamela almost purred.

Silence, and then Pamela said, "Okay, girls. You can come out now."

All four of them poured out of the closet. Tara and Laura rushed to fasten his ankles to the bedposts. They were so quick, he didn't have time to fight them off.

"What are you doing?" Kyle asked.

His face and neck are as red as the roses growing in my backyard, Tara thought.

"Let me go!" Kyle said. "This isn't funny."

Tara ran into the closet to get Pamela a mask and a wig.

She tucked her blonde hair into the wig first, then stretched the elastic band over her head.

Kyle struggled to get free. "I want out of here. Now!"

Rachel turned as white as the shag carpet and ran from the room.

Laura ripped off a piece of duct tape and covered his mouth. It took another two pieces of tape to shut him up.

Tara hurried over to the camera and hit record. She then retrieved two pairs of scissors from her desk drawer and handed a pair to Pamela. They both worked on cutting his jeans from his body. Tara looked at Kyle with narrowed eyes. "You never should have raped my friend," she growled. "We're going to make sure you never do it again."

Kyle squirmed, pulling on his restraints, trying to get free.

Mandy ran out the door. A few seconds later, she ushered Rachel back into the room just as Pamela cut off Kyle's underwear.

For a moment, they all stared at his junk.

Rachel looked disgusted.

"Haven't you ever seen a penis before?" Laura asked her.

Rachel shook her head. "It's ugly."

They all burst out laughing.

Tara had almost forgotten the curling iron! She ran to the bathroom, then brought it to the bedside table and plugged it in. Holding it up in view of the camera, she opened and closed the clamp for fun. Just the idea of using a hot curling iron on Kyle's most vulnerable parts would make for good tension on YouTube.

When Tara noticed Rachel still staring at Kyle's dick, she found a pen and then leaned over the side of the bed and used the pen to lift up his penis. "See that! Those are his ball sacks."

Laura laughed. "Also known as testicles."

Pamela reached into the desk drawer and pulled out a carving knife and a honing steel. As practiced, she made a big show in front of the camera of scraping the knife against steel, sharpening the blade.

"It's time to make Kyle squeal," Pamela said in a matter-of-fact tone that caused chills to crawl up Tara's spine.

That line hadn't been part of their plan, but Tara liked the effect, since she knew they weren't going to harm him.

Kyle's eyes widened. Snot dripped from his nostrils. His words were muffled beneath the tape, making it impossible to understand what he was saying.

Pamela set the sharpener down before climbing on top of the bed. Positioning herself at Kyle's side, she made sure she wasn't blocking the camera's view before she picked up the knife.

Kyle struggled to get loose until Pamela slid the long, sharp blade of the carver's knife beneath the stem of his penis. Then he froze.

The angry, determined look on Pamela's face worried Tara.

"Are you sorry for what you did to me?" Pamela asked Kyle.

His head bobbed up and down like one of those bobblehead dolls, while his body remained stiff; he was most likely afraid of making any sudden moves.

"When I told you to stop, you shoved your tongue down my throat," Pamela told him. "I could hardly breathe. I was suffocating, but you didn't care. You were determined to do whatever you wanted to. I begged you to stop. When I reached for my phone, you grabbed it from me and tossed it aside. Your slobbering tongue and your hands were all over me. I kicked my legs, but every time I tried to scream, you covered my mouth with yours. I almost got away." She exhaled. "But you caught up to me, didn't you? You threw me to the floor, ripped off my shirt, pushed up my skirt, and climbed on top of me."

Pamela's head fell forward, her chin nearly resting on her chest as she sobbed.

Tara wanted to go to her, but she could tell by the way her friend was trying hard to collect herself that Pamela had more to say, so she stayed where she was and remained silent.

Pamela lifted her head and said through her tears, "I've hardly slept since that night. I keep my bedroom door locked at all times, and I jump at every little sound. Night after night, I relive what you did to me." She used her left forearm to wipe at the tears. "I tried to forget what happened, but I can't. You had no right to do what you did." She swallowed. "I brought you here because I wanted you to know what it feels like to be completely powerless to stop someone from hurting you. Do you like feeling powerless, Kyle?"

He shook his head, his bloodshot eyes rapidly blinking.

"You'll be glad to know I was too scared to go to the police or the hospital, and I was too ashamed to tell my parents."

Tears rolled down both sides of her face and onto the pink duvet, leaving a trail of wet spots. Her hands began to tremble. "I've never hated anyone like I hate you."

Laura came up behind Tara and whispered into her ear, "She doesn't look right. Stop her before she does something we might all regret."

Tara didn't know what to do. Once Pamela finished her speech, she would give her friend the sign that it was over and then shut off the camera.

"After you got off me," Pamela told Kyle, "you looked at me as if I were a piece of trash. That's when I knew you had done this before. I also came to realize it would be up to me to make sure you never raped anyone else."

Pamela grabbed hold of his penis with her left hand and brought the sharp blade of the knife snug against the base.

Kyle's eyes bulged, and sweat dripped down the sides of his face.

Laura shouted for Pamela to stop as she lunged for the bed.

Tara couldn't tell if Pamela had purposely cut Kyle or if the movement caused by Laura pouncing on the mattress had made things spiral out of control. But either way, she knew they were in trouble when she saw blood spurting everywhere.

Rachel screamed, then collapsed to the floor like a rag doll.

Mandy shouted Rachel's name and ran to her side.

Tara couldn't wrap her mind around what she'd just witnessed. This couldn't be happening. Her ears were buzzing. She felt faint. "No," she said. "Stop!" But it was much too late for that.

Blood pooled between Kyle's legs.

Pamela climbed off the bed. She looked like a zombie.

Laura plucked the knife from Pamela and took it to the bathroom, where Tara heard it clang against the sink. And then Tara saw two beams of light from the street below shoot through the window and sweep across the room.

Tara ran to the window and looked out.

Her parents had come home early.

Chapter Four

At work in her cubicle the next day, Sawyer read through news headlines, dismayed to see just last night a group of teenaged girls in the nearby town of Rocklin had decided to teach a boy a lesson. The scene was described as bloody and frightening, but the wound had turned out to be a nick that would heal quickly.

Thank goodness.

What was the world coming to?

First, the Black Wigs, then The Slayers, and now young girls taking matters into their own hands right inside the comfort of their home.

The Black Wigs, purposely or not, had created a monster. Revenge was not the answer.

Sawyer moved on, sorting through notes and articles she had previously saved and written about the Black Wigs. Inside an eight-by-ten envelope was a copy of the flash drive Sean Palmer had given her with instructions to have the homemade video lightened since it had been taken at night and was grainy and pixelated. Palmer's source was unknown, but he'd said the video had been taken in West Sacramento on the same night Otto Radley had been released from prison.

Otto Radley had abducted a twenty-one-year-old woman named Christina Farro and held her captive for three years. Pulled over for a traffic violation, he was arrested when the police found evidence inside his car that led them to Christina Farro. Twenty years later, Otto Radley was released and hadn't been seen since. Poof! Gone in the blink of an eye.

The answer to what happened to Otto Radley could be on the tiny flash drive sitting right in front of her. Although the video was dark and blurry, Otto Radley was a giant of a man. Just like the shadowed figure seen on the video. If she squinted her eyes and focused really hard, she could see the figure approach a woman sitting on a bench, a woman with short dark hair. A moment later, another figure with the same short dark hair appears from behind a tree.

Before Sawyer had a chance to do anything with the video, Palmer had been attacked and was still recuperating. She had, however, upon her return to work, copied the video and then taken the original flash drive to Detective Perez, leaving it with the person at the front desk since the detective had been too busy to see her.

Sawyer spent the next thirty minutes watching how to enhance videos on YouTube. She finally gave up and did a search for video-enhancement companies in the area. She called the one with the best reviews: Purple House Digital in Midtown.

Minutes later, her problem was solved. The owner said he would be happy to take a look at the video and see what he could do.

Sawyer played with a rubber band, rolling it around her index finger while she stared at her notes. As far as investigators could tell, Brad Vicente had been the Black Wigs' first target. That was three months ago. According to reports, five women wearing black wigs and masks had kept Vicente trapped in his own home while subjecting him to torture. But when an anonymous call led the police to a bound and bloodied Brad Vicente, they also found a collection of rape videos Vicente had made for his own private viewing. Although the police were actively searching for the female vigilantes, Brad Vicente was found guilty of being a serial rapist, and he was locked up.

The Black Wigs' second target could be Otto Radley. If Otto Radley did turn out to be the man on the video, then where was he? Were the

Black Wigs holding him captive somewhere? Was he dead? Or had the big man simply run off?

Victim number three was Myles Davenport, a man taken from the parking lot outside the high school where his ten-year reunion had taken place. Security cameras had caught members of the Black Wigs at work. Myles Davenport was found in the woods surrounding Placerville. Autopsy reports revealed that he'd died of a heart attack.

What tied these men together was that at some point in their lives, Brad Vicente, Otto Radley, and Myles Davenport had all been accused of rape.

Sawyer tapped the tip of her pen on Nick Calderon's name. A quick search revealed no record of any sort. No one had ever accused the man of rape. Geezer had told Sawyer that one slender person of average height was seen on the neighbor's home security camera.

One person.

If the Black Wigs were responsible for the death of Nick Calderon, then why would only one of them be seen coming and going?

Geezer had also mentioned that the person appeared to have been wearing lipstick. Nobody would have made note of that unless it stood out. He also told her that the black wig fell to the intruder's shoulders.

Sawyer skimmed through articles about the Black Wigs written by other sources. Lipstick was never mentioned. Not once. The wigs, though, were talked about many times as being short—cut close to the ears.

There it was again. A tingle. More of a niggling. Could they be dealing with a copycat?

Anything was possible, especially considering the rippling effect the Black Wigs appeared to be having on young females around the country.

She grabbed a new manila file and wrote "Nick Calderon" on the tab. Using the notes she'd taken on her phone, she found a fresh pad of paper and wrote down the residence where Linda Calderon said her ex-husband had lived during much of his childhood: Children's Home of Sacramento.

The next few hours were spent scouring the internet.

Nick Calderon had been abandoned at a young age. A troubled child, he'd kicked and bitten his way through the foster system until he'd eventually ended up at the Children's Home of Sacramento.

An article she found on the school talked about how a professor of public policy had tried to close down residential homes in Sacramento altogether, since she and others believed strongly in the government-funded foster system in the hope that the children would eventually be reunited with their families. But the other side of the coin was that not all children had families that would take them back. And not all children were emotionally, physically, or mentally equipped to deal with a smaller family unit. That's where a government-funded residential treatment facility in Sacramento came into the picture. The children were put in an environment where they were provided family meals. Many children, boys and girls, came to consider others at the facility to be like siblings.

Next, Sawyer checked Facebook. Nick Calderon had an updated profile. From the looks of it, he'd been fairly active on social media right up to his death. He was an insurance salesman. He also liked to hunt. There was a picture of him with two other men, taken last year. They all wore what looked to Sawyer like standard camouflage duck-hunting gear.

The guy standing in the middle was the tallest and thinnest of the three. His face was half-hidden beneath the bill of his hat. The guy on the far right had a large belly and a full beard.

Sawyer moved on, scrolling through inappropriate memes and silly jokes. She kept skimming until she got to a black-and-white Polaroid picture: three boys standing side by side in front of a nondescript, two-story building that was half-brick, half-stucco. The sign next to the boys read **CHILDREN'S HOME OF SACRAMENTO**. The names Bruce, Nick, and

Felix had been scrawled across the bottom in permanent black marker with the year 1992 written beneath the names.

She looked through Nick's list of friends. No Bruce or Felix. No last names mentioned on any posts, leaving her no choice but to concentrate on learning more about the home, which also had been a school. No fewer than seven links popped up on her screen. There had been a fire at the school. The historic building had burned to the ground in less than twenty minutes. Oil, gasoline, and other supplies kept in the basement had fueled the fire. Another link to the school showed various black-and-white photos, groups of kids huddled together like they do every year at most grammar schools. There was a picture of a woman pushing a young girl on a tire swing in front of the building; another picture had been taken in the dining room, which consisted of one long table that seated twenty children at once. At the end of the table was a woman. She was standing. Hands on hips, she wore an apron and a smile.

Hoping to learn more about the kids and staff who once resided there, Sawyer called the Sacramento County Clerk's Office. After being directed to the Department of Social Services and then to Foster Care Services, and receiving little help, she skimmed through the articles again until she found a name. Nancy Lay was listed as a staff member at the children's home. Sawyer put the woman's name into a database. Bingo. Nancy Lay was eighty-nine and lived in Auburn.

She called the number listed. Nobody answered, so she left her name and number and asked Nancy Lay to please give her a call back. After she hung up, she called again and left her email, just in case. Next, she printed off the black-and-white photos for her file.

"Sawyer! There you are."

Sawyer spun her chair around, surprised to see Lexi Holmes filling the entrance to her cubicle. Sawyer had been working as a crime reporter for only a few months. Lexi had been reporting crime for nearly two decades, but you wouldn't know it since she didn't look forty-one. Lexi was small-boned and stylish, her dark hair pulled back tight into a bun at her nape. Her eyes were the color of nutmeg, and her high cheekbones looked as if they had been chiseled from marble. If Lexi ever showed up to work in jeans and a T-shirt, Sawyer wasn't sure she would recognize her.

Admittedly Sawyer hardly knew the woman, but she didn't trust her. Nor did she like her very much. At every editorial meeting, Lexi and the others made certain Sawyer was left covering stories about minor crimes—petty theft, intent to sell drugs, disturbing the peace. Sawyer knew she wasn't being fair; the truth of the matter was that sometimes there just wasn't enough real crime to go around. "What do you need, Lexi?"

"I need you to help a girl out. I'd like you to give me everything you have on the Black Wigs story."

"Um, that would be a big no."

"Excuse me?"

Sawyer smiled despite the nerves swirling around in her stomach. "You had your chance. A few weeks ago, you and David wanted nothing to do with the Black Wigs story. I said no."

"Maybe this will change your mind." Lexi stepped forward and plopped a manila file on Sawyer's desk.

Sawyer swiveled around so that she was facing her desk and opened the file. It was a copy of the police report for the Nick Calderon case. She skimmed the basics—victim's name, date and time, address, ethnicity, birth date, marital status—then quickly moved on to the narrative section. No witnesses or suspects at this time. The police had retrieved a recording from the neighbor's security camera. The dog, a male, medium size with brown fur, according to the neighbors, was missing.

Sawyer shut the file. "How could you possibly get a copy of that police report so soon?"

Lexi's eyes did a half roll. "Every decent reporter I know in this building has multiple sources at almost every government agency at their disposal. You don't?"

"Those aren't called sources. A copy of a police report from an ongoing case is considered a 'leaked document.'"

Lexi snorted. "I would consider this report to be nonattributable. As long as I don't attribute any of the information in the report to the police, no foul."

Sawyer narrowed her eyes. "I've been working with you and the others for months, and this is the first time you've said more than two words to me. What do you really want?"

"I've been watching you. If you ask me, you're an investigator, not a reporter. And I want to help you take this group down."

"Take them down?"

"Yes. I want to find them and then watch them squirm as they're escorted to jail. One after the other," she said with much relish.

"The Black Wigs could very well be victims of assault. Why else would they go after these guys?"

"Are you condoning what they've done?"

"Of course not, but I also refuse to judge the Black Wigs until I know the whole story."

"I'll tell you the whole story. The Black Wigs are creating havoc in our society. We've got young girls everywhere thinking that these women with their masks and wigs are superheroes. Secret groups are popping up all over social media. And now my sixteen-year-old niece—my beautiful, innocent niece—has been drawn into the insanity."

Sawyer frowned. "Your niece?"

"Tara Alcozar. She and her friends decided to mimic the Black Wigs and try and teach a boy a lesson. Things got out of hand, and now my sister and her husband are being sued."

"I saw it on the news. The girls never intended to hurt the boy. And it was only a nick. Even minor cuts in the genital area bleed a lot. The boy will be fine, and I'm certain the case will be dismissed."

Lexi crossed her arms. "I want this story. If you won't give it to me, I'll either jump on it and write my own story, or we can work together."

"You want to work on the Black Wigs case with me?"

"Not even a little bit. But those female vigilantes," Lexi said, uncrossing her arms and wagging a polished nail at her, "are a hot commodity right now. And I want a piece of the action."

"Action?" So it wasn't all about her niece after all, Sawyer thought.

"These lady vigilantes are a big deal right now. Everyone is talking about them. Halloween is a month away, and black wigs are flying off the shelves."

"You're kidding me."

"I don't kid about things like this. In fact, I don't kid around. Period. So what do you say? Either we collaborate or we rush competing stories into publication. What's it going to be?"

The woman was threatening her, and Sawyer didn't like it. "I need to talk to Palmer."

"I already did. He's the one who suggested I talk to you."

What the hell? Sawyer knew it wouldn't look good if she lost her temper. Instead she took a calming breath. If she didn't include Lexi on the case, things could get ugly, and difficult. She drew in a breath. "If I agree to let you join me, we do things my way."

Lexi came forward and took her file back. "Sure, sure. We do things your way. Meet me in Conference Room G on the second floor in thirty minutes."

"What for?"

"We need to share information and strategize. I want the Pulitzer Prize."

"The Pulitzer Prize? I thought you didn't kid around?"

"I don't."

Sawyer reeled in the urge to laugh. "I have a full schedule today. We'll meet tomorrow at ten a.m."

Lips pursed, Lexi gave a subtle eye roll, nodded her agreement, then walked away.

Sawyer organized the notes and files scattered about, then put it all in her desk drawer and locked it. Her phone buzzed. There was a text from Derek, her boyfriend, who also worked at the paper. His office was on the same floor, right around the corner.

The text read: What time are we supposed to be at your sister's house for dinner?

Damn. She'd forgotten all about dinner at Harper's. She looked at her calendar. Sure enough, there it was: *Dinner @ 7 pm Harper's.*

She texted him back: Can you pick me up at 6:45? ♥

Derek: Great. Excited to finally meet your sisters. See you tonight.

Sawyer: Don't get too excited! See you soon.

She had an appointment with her new therapist. She also wanted to stop by Palmer's house and have a chat, but that would have to wait since she didn't want to be late for dinner.

As she headed for the exit, her thoughts quickly ping-ponged back to Lexi. There was no way she was going to let Lexi Holmes get the best of her. She would share most of what she had . . . but not all of it. She needed to keep the last puzzle piece in her pocket . . . just in case.

CHAPTER FIVE

Sawyer took a seat on the small, comfortable sofa, placed her hands on her lap, and waited for her therapist to get things rolling. Jane Thomas was a licensed mental health counselor who worked in a private practice. Standing at full height with shoulders pushed back, Jane didn't come close to hitting the five-foot mark. Her eyes were as brown as the unused-but-well-oiled mahogany desk by the window at the far corner of the room, her shoes were always flat and sensible, and her polyester tops were always colorful and swingy.

Sawyer's favorite thing about Jane was that she didn't take notes while Sawyer talked. She simply listened.

Jane sat in her upholstered wing chair, legs crossed. "Last week we talked about your relationship with Derek. Did you have a chance to talk to him about your concerns?"

The concerns she'd spoken of had to do with intimacy. She and Derek had been dating for a few months now. He was a childless, thirty-five-year-old widower, and yet they hadn't slept together. Lately, Sawyer found herself wondering whether Derek didn't like sex. Or maybe he just wasn't interested in having sex with *her*.

"Not yet," Sawyer said. "But we're going to dinner on Friday night, so I'll let you know how that goes next week."

Jane nodded. "What about your nightmares. Any improvement?"

Every week, Sawyer found herself wondering why she was there. She was fine. She didn't have time for therapy. But before Sawyer's mind could wander too far, Jane would find a way to reel her in and make her wish their time together would continue for another hour.

At the moment, Sawyer was at the regret stage, wondering why she bothered. "No improvement," she said.

"What are the nightmares about? Any reoccurring themes?"

"Lately they have all been the same. I'm ten, maybe eleven, when I hear footsteps in the hallway. Drawing the covers over my face, I stiffen as I hear the floor creak right outside my bedroom door. But whoever is there soon moves on. I know this because I hear a door at the end of the hallway open quietly. It's the door to my older sister Harper's bedroom." Sawyer's leg began to bounce. She rolled her fingers into tight fists.

"Do these nightmares scare you?"

"No. They make me furious, so angry I wake up with a sore jaw after clenching my teeth all night. I had no idea until recently that my father was raping my sister. How many times did that man walk past my door and make his way to Harper's room?"

Sawyer took a breath, but it didn't help. She felt tense and jittery. She and her sisters had gotten the short end of the stick when it came to parents. Neglect and sexual abuse ran deep in their family, as did the scars she and her sisters still carried with them and probably always would.

"When I hear those overly cautious and disturbingly quiet footsteps," Sawyer went on, "I do everything I can to try and wake up, but I don't and I can't."

"What would you do if you woke up?" Jane asked.

"I would get out of bed and go straight to the kitchen, pull the sharpest knife from the drawer, and then make my way to Harper's room and plunge the blade into my father again and again until I was sure he was dead."

Judging by the blank expression on Jane's face, the words that poured out of Sawyer's mouth were of more surprise to Sawyer than they were to her therapist. Sawyer didn't consider herself to be an angry person. But suddenly she wasn't so sure.

"In the past," Jane said, "did you fantasize about doing the same thing to the men who hurt you?"

"No. I've never dreamed of killing anyone but my father." Sawyer rubbed her knee, pressing down to make it stop jumping. "I also have nightmares about the Black Wigs. Have you read about them?"

"The vigilantes?" Jane asked.

"Yes." After a pause, Sawyer said, "I recently dreamed about the Black Wigs. I'm not sure if I was wearing a wig, but I was definitely in the woods with a group of women who were wearing wigs and masks. There was a naked man tied to a tree. He was crying, blubbering about how sorry he was. One of the vigilantes kept waving a gun at him. Her hand was shaking. I didn't know what to do, so I simply stood there, watching. Through it all, my mind was clear. I knew that what they were doing to the man was wrong. But I also understood why the women were so damn pissed off."

"How did the nightmare end?"

"Just like that," Sawyer said. "Me standing there like a useless wooden post, not knowing whether to run for help or stay and see how it all played out. Before I could make a decision, I woke up."

"You're conflicted."

"Yes, I am. I'm investigating—I mean, I'm writing a story about the Black Wigs. I'm supposed to be unbiased, but I'm not. I hope Brad Vicente rots in jail. I hope Otto Radley is trapped without food or water in a room so small he can't stand up. And I hope beyond hope that Myles Davenport's heart attack was caused by severe trauma."

Sawyer met Jane's gaze, waited for her to say something.

Nothing.

Sawyer let out a breath so long and heavy she felt her body sink an inch lower into the couch. "If the Black Wigs had a sign-up sheet," she went on, "I guess my name would be at the top of the list. I'm weak and broken, aren't I?"

"You're neither," Jane said. "I think you're going to be all right."

Chapter Six

Harper Pohler drank a glass of water to alleviate the morning sickness, something she'd experienced when she was pregnant with Lennon and then Ella. *This too shall pass,* she thought as she glanced at the clock in the kitchen. It was just past noon. She still needed to make lasagna for dinner tonight, take a shower, and then pick up Ella at two forty-five. She also needed to clean the house. It was a mess. Before she could grab the noodles from the pantry, she received a text telling her to log on to her computer.

The phone number was unfamiliar, which meant the call was likely coming from a throwaway phone used by a member of The Crew—five female vigilantes who had found each other on the dark web and then formed their group. Early on, they had decided to use nicknames: Psycho, Cleo, Lily, and Bug. Harper was known as Malice.

Weeks ago, after The Crew helped Bug kidnap a rapist, the man had suffered a heart attack and died. Days later, Bug disappeared, leaving the rest of them to deal with the aftermath.

The Crew, referred to as the Black Wigs by the media, was now down to four.

The television remote was on the side table next to a framed picture of Harper; her husband, Nate; and their two children, Lennon and Ella. The picture had been taken on their front lawn two years ago when Lennon was thirteen and Ella was only eight. She laid the picture flat so she didn't have to look at Nate. Not because she didn't love him, but because looking at him made her feel things she didn't want to feel. Three weeks ago, he had confronted Harper about her comings and goings. When she told her husband she wasn't ready to talk to him about what she'd been doing in her free time, which would mean telling him about her involvement with The Crew, he had packed up and left to work a construction job with his father in Montana. It was a temporary move meant to give them space to think things over. She loved Nate and he loved her. When he did finally return, she would need to tell him everything. Before it was too late. If she wanted to keep her family together, she needed to help The Crew finish what they'd started and be done with it.

Harper walked to her bedroom to get her laptop. She brought it to the living room, powered it on, and then used her nickname, Malice, to log on to their private group. The other crew members had already signed on.

LILY: Did everyone see the story on the news about the insurance salesman who was killed last night in the Tahoe Park area of Sacramento? A person of interest was seen leaving the premises wearing a black wig, and the police are now linking the murder to us.

Malice and Psycho answered in the affirmative. Everyone had seen the news.

CLEO: Copycats are coming out of the woodwork. A group of young women who call themselves The Slayers are also in the news.

LILY: I saw that. They've already posted quite a few videos on YouTube.

PSYCHO: I think it's all good. Rape and assault are becoming commonplace, and we've helped shed light on something that has been going on for far too long. People in authority are using their positions to do the unspeakable, and they're getting away with it.

CLEO: I read about a bus driver who admitted to raping a fourteen-year-old, but he won't be spending time in prison.

PSYCHO: Women are tired of being the ones held accountable after they've been harassed and raped. These random players who are taking matters into their own hands—copycats, or whatever you want to call them—only help take the pressure off us. The police don't have enough resources as it is.

LILY: Good point. Cleo, are you ready to tell us who we're going after next?

In Harper's opinion, Cleo was the most damaged and fragile of the group. Her tough exterior was a shield. Cleo had been gang-raped at a fraternity house when she was seventeen. When she finally escaped her nightmare, she had done everything right. She'd gone straight to the hospital. She'd told her parents. They had taken the assholes to court. And all the boys she'd named had walked free.

CLEO: I'd like to go after every single boy who touched me. But I know you're all eager to move on now that Bug has left town and Malice is pregnant. So I've whittled my list down to three men: Eddie Carter, Don Fulton, and Felix Iverson.

Harper brushed a hand over her swollen belly, thankful for Cleo's decision to go after only those three.

LILY: One at a time?

CLEO: Yes. We'll start with Eddie Carter, a numbers guy at EFK Financial. He's married with two kids. Every day of the week, he works out at the gym close to his house.

MALICE: Is that the same Eddie Carter who started the non-profit program in California to help get families off the streets?

CLEO: I don't care if he gives scholarships to every young person in America. It's guilt that's driving him. Eddie Carter was the leader of the pack. He makes all the other guys we've gone after, with the exception of Otto Radley, look like wimps. He raped me and then held me down while others took their turns. He laughed, he jeered, and when it came time to get up on the witness stand, he told the judge and jury that he and I had had sex multiple times prior to the fraternity party. That was a lie. He and the others were let go without so much as a scolding.

LILY: Eddie Carter must be punished.

PSYCHO: I have to leave for work soon. What's the plan? When and where do we meet?

CLEO: Saturday. After he works out, I'll be inside his Ford Escape, waiting for him. With the help of my Glock, I'm going to convince him to drive to the same abandoned warehouse off Power Inn Road where we took Otto Radley. And that's where he'll stay for a night or two.

PSYCHO: How do you plan to get inside the car without a key?

CLEO: Easy. I have a mini airbag and a long reach tool. I watched a how-to video on YouTube.

PSYCHO: Nice. I'll stay close to the gym early Saturday, then follow you to the warehouse.

LILY: What happens when you arrive at the warehouse?

CLEO: My target will be blindfolded and his wrists bound when we get to where you and Malice will be waiting. Be ready to toss questions his way, one after another. We're going to cross-examine him, make him sweat, let him know he's scum. I want to scare the shit out of him, threaten to do to him what we did to Brad Vicente. When it's over, I'm going to let him know that his cushy little life is over. I'm going to video his face up close as he admits to everything he did. Then I'll send a copy of the video to his wife and the police. Once he's good and scared, we'll leave him alone for the night.

LILY: What about his car?

CLEO: I'll take care of it. Don't worry.

MALICE: That's it? Just leave him alone in the warehouse?

CLEO: That's it. See you all Saturday.

After everyone signed off, Harper did the same. She then did a quick search on Eddie Carter. He had attended UCSD and was a part of Delta Sigma Phi. A friend of his on Facebook had posted an old photo that showed well over a dozen young men standing in front of a large colonial house with a wraparound porch.

She had to dig deeper to find anything about the time Eddie and his friends spent in the courtroom. But there it was at the end of an article about fraternities in Chico. Just a small paragraph titled Frat Boys Wrongly Accused. The header said it all.

And just like that, quick as a wink, images of a shadowy figure popped into her mind: Harper lying in bed, praying he wouldn't come tonight. But that didn't stop the man from walking into her room, slipping out of his clothes, and climbing into bed with her. The smell of whiskey clung to him. He brushed his stubby fingers through her hair, pressed his nose to her neck, and inhaled. "My sweet Harper. You'll always be Daddy's little girl."

Her brain shut down. Her body stiff, she closed her eyes.

A few minutes passed in silence. And then like a bomb that had been detonated, Harper jumped up from the couch, marched through the kitchen, and opened the door that led to a small shed in the side yard where she kept cleaning supplies—bucket, brush, scouring pads, ammonia, and liquid bleach.

The lasagna would have to wait. It was time to get to work. The house was a mess. Sheets needed to be washed. Mattresses needed to be turned over, and bathrooms needed to be scoured.

Chapter Seven

For too many reasons to count, it had been months since Sawyer had sat at her oldest sister's dinner table. But here she was, her heart beating so fast she wondered if it might explode.

Harper had wanted to meet Sawyer's boyfriend, Derek. Sawyer never should have accepted the invitation. It was too soon in their relationship. Chances were good she'd never see Derek again after tonight. But then again . . . if he couldn't accept her family for who they were, then why would she care?

Derek looked at her. "Are you okay?"

"I think I'm having a heart attack. We should go."

He smiled. "Take a breath. It's going to be fine. It looks like both of your sisters have gone to a lot of trouble."

It was true. The house was cleaner than ever, which was saying a lot. Harper's best dishes and a vase of fresh flowers adorned the table. And both her sisters were in the kitchen, where Sawyer could hear pans clanking and knives chopping.

She and Derek had arrived five minutes ago. Harper and Aria had looked slightly frenzied as they introduced themselves. Aria then ran back to the kitchen, muttering something about the bread in the oven, while Harper explained that the kids were washing up. She'd told them to take a seat at the table and they would all be joining them in a minute.

"Maybe we should offer to help," Derek said.

Sawyer shook her head. "She's a control freak. She wouldn't allow it."

"Lennon! Ella!" Harper shouted from the kitchen. "It's time to eat."

Ella was the first to appear. She ran to Sawyer's side and squeezed her tight. Lennon joined them too and took a seat at the table across from Sawyer.

After Ella pulled away Sawyer said, "I'd like you both to meet my friend, Derek."

Lennon and Derek shared a nod.

"Friend or boyfriend?" Ella asked, her eyes scanning every inch of him.

Derek looked at Sawyer and lifted a brow in question.

"I don't think there's a difference, is there?" Sawyer asked. "I mean, he's a boy and he's a friend."

Lennon laughed.

Sawyer wrinkled her nose. "What?"

"There's a big difference," Lennon said. "Friends hang out. Girlfriends do more than that. They don't just hug."

"They kiss too!" Ella said.

Derek laughed.

"Exactly," Lennon told his sister. "Girlfriends also expect you to support them emotionally and spend time with them. They like to talk about the future and stupid things like that."

Derek and Sawyer exchanged looks, both struggling not to burst out laughing.

"Do girlfriends want to get married?" Ella asked.

"Some of them do," Lennon said, his eyes wide. "It's scary. That's why I don't have a girlfriend."

Harper walked into the dining room, wearing oven mitts and carrying a steaming dish of lasagna that she set on the table. "This is hot, so don't burn yourself. Ella, could you please grab the basket of garlic bread from the kitchen and bring it out here?"

Ella ran off just as Aria appeared with a wooden bowl filled with salad and placed it next to the lasagna.

Ella returned with the bread and then took a seat next to Derek. "Girlfriends dress up more than friends do, I think," she added as if she'd never left the room.

Harper took a seat at the head of the table. "What is she talking about?"

Derek chuckled. "She asked Sawyer if I was a friend or a boyfriend, and we still haven't gotten an answer, have we, Ella?"

Ella shook her head. "No. Aunt Sawyer has not answered."

Before Sawyer could say a word, her brother-in-law walked through the front door. Nate had spent the past few weeks working on a project in another state. His hair was longer, his beard fuller. Sawyer had heard through the grapevine—Aria—that Nate and Harper weren't getting along and needed a break from each other.

"Dad's home!" Ella jumped out of her seat and ran to him. Her thin arms curled around Nate's legs.

Nate dropped his duffel bag to the floor and knelt down for a proper hug.

Lennon joined them.

And then Harper.

"Did you know he was returning tonight?" Sawyer asked Aria in a low voice.

Aria shook her head.

Before Nate could get situated, Ella explained what was going on. "Mom invited Sawyer and Derek to dinner. I think they're boyfriend and girlfriend, but Sawyer isn't sure."

They all laughed at that.

Derek stood. Introductions were made, and the two men shook hands.

After a while, Nate told everyone to go ahead and eat while he cleaned up. It wasn't long before he rejoined them. He was dressed in jeans and a T-shirt. As he filled his plate, he said, "It's good to see you, Sawyer. What are you working on these days?"

Happy to play along and pretend everything was fine, Sawyer dived right in. "I'm working on a few stories, but mostly the one about the female vigilantes."

"The Black Wigs?" Lennon asked.

"That's right," Sawyer said.

Lennon looked at his dad and said, "These crazy women are everywhere, and now a group called The Slayers are joining the cause."

"How do you know this?" Nate asked.

Lennon's eyes were as wide as ever. "Because they videotape the whole thing and upload it on social media."

Sawyer kept quiet, but her nephew was right. The Black Wigs seemed to be inspiring females across the country to go after men who sexually harassed and objectified women. Sawyer had watched a few of the videos herself. The Slayers claimed the men they held hostage were rapists and molesters. The women made their victims sweat by sharpening knives and making threats. If their captive showed little or no emotion, The Slayers used waterboarding techniques to draw out the man's fear. It wasn't until their victim broke down and begged forgiveness that they released him. As far as she knew, all their victims had been released unharmed. And yet authorities had no idea who was behind it all or where the men had been taken since they were drugged and blindfolded. The few men who had come forward had said they'd passed out at a party or gathering and awakened tied to a cot in a dark room that resembled a cave.

Nate looked at Sawyer. "Is this true?"

"Yes," Sawyer said. "There's a group of girls who call themselves The Slayers."

"How can I help?" Aria asked. "Work at the shelter has been slow, and I have plenty of time on my hands. Surveillance, phone calls, research. You name it. I'll do it."

The pleading look in Aria's eyes warmed her heart. In Sawyer's opinion, Aria had suffered the worst abuse of all three sisters combined. But Aria had somehow pushed all her trauma inward and downward and locked it up tight. Instead, Aria channeled her energy toward protecting the vulnerable. She tended to steer clear of human interaction, which was why she'd been working for an animal shelter for as long as Sawyer could remember.

"I'm sure I can find something for you to do," Sawyer said. "If you're absolutely sure you have time?"

Aria smiled. "Wonderful!"

"Is this a paying job?" Lennon asked.

"Afraid not," Sawyer told him.

"That's enough chitchat about work," Harper said before turning her attention on Derek. "I heard you have a big family."

"I do," Derek said. "I'm the youngest of seven kids. I have four sisters, two brothers, and fourteen nephews and nieces."

Ella gasped. "That's a lot of people."

"You're right about that," Derek said. "When we all get together, it feels like a hundred people."

"Do you have a favorite brother or sister?" Ella asked.

"No," he said. "They're all equally annoying."

Ella laughed. "Just like Lennon."

Lennon flicked a pea at his sister.

"No throwing food around," Harper said.

"Let them have some fun." Nate flicked a pea at Lennon, hitting his son square in the forehead.

"You kids are cleaning it all up, including every dish when we're done. That includes unloading and loading the dishes and—"

Before Harper could finish, a pea hit her smack in the chest.

Nate was the culprit.

Sawyer glanced at Aria. They were both frozen in place, waiting for Harper to lose it completely. Derek must have sensed the tension in the air, but he just kept eating, pretending not to notice. *Nothing to see here.*

They all looked up, though, when Harper stood. She walked over to where Lennon was sitting, leaned over his shoulder, and picked up the bowl of peas, then continued on to the end of the table where Nate sat, raised the bowl a few inches above his head, and turned the bowl upside down. Peas rained down on his head, where they made a little pea-green mountain. Some of the peas rolled off his head and down his chest, quite a few of them disappearing between the gap at the top of his button-down shirt.

Before Harper could walk back to her seat, Nate pushed out his chair, which prompted Harper to run for her life. They disappeared down the hallway, where they all heard a door close.

"I don't come to dinner as often as I used to. Should we be worried?" Sawyer asked.

"No," Ella said. "They're probably making up."

Sawyer raised a brow.

Aria was on the floor, crawling around on all fours, picking up peas, telling everyone not to move because she didn't want to clean up mashed green peas.

Sawyer leaned close to Derek. "Sorry about all the chaos."

"Chaos? Wait until you meet my family. This was nothing."

Lennon laughed.

"I want to meet your family," Ella said. "Don't you, Sawyer?"

Derek nudged her with an elbow. "What do you say?"

Sawyer didn't need to look around to know that all eyes were on her. "Of course I do. I can't wait."

Sawyer waved as Derek drove off after walking her to her apartment door and kissing her good night. Not for the first time, she questioned why he hadn't even hinted at taking her home with him. She knew he lived in a quaint one-story home off Marty Lane in Land Park.

A sudden movement caught her attention. Looking to her left, she craned her neck for a better look. Someone was sitting behind the wheel of a small green car parked down the block on the wrong side of the curb. Thinking it could be a neighbor having car trouble, she stepped that way.

Tires screeched as the driver made a U-turn in the middle of the road, taking off in the other direction.

A chill washed over her. Was someone watching her?

Inside her apartment, she locked the door, then turned her back to it so that she was peering into the semidarkness of her apartment.

Her heart was racing. What was wrong with her? She wasn't usually skittish or fearful, but for some reason she suddenly felt vulnerable.

She knew—she could feel it inside her—that it wasn't just the possibility of being watched that bothered her. It was everything. But mostly it was Derek. Years of childhood trauma had damaged her. When it came to relationships of any sort, she had built walls. Lots of walls. Those walls had made it possible for her to move on with her life.

If she intended to build a better life for herself, the walls had to come down. The passing of time did not heal all wounds. Her recent nightmares were proof of that.

Before her eyes adjusted to the dark, something lunged for her. She screamed and then let out a shaky laugh when she realized it was Raccoon, her cat, just jumping off the couch.

"Come on, Raccoon," she said, brushing her fingers through his fur. "Let's go to bed."

Chapter Eight

The next morning before leaving for work, Aria Brooks logged on to her computer while she drank her coffee and was excited to see that Sawyer had already sent her an email with an update on the Black Wigs case. She mentioned a coworker named Lexi Holmes, who had weaseled her way into working on the story with her. Sawyer told Aria about a recent homicide, a man named Nick Calderon, and how she believed his murder could be the work of a copycat.

If Aria was still interested, Sawyer wanted her help in learning more about Nick Calderon's life. His ex-wife had told Sawyer that Calderon didn't have any friends, but what about the people he worked with? Sawyer questioned. Bottom line: Who were Calderon's enemies? Who hated him enough to kill him?

Aria's entire body thrummed at the idea of having something else to occupy her time. She loved her job at the shelter, but she worked only when they needed her, and she liked to keep busy—something all three of the Brooks sisters had in common.

Hours later, while Aria hosed down the dog runs at the animal shelter where she worked, she couldn't stop thinking about Nick Calderon's death. The first thing she wanted to do was talk to his coworkers and get an idea of who he was. As she shut off the water to the hose, she heard her name come over the loudspeaker outside: *Aria Brooks. Please come to the front right away.* The voice belonged to her boss, Tiffany Sparks.

Aria used her forearm, the only part of her not covered in dog hair and dirt, to push flyaway strands of hair out of her face. A part-timer and a volunteer had failed to show up, which had made for an unusually busy morning. Based on the rattled sound of desperation in Tiffany's voice, things were not improving.

Inside the shelter, chaos abounded. A couple of dogs were barking nonstop. Two people stood in line, both with dogs.

Tiffany stood behind the front counter with a phone pressed to her ear. On the counter was a filthy cage with a cat and her four kittens. The poor mother looked exhausted, probably hungry and dehydrated too.

A Doberman pinscher in one of the cages nearby was upset about something, and he wouldn't stop barking. He was a newcomer and he wasn't happy. As Aria approached, Tiffany muted the call, gestured to the waiting room, which was three plastic chairs pushed against the wall, and said, "Could you help the man over there? He was first."

Aria nodded and headed that way.

The man, midthirties, was sitting in the middle chair. His wavy, overly long, light-brown hair looked windswept, covering most of one eye. He wore dark fitted jeans and chunky boots with combat-style treads. At the end of a long rope was a German shorthaired pointer, one of the top breeds for competitive hunting because of their reflexes and speed.

The man stood as she approached.

"Hi," she said. "I'm Aria."

"Corey."

Her gaze settled on the dog. Aria let the animal sniff her hand before she knelt down and stroked the animal's neck and back. The dog was too thin, with jutting ribs. There was no collar. Just a rope tied around his neck. "Who do we have here?" she asked.

Corey shrugged. "No idea. I found him running around the street in front of my apartment. No pets allowed, so I brought him here."

"Ah, such a sweet, handsome boy."

"Thank you."

Aria looked up at him. "I was talking about the dog."

"I know."

Her cheeks flushed. She pushed herself back to her feet. "You did the right thing, you know, bringing him in." She gestured toward the counter, where Tiffany struggled to keep the phone propped between her chin and shoulder while also trying to contain a golden retriever that kept jumping up so that his paws were on the counter, upsetting the cat in the cage. "If you don't mind," Aria told Corey, "I'll need you to fill out a form."

"That's fine," he said.

Aria returned with a clipboard and pen. She took the end of the rope just as the door opened and another man walked in. His eyes were the same dark blue as his grease-stained coveralls. The name tag said his name was Nolan. Red in the face, Nolan yanked hard on a leash, making the poor dog in his care let out a high-pitched yelp as he cut to the front of the line.

The animal, Aria noticed, looked like a pit bull mix.

The Doberman increased his volume, which prompted the pit bull to bark too. Nolan yanked the leash again.

"You're hurting the animal," Corey said.

"Mind your own business." Nolan pulled up on the leash, so hard and so high that the dog's two front feet left the ground.

Aria gasped.

Tiffany hung up the phone.

The cat hissed.

Corey, the man with the combat boots, moved fast. In the blink of an eye, he had Nolan up against the wall, his arm pressed against Nolan's neck so the man couldn't move. The pit bull took off down the wide cement aisle, heading for the open door at the other end of the building. All the dogs were barking now.

With the German shorthaired pointer at her side, Aria took off running for the other dog. The shelter backed up against forty acres of what she considered to be an urban forest with lots of meandering trails shaded by alders and ash, walnuts, and willows. Relieved to see that the gate leading to the trail was closed, she didn't have to go far to find the pit bull. Sorely neglected like so many of the animals brought to the shelter, the poor dog sat near the fence, shaking and panting. He had scabs all over his body, and he was too thin.

Aria pulled a couple of dog treats from her pocket, gave one to the pointer, and then used the other to try to get the pit bull to come to her. She could tell he wanted to trust her, but too many years of abuse had left him wary of humans.

Aria was within a few feet of the dog when Corey came to her aid.

"You're still here," Aria said, surprised.

"I wasn't going to leave you or the other lady here alone with Nolan."

"Is he gone?"

Corey nodded. "He threatened to call the police and charge me with assault."

"Oh, no."

"It's okay. I called his bluff. Turned out that Nolan was all bark and no bite."

Aria smiled, then watched him get real close to the pit bull, kneel down, and talk to the dog in a soothing voice, telling the animal that everything was going to be okay.

She thought for sure the dog would run off when he got too close, but the pit bull didn't move. It wasn't long before Corey was petting the animal's head and rubbing the sweet spot under the dog's chin.

"Do you need a job by any chance?" Aria asked, teasing since the shelter preferred volunteers.

He laughed. "I actually have one. As delightful as this has been, I should get back to it. Come on, boy," he said to the pit bull. "Let's get back in there and fill out some paperwork."

Soon the dogs were placed inside clean cages with plenty of food and water and the paperwork was done.

Aria and Tiffany both thanked Corey for all his help.

"We have lots of trails around here. If you ever want to take a dog for a walk, you know where to come," Aria told him.

He smiled as he waved goodbye.

The minute the door closed behind him, Aria released a pent-up breath. "That sure was nice of him to help us."

"Yes, it was," Tiffany said. "I'm going to feed the animals in the back and then take Chompers for a walk."

"If it's okay with you," Aria said, "I'm going to take an early lunch after you get back from your walk."

"That's fine."

Aria went to the counter and flipped through the forms on the clipboard. Corey's last name was Moran. He lived on T Street.

She shook her head, inwardly scolding herself for being curious about his name and address since she wasn't interested in pursuing any sort of relationship with the guy. With that in mind, she decided to focus on Nick Calderon's death. Pulling her phone from her back pocket, she looked up the address for the insurance company in Elk Grove where he had worked before he was killed.

Chapter Nine

It was a few minutes before nine when Sawyer was greeted at the door by a woman named Debbie, then led into Palmer's home on H Street in East Sacramento. She wanted to talk to her boss before her scheduled meeting with Lexi Holmes.

She was led into a large room with lots of windows but not much light since the curtains were drawn tight. Palmer looked over his shoulder at Sawyer and then raised the remote and shut off the television. "I was wondering when you would come."

Debbie walked away.

"Get over here where I can see you without straining my neck."

Sawyer did as he asked. Ten days had passed since Palmer had knocked on the door of a serial killer's house and left in an ambulance. He was fond of telling people that he would be dead if Sawyer hadn't shown up with a gun and taken aim at the madwoman. One shot had saved his life.

In many ways, Palmer had saved her life, so now they were even.

"Nice setup," she said. He not only had a hospital bed in the middle of his living room but also one of those rolling metal food trays. But as she walked closer, she noticed that his skin color was ashen, and his arms appeared thin. *Fragile* had never been a word she would have used to describe Palmer until now. She had thought, or maybe hoped, he'd look a little better by now—stronger and healthier.

Palmer frowned. "Not a pretty sight, huh?"

Sawyer cleared her throat. "What do you mean?"

"I look like I'm on my deathbed. Your face is like a mirror, and the horror is scrawled all over it. You don't need to say a word. I can see what you're thinking."

"God, you're a pain in the ass."

He tried to laugh, but it came out sounding like a cackling witch. He reached for his cup of water and took little sips through a straw.

Sawyer sat down in the cushioned chair facing him so they could better see each other. "So you knew I was coming?"

"I did."

"Are all those drugs making you psychic?"

"You're here because Lexi told you she talked to me about handling the Black Wigs case, correct?"

His words quickly renewed her anger, and she jumped to her feet. "That's right. Lexi threatened to rush her perspective on the Black Wigs story to publication if I didn't collaborate with her."

He chuckled.

"Why is that funny?"

"Because it's way too easy to get your goat. She came to me, asking permission to take over the story. I told her it was yours and that she should talk to you."

Sawyer waited for more, but nothing was forthcoming. "That's all you told Lexi?"

"That's it."

Sawyer plopped back down into the cushioned chair. Elbows propped on knees, she rubbed her palms over her face.

"You're an easy target." Palmer stated the obvious.

"You could have warned me."

"Why would I do that?"

That was a very good question. Sawyer and Palmer weren't related. He wasn't her friend in the true sense of the word. He was her mentor and her boss, and she looked up to him. In quick succession she'd solved a couple of cases, and apparently it had gone to her head. "I'm an idiot," she told him.

"I wouldn't go that far. Impulsive, imprudent, rash—"

Sawyer raised a hand to stop him.

It worked.

"Just to be clear," Sawyer said, "if I'd had the good sense to hold strong and tell Lexi no, you would have stood by my decision?"

He nodded, but she didn't miss the self-satisfied smirk on his face. He was gloating. He'd known she'd crack like a hard-boiled egg. He'd also known that she would race to his home, uninvited, to give him a piece of her mind. Not only was she an idiot—she was all those other things he'd called her too.

Sawyer took a breath. "So, any suggestions on how to handle working with Lexi Holmes?"

"Yes. Be prepared to work three times as hard, or she'll make mincemeat out of you."

"Is mincemeat really a thing?"

"It most definitely is. And trust me. You don't want to be chopped and diced and served for dinner in a boozy concoction of overcooked meat and apples seasoned with cinnamon."

"Great." She looked around the room, twiddling her fingers, trying not to let it all get to her. It was one big learning experience. One of these days, she would be confident enough to stick to her guns. "Nice place you got here," she finally said.

"All decorating credit goes to Debbie."

"Is she your caretaker?"

"She's my wife."

No way. He was teasing. "You told me you were divorced."

"I was."

"It was only a few weeks ago when you told me you were divorced."

"Correct."

"Two days after you told me you were divorced, you were stabbed by a lunatic."

"You have the memory of an elephant."

She shook her head at him.

"After the incident," he said, making it sound more like a slip and fall and less like attempted murder, "I realized life was short, and while I was doped up on Percocet and feeling no pain, I asked the lucky lady to marry me."

"And she said yes?"

His smile made his eyes sparkle.

"She's not wearing a wedding ring."

"We'll go shopping as soon as I'm up and about."

"No church wedding, I guess."

"Only the best for my girl," he said. "A good friend of mine came over, pinned a bow tie to my undershirt, and officiated the thing right here in the living room."

Silence.

"Something wrong?" he asked.

"Truthfully," Sawyer said, "you just never struck me as the type to do something so spontaneous. I mean, the doped-up thing makes sense, but there's a part of this whole love story that makes zero sense."

"Which part?"

"The beautiful and kind Debbie part."

"What? You don't think I'm good enough for her?"

"No. I don't."

"What if I told you that she's not as nice as you think?"

Sawyer laughed and then pushed herself to her feet. "I better go and let you get your rest." She walked to his side and gave him a long look.

"Quit looking at me as if I'm a goner. I'll be back in the office sooner than you think."

"You better be," she said before heading for the exit.

Chapter Ten

It was five minutes after ten when Sawyer walked into the conference room at work. Lexi Holmes was already seated at the rectangular table, surrounded by papers and a three-ring binder. "You're late."

Ignoring her, Sawyer took a seat, reached into her bag for her own file and notebook, and set it on the table in front of her.

Lexi leaned forward and handed Sawyer a piece of paper. "I think it would be a good idea if we talk to the victims of the Black Wigs. We need to make it clear to the community that what these vigilantes are doing is wrong."

"We don't know if that's true," Sawyer said.

Lexi's hand went to the base of her throat. "Cutting off Brad Vicente's appendage was the right thing to do?"

"Well," Sawyer said, "the man is in prison for doing unspeakable things to women whose names we still don't know."

"I'm not sure I understand exactly what you're trying to say."

"I'm saying it's possible, if not probable, that the Black Wigs were victims at one time. It's a well-known fact that only five out of every thousand rapists go to—" Sawyer stopped herself. No need to give her opinion. Opinions were like assholes . . . everyone had one. "Although we must remain unbiased, I would like to write about this from the vigilantes' point of view."

Lexi's gaze was fixated on the pen she kept tapping against the table.

When Lexi failed to say anything, Sawyer added, "Clearly, the vigilantes are going about it all wrong, but what I want to know, as I'm sure many readers would too, is *why* the Black Wigs are doing this. These men are being chosen for a reason. And so far, their attacks were carefully planned."

"How can you be so sure?" Lexi asked.

"Because otherwise the Black Wigs would be in jail already. Take Brad Vicente as an example. It would require organization and preparation to kidnap a man, keep him tied up in his own home, then cut off his dick and escape unseen."

"Are you open to giving our readers the whole picture?" Lexi asked.

"Do you mean let our readers see what's going on through the lens of both the vigilante and the victim? Of course."

"Good." Lexi handed Sawyer a piece of paper. "I'll handle the story from the perspective of the Black Wigs' victims." She gestured toward the paper in front of Sawyer.

Sawyer studied the names: Brad Vicente, Otto Radley, Myles Davenport, and Nick Calderon. Beneath every name was the date and place of birth, social security number, schooling, and employment information, if any, and names of friends and relatives, including phone numbers and addresses.

"I want to handle the Nick Calderon case."

"But he's a victim of the Black Wigs," Lexi said.

"I don't think so."

Lexi straightened in her chair. "I talked to Detective Perez over the phone. The person seen on the security camera was wearing a black wig. Can you explain that?"

"I think it's a copycat."

Lexi looked as if she wanted to say something but was holding back. She finally angled her head and said, "You're a real go-getter, aren't you?"

Sawyer said nothing.

"Just because you're not afraid to get out there and talk to people, doesn't always mean that you should."

"Why not?" Sawyer asked.

"Because you tend to step on people's feet. People who matter. People like Detective Perez. He doesn't appreciate you getting in the way. Up until now, you've been lucky. It's as simple as that."

Sawyer knew Lexi was talking about her involvement in a recent case concerning a string of missing girls. "I don't believe hard work and long hours has anything to do with luck."

Lexi went back to tapping the end of the pen against the table. Her brow furrowed as she met Sawyer's gaze. "So we'll split this Black Wigs story right down the middle. I'll tell it from the victims' side . . . except for Nick Calderon . . . and you tell it from the vigilantes' side." There was a pause before she added, "It's your career on the line, not mine."

"You don't think it's reasonable to assume that the women who make up the Black Wigs might have been abused by the men they have chosen to go after?"

"I don't think it's a good idea to ever assume."

"Aren't you curious to know why these women are doing what they're doing? Don't you want to know how society got to the point where young girls are imitating the Black Wigs on social media?"

Lexi sighed.

"What?"

"When it comes to telling the story, I'll remain unbiased. But do you want my honest opinion about all this?"

"I do."

"The Black Wigs are nothing more than thugs. Nobody should take the law into their own hands. It's not up to them to punish these men, no matter the circumstances."

"It's happening, though, and I think it's pretty clear that people are mimicking the Black Wigs out of frustration. Rapists are ruining lives and getting away with it."

Lexi didn't look impressed.

"Every day," Sawyer went on, "somewhere in the world, a doctor sedates and then assaults a patient. A coach takes advantage of a student and is never arrested. Just last week, a young high school girl in Sacramento was raped. She reported the assault immediately. Nothing was done to the boy who attacked her."

Sawyer took a calming breath. "You focus on the victims, and I'll concentrate on the Black Wigs, The Slayers, and every woman out there who has been victimized. But nothing you write gets published until I give approval. We're doing this story my way. If you want out, now would be the time to say so."

Lexi sat back in her chair. "I'm in."

"Good. I'm going to start by interviewing the women who filed complaints and/or brought the men on your list to court years ago. Then I'll move on to anyone who knows the abusers—friends, coworkers, neighbors, and family."

"That's a lot of people to talk to."

"Is that a problem?"

"It could be. The Black Wigs story is huge right now. Everyone is talking about them. We need to get something out there. Pronto."

Sawyer shook her head. "If we rush it, it'll look like every other hack story out there. It might take some time, but we're going to do this right."

"Fine," Lexi said. "There's one more thing we need to discuss."

"Okay."

"We have an appointment at the California State Prison, Sacramento, at noon."

Sawyer wondered how she was able to arrange an interview in such a short amount of time, but she didn't say anything since she wanted to avoid the whole I'm-a-pro speech.

Lexi glanced at her watch with its gleaming yellow-gold band. "Meet me in the lobby in forty-five minutes. We'll drive together. My car."

Sawyer nodded. She could insist they take her car, but it was dirty and she needed gas.

"We'll only have thirty minutes to interview him," Lexi said. "I have a list of questions ready to go."

Of course she did.

"We won't be allowed cameras or recording devices, so be prepared to take notes."

They both stood at the same time.

Sawyer realized the collaboration would never work unless she let Lexi do what Lexi did best—collect, verify, and analyze the information—while Sawyer concentrated on the Black Wigs, women she empathized with. There was no doubt in her mind that they had been wronged, their lives most likely left in tatters while the perpetrators walked free.

Chapter Eleven

Valerie Purcell slipped on her leopard leggings and black tank top with the crisscross straps and then went and stood before the full-length mirror. She turned to her right and then her left. Not bad for a seventy-four-year-old broad with silver hair and hardly any muscle tone. At least, not yet.

Two weeks ago, she'd decided to make Henry's old office into a workout room. Her daughter had helped her go through his things, but the built-in bookshelf was still lined with books and knickknacks and silly awards that had made him feel as if he were someone when, in fact, he'd been no one.

Two months had passed since her husband suffered a major heart attack and died on the spot. Henry's death replayed in her head a couple of times a week. When would that stop? *Hopefully sooner rather than later,* she thought as she picked up the five-pound dumbbells.

Henry had been seventy-five when he died. A year older than Valerie was now. He'd been a personal injury lawyer, also known as an ambulance chaser, which was something he actually did all the time.

Before she knew of his betrayal, she had tried to get him to retire. Mostly because she'd wanted to travel before they got too old, but Henry wouldn't think of it. He'd said he would rather die than sit home all day with nothing to do. And that's exactly what had happened. They'd been in the kitchen when it happened. As he worked on cutting the foil below the lower lip of a bottle of Cabernet from Napa Valley, a serious expression had crossed his face before he told her he had something very important he needed to discuss with her.

Her heart had begun to race. Was he finally going to retire? Where would they travel to first? Italy? France? New Zealand? So many options. It would be difficult to choose when the time came to book their flights. She'd been badgering him about taking her somewhere for so long she'd started to think it might never happen.

He began to rotate the corkscrew. A sheen of sweat had made his forehead shiny, as if the task at hand was too much for him. And then he'd said, "I want—"

"What do you want, dear?" she'd asked him, waiting for him to finish his sentence.

He grabbed a tissue from the counter and dabbed it over his face. "It's hot in here."

"It's fine," she told him. "What do you want?"

He picked up the corkscrew and made a half turn and then another. "I want a divorce."

"What? Why?"

"I've fallen in love with someone else." He usually gave the corkscrew six half turns, but he'd managed only four before his hands dropped to his sides and he fell backward, his head bouncing off the marble countertop on his way down.

She ran to his side and felt for a pulse. He was hanging on but barely, his clawlike hand clutching at his chest. She thought about calling for help, but she couldn't shake loose his declaration of love for another woman. Who was it? she wanted to ask, but didn't.

"Help," he squeaked. Tiny bubbles of spit formed at both sides of his mouth.

"You just professed your love for another, and you want me to help you?"

No answer. His face was extremely pale now, his lips a grayish blue.

She took a couple of breaths to calm down and hopefully put to rest the urge to give him a good kick or two.

She would call for help. Eventually. But first she finished opening the bottle of wine, poured herself a glass, and took a sip. *Nice.* Henry was missing out. She then walked to the family room, picked up the remote, and flipped through the channels. By the time she returned to the kitchen, he had passed on.

The sound of a timer going off downstairs brought her back to the present. Dumbbells in hand, she stood still for another second or two, listening. The sound was familiar. It was the timer on her oven. But she hadn't put anything in the oven. In fact, she rarely cooked anymore. She left the workout room and went to the hallway, where the beeping grew louder.

A crash followed.

At the top of the stairs, she leaned over the banister. "Who's there?"

Silence followed.

Hurrying down the steps, wondering whether the neighbor's cat had somehow gotten inside the house, she tripped suddenly and flew headfirst down the stairs. She hit the landing hard, and tasted blood.

Seconds passed before she attempted and failed to move her arms and legs. Her neck was crooked in such a way that she could see her left leg. There was blood everywhere. A broken, twisted bone protruded from her calf. "Help," she said when she heard movement and then quiet footfalls.

She closed her eyes. When she opened them again, someone was standing over her and leaning low. Black hair and red lipstick. Cleopatra? It wasn't Halloween, was it? "Who are you?"

"You might remember me as Cockroach."

Cockroach? "From the Children's Home in Sacramento?"

"That's right."

She struggled to swallow. "What are you doing in my house?"

"I'm making the rounds. Paying all my old friends a visit. I've already seen Nick Calderon."

"But he's dead."

"Yes, he is. I'm pretty sure he went to hell, where he belongs."

Valerie's chest tightened as images of her husband lying on the kitchen floor took hold in her mind's eye. He'd looked so pale, so old. It had all been for the best. But she was young and vibrant. She was going on a Caribbean cruise next month. She couldn't die. Not now. Not yet. "When those bullies picked on you," she said to Cockroach, her voice trembling, "I tried to stop them. I always wanted the best for you."

"Is that why you made me mop the floor whenever I cried? Then kicked me in the ribs, over and over, if I missed a spot?"

Her heart was racing now. She tried to move her leg, hoping she might be able to crawl out the door and scream for help, but just that tiny movement sent a searing-hot pain through her middle. She let out a whimpering cry. "Imagine trying to take care of dozens of troubled children," she tried again. "Kids need discipline. I had to do whatever was necessary to keep order."

Cockroach stepped over her and walked up the stairs.

"What are you doing?"

"Just removing the rope I tied from one railing to the other in the hope that you would trip over it when you heard someone in your kitchen. It worked perfectly."

Cockroach was back beside her, holding a syringe, examining it closely before reaching for her foot. She could feel the needle pinching the skin under her toenail. The pain was excruciating. "Let me go. Please stop."

"I remember saying those exact words to you all those years ago."

"I'm sorry," she said. "Is that what you want to hear?"

"A little too late for apologies, I'm afraid. Sleep tight. You'll be with your husband soon."

Valerie groaned. Henry was the last person in the world she wanted to see again. She licked her dry lips. Her breathing grew shallow. She felt nauseated.

So this was what it felt like to die. She'd always wondered what thoughts or life events might flash before her in those last moments.

But there was nothing.

No bright light in the distance calling to her. Only blackness.

No thoughts or consciousness. No kind faces smiling upon her as she took her last breath.

Just a big gaping hole of nothingness.

Chapter Twelve

The drive to the prison was spent listening to Lexi talk on the phone about other stories she was working on, including one about a domestic murder and the confession made by the wife on social media. If she had not been on the phone, Sawyer might have told her that she'd called Brad Vicente's sister after their meeting this morning. The woman had nothing good to say about her brother—a few choice words before hanging up—but it was something she might be able to use to get Brad Vicente talking.

Once they arrived, everything went quickly. After signing in, they were ushered down a long hallway. Surrounded by stark-white plaster walls and sanded cement floors, Sawyer stiffened at the sounds of alarms, yelling, and someone pounding on the wall.

Inside a ten-by-ten, windowless room, Brad Vicente sat at a rectangular metal table. He wore a state-issued T-shirt and jumper and no restraints.

Lexi pulled out a chair across from Vicente and took a seat. Sawyer did the same. Armed with paper and pen, Sawyer glanced at the tall security guard standing off to the side. His arms were crossed, and his gun holster was visible. His presence provided comfort, and yet the jittery feeling in the pit of her stomach wouldn't leave her.

She'd never interviewed a prisoner before. First time for everything. Sawyer looked across the table at Brad Vicente and said, "I'd like to start by thanking you for allowing us to talk to you."

Brad Vicente looked like a regular guy, leaning toward handsome. His head had been shaved, leaving an outline of dark shadows where his hair had once been. His jaw, on the other hand, was bristling with new growth. His smile was disconcerting. The twinkling eyes and flash of straight teeth made her feel like prey. Or maybe nerves were simply getting the best of her. Forgetting her question, she looked back at her notes.

"I've been in business for many years," he said as she flipped a page. "One of the things I learned early on was that getting right to the point of the matter is usually the best way to go."

He was right. Sawyer raised her gaze to meet his. "Do you have any idea who cut off your penis?"

He smiled.

She waited.

His smile turned sour. "Don't you think I would have told the world who did this to me if I had a name?"

"You were locked in your house with five women for days. You didn't recognize any of their faces?"

"I was born a ladies' man. They flock to me like bees to honey. I've been with a lot of women." He laughed. "I was also blindfolded."

"How many women have you been with?"

Lexi appeared to shift uncomfortably in her seat.

Brad Vicente lifted a shoulder. "Too many to count."

"Whoever took a knife to you," Sawyer said, "must have been angry. These women tied you up and then cut you. That makes what happened to you seem very personal. Don't you think?"

"Women are overly sensitive. Maybe one of them didn't like something I said in passing. Who knows? It's not easy being a single man in today's world. You have to buy a woman dinner and drinks just to get an opportunity to try and get to know them. Because of who I am, I'm able to get reservations at the best restaurants. Maybe I didn't tell my date at the Blue Fox that she was hot enough. If you want to get anywhere with a woman, you have to dish out the compliments. It's ridiculous."

"Is that where you took your dates? The Blue Fox?"

He fidgeted in his seat, making Sawyer wonder if the question had made him nervous.

"No," he said. "I don't remember."

It was clear by his sudden difficulty with keeping eye contact and the way his lips pursed that he was lying. She wanted to keep him talking, though, so she made a mental note to go to the Blue Fox and find out if anyone recognized his name or picture. "Do you ever go out with a woman more than once?"

"Sometimes."

"Do you usually have sex on the first date?"

Lexi coughed into a fisted hand.

Sawyer ignored her.

"Yes," he said. "If the woman passes my tests, then we usually have sex. Why go on a date otherwise?"

"What sort of tests does she need to pass?"

He blew air out of the side of his mouth. "Isn't it obvious?"

"Not to me."

"Most importantly, she needs to be good looking. When we finally meet up, she better look like her picture."

"Her picture?"

"Yes. The one she posted on the dating app. A lot of women post pictures from years earlier when their skin was as plump and firm as their breasts."

Sawyer glanced at Lexi, but she was looking down, making notes. "So if your date looks like her picture, she passes the test? That's it?"

"Not necessarily. If she's a bitch, then it's a no-go. Bossy or too abrupt would be a game changer."

"Meaning you wouldn't ask her to your place?"

"Exactly."

"What dating app did you use?"

"Zoosk. Match. Tinder. Whatever's out there."

Sawyer jotted the names down. "I've read reports from two women who went out with you. They both had similar stories. You asked them to your house for a nightcap. They agreed. Both women began to feel woozy, as if they'd been drugged. As soon as they walked into your house, you locked the door and forced yourself on them, pushing one woman against the wall so hard she suffered a concussion."

"Liars." He jabbed a forefinger into the tabletop. "If they made it through dinner and came to my house, they wanted a piece of me. Every single one of them."

He was upset, off balance, and she wanted to keep it that way. "Do you get along with your mother?"

His face reddened.

"I talked to your sister," Sawyer said, on a roll now. "She said you've always been an angry man, distrusting and—"

He slapped both palms flat on the table in front of him. "I was framed. Her name was Li. And yes, we were at the Blue Fox. She was beautiful. Exotic. Long blonde hair. Find her fucking ass and take her and her friends down." He stood. "This little party is over."

"Why?"

"Because I was told this session would give me a chance to tell the world that I've been wrongly accused."

"A jury found you guilty," Sawyer stated matter-of-factly. "They have videos showing you raping multiple women."

"Fake. Photoshopped. Someone is trying to frame me." He held up a hand to inform security he was ready to go.

"We're on your side," Lexi cut in. "We want to expose these women in black wigs and see that they are punished for what they did to you."

His jaw twitched. As he plopped back down into his chair, he kept his gaze on Lexi. "Go on."

"I also talked to people who know you," Lexi said. "A few close friends of yours, including Margo Kensington. She said the two of you once dated. She and others were adamant about you being wrongly accused."

His shoulders relaxed. "Because it's true."

"Margo said you were always thoughtful and kind."

He drew in a steady breath. "She was a sweet girl."

Sawyer watched the exchange. Lexi kept her gaze directed at him the entire time.

Lexi angled her head. "The two words that came up the most to describe you were 'compassionate' and 'generous.'"

"That's right. I once stopped a dog from attacking a neighbor's kid." He pulled up the right sleeve of his jumper. "The animal bit me. Twenty-three stitches." His chest puffed. "But the kid got away." He laughed. "They called me a hero for months."

"That's what I mean," Lexi said. "You're smart, good looking, and you care about others, which is why none of this makes sense to me or the people who know you best."

His eyes widened, and he leaned forward. "It's refreshing to finally talk to someone who understands what's happening here. I've been wrongly accused and nobody seems to care."

"You have a lot of followers out there rooting for you," Lexi told him, her voice soft and soothing. "People who care about you and who want to see you released."

"Glad to hear it."

"And that's why we're here." Lexi placed her forearms on the table and leaned closer. "This is your chance to tell us, in your own words, what happened."

"It was horrible," he said. "A nightmare." He raked his fingers over his head. "Imagine being in a room with five aggressive women, all wearing wigs and masks, stripping you naked, then tying you up with rope and duct tape. I was freaked out."

"Did you recognize a voice, anything at all?"

"No. They all called each other by weird names, like Bug and Psycho."

"Did they tell you why they were there?"

"That's a good question, but no. They never did tell me why they came after me. I think they might have had me confused with someone else. They tore my house apart. I still don't know what they were looking for."

"Videos," Sawyer said. Brad Vicente was full of shit, and she couldn't take it anymore. "They were looking for video content you took of the women you bound and raped. That's why you're sitting here now."

He angled his head back toward Sawyer and gave her a look that shouted *psychopath*—eyes wide, eyebrows elevated, nostrils flared. But the rest of his face was relaxed. A chill swept up her spine.

Facing Lexi again, he hooked a thumb like a hitchhiker at Sawyer and said, "I don't think she's on my side."

"She's on the same team," Lexi said matter-of-factly, leaving no room for argument.

"Time to wrap it up," the guard said.

Lexi nodded at the guard, then returned her attention to Brad. "You said the women wearing wigs used nicknames. Were there any other features that stood out to you?"

The guard approached the table.

Brad stood. His eyes flashed. "Tattoos," he said. "I couldn't see much through the blindfold, but every now and then I got a glimpse. One of the women had weird markings on her neck and arms. I thought they were tattoos, but they could have been birthmarks. Or maybe she'd been disfigured in a fire. Who knows?"

"Were all the wigs the same length as far as you could tell?" Sawyer asked.

He gestured to a spot just past his chin.

"Lipstick?"

He shook his head.

Lexi cut in. "If we need to talk to you again, would you be willing?"

His gaze roamed over Lexi. "I might talk to you again," he said. "But not your friend."

Sawyer mentally flipped him off as he was ushered out the door.

Lexi slipped her notepad and pen into her bag. As they strolled out of the room and back toward the front of the building, Lexi said, "Overall, I'd say that went well."

Sawyer wasn't so sure. Her adrenaline was at max speed. She felt riled up. "That was intense."

"You did good. Now we just need to find Li on Tinder."

Sawyer appreciated her kind words. She had interviewed a lot of people over the years. She knew that if she wanted someone to talk that she needed to make her subject feel at home. And yet the dirty, lying bastard had managed to strike a nerve. "When did you talk to Margo Kensington?"

"I called her yesterday. She told me that Brad Vicente was scum and to never call her again."

"So you made up that whole story about talking to Margo and friends," Sawyer stated rather than questioned. "And now he's putty in your hands."

Lexi smiled.

The sound of their footfalls slapping against the concrete floor was nearly drowned out by the sound of too many men crammed into not enough space. Sawyer and Lexi took turns signing out.

The air outside warmed the back of Sawyer's neck. Her gaze immediately fixated on the car parked across the street from the prison. It was shiny, mint green, small, and hard to miss—the same car she'd seen at her house after Derek had dropped her off. She was about to mention it when the vehicle merged onto the road and drove off.

"Everything all right?" Lexi asked.

Sawyer didn't say anything about the car since she didn't want to come across as paranoid. Instead she said, "I was just thinking about Brad Vicente. He's a narcissist and a liar," she said as they walked. "I think I'll leave the prison visits to you."

"Perfect. Maybe next time I see him, he'll propose."

Sawyer looked at Lexi as if she'd lost her mind.

"That was a joke."

"Ah. Funny. I guess we're going to learn a lot about each other."

"Not if I can help it," Lexi said.

Sawyer laughed again before noticing the grim expression on Lexi's face. Something told her the next few weeks were going to be anything but enjoyable.

After she was buckled up and Lexi was back on her phone, talking about a case unrelated to the Black Wigs, Sawyer texted Aria, telling her what Brad Vicente had said about one of the women who held him captive having scars or burns, which reminded Sawyer of Christina Farro. *Perhaps it's time I pay her another visit.* She also told Aria about the exotic blonde-haired woman named Li, whom Brad Vicente had been matched with on one of the dating apps.

This Li could be the answer to all their questions. Too bad they didn't have a surname.

Sawyer's shoulders slumped. If Li was involved with the Black Wigs, there was no way she would have used her real name on a dating app. But still . . . if they could find the profile, it would be something.

And something was almost always better than nothing.

Chapter Thirteen

After checking in with the receptionist, Aria sat in a waiting area at the insurance company in Elk Grove where Nick Calderon used to work before he was killed, and she found herself thinking of Corey Moran, the nice man who had brought the dog to the shelter and then helped her and Tiffany deal with Nolan, the weirdo.

Enough of that, she thought as she flipped through the pages of a *People* magazine, hoping the receptionist would tell her Nick Calderon's boss would talk to her. Her phone vibrated, letting her know she had an incoming text. It was an update from Sawyer, telling her about her visit with Brad Vicente and asking her to look into Li and Farro.

Aria was about to use her phone to search the internet and see what she could find on Li, if anything, when a young woman dressed in slacks and a blazer appeared and told her Mr. Panfili could see her, but he had only a few minutes.

When Aria entered Mr. Panfili's office, he stood. He was at least six feet tall and had a receding hairline. He looked friendly, and she instantly felt at ease. His office was made up of floor-to-ceiling windows that provided a stunning view of downtown Sacramento. She leaned over his desk and shook his hand, then took a seat in a leather chair opposite him.

"You're a reporter for the *Sacramento Independent*?" he asked after they were both sitting.

"I'm actually an assistant," Aria told him. "I know you don't have a lot of time, so I'll get right to it."

He nodded.

"Nick Calderon worked here for the past ten years, is that correct?"

"Yes."

Aria wanted to sound professional. She thought about what Sawyer might say under these circumstances. "I'm sure you've already chatted with police detectives, and I know it can get redundant in cases like this, but—"

"Nobody has come to see me about Nick."

That was surprising.

"I did hear through the grapevine that he was found on the floor inside his home," he said. "Any possibility that he had a heart attack?"

"I'm afraid not. His death has been ruled a homicide. His ex-wife, Linda, said that Nick didn't have many friends, if any, which is why I'm here. He does—or at least he used to—post on social media, but there wasn't much to go on."

Mr. Panfili lifted a finger to quiet her and then picked up his phone. "Hey, Adam, could you come to my office for a minute? Thank you."

He hung up. "Adam Masters is the one you should be talking to."

Before she could respond, there was a knock on Mr. Panfili's office door.

"Adam, this is Aria from the *Sacramento Independent*. She was wondering if Nick Calderon had any friends."

Aria noticed a look shared between them, a look she couldn't decipher. But as soon as Adam opened his mouth, the mystery was solved.

"Should I tell her the truth?" Adam asked Mr. Panfili.

"Nothing but," he answered, leaning back in his swivel chair.

Adam remained standing. "Nick Calderon was written up too many times to count. He has more complaints on record than every employee in this building put together. He was a troublemaker and a bully."

Aria lifted an eyebrow. Adam didn't beat around the bush. "And yet he wasn't fired?"

Again, Adam exchanged a look with Mr. Panfili, who simply nodded as if to say, "Go ahead and tell her."

"Let's say we were in the process of doing just that."

Aria let out a breath. *Wow.* "So it would be safe to say that Nick Calderon had few friends but plenty of enemies."

"People who might even wish him dead?" Adam asked. "Unquestionably."

Aria found his candor almost shocking, but still, yes, that's exactly what she was looking for. "Can you give me any names?"

After a quick glance at his boss, Adam smiled and said, "I shouldn't have been so flippant. It's just that Nick tended to rub people the wrong way."

When it became clear that no names would be forthcoming, Aria thanked both men for their time, and then Adam walked her out of Mr. Panfili's office and to the main exit.

Aria was walking across the parking lot when she heard someone calling out to her.

"Miss! Miss!"

Aria stopped and turned around. The woman was short and overweight, and she was winded by the time she caught up to Aria. "I heard you were here asking about Nick Calderon."

"That's right."

"Adam said he told you that Nick didn't have any friends."

Aria nodded.

"I thought I should tell you that he did have one friend."

Aria perked up at that.

"Long story short, it was Nick's birthday last month, and he made sure everyone knew it, telling everyone who passed by his desk that drinks were on him at a bar not too far from here. I knew nobody would go, and that made me sad."

"So you joined him?" Aria asked.

She snorted. "Yep. Despite all the warnings, I went. Big mistake. I met Nick's friend, Felix Iverson, and I wish I hadn't. He was one of the most unsavory characters I've ever met, and that's saying a lot."

Aria wrote down the name. "Anything else I should know?"

"No," she said, "not really. Just that I feel sort of bad for Nick. You could tell that he needed help but didn't know how to reach out or communicate with people. I think he had a lot of demons inside that head of his. You want to know what the worst of it is?"

Aria waited.

"When everyone in the office found out he'd been killed, I didn't see an ounce of sadness on anyone's face. I saw relief."

Chapter Fourteen

Bruce Ward held a cold bottle of beer in one hand and his cell phone in the other. Using his thumb, he hit call for the third time in a matter of minutes. His wife didn't pick up.

His recliner was so old it had a crater almost a foot deep. He set his beer on the side table and used both hands to push himself to his feet. He went to the kitchen where he poured himself a shot of whiskey. Staring out the window over the sink, he downed the whiskey as he watched a hawk dive toward the ground for a mole.

The mole got away. The hawk looked dazed.

Bruce returned to his recliner. He checked for any incoming texts or emails. Nada.

He rubbed his jaw. Every muscle in his body felt tense and sore. When Sandra got home, he'd make her give him a massage with a happy ending, of course. The thought of Sandra's warm fingers kneading his shoulders made him feel a little less tense.

A muted tinkling noise, like silverware clinking together, grabbed his attention and held tight. He turned down the volume on the TV, listened closely for a moment, then hauled his butt out of the chair. No small feat, considering he'd put on a few pounds over the past year.

The house was small. Two bedrooms. One bath. It took him under a minute to make the rounds. Nobody was there. He walked into the kitchen, opened the door leading into the garage, and peeked inside.

His old Buick was there. The car smelled like motor oil and dust. Despite the fact that the engine sounded like a dryer with shoes in it, he loved that car.

Back inside, he pulled his phone from his pocket, plopped down into his recliner, and checked for messages. There were none. He called Sandra, growing impatient as he waited for her voicemail. "If you need to talk, leave me a message." By the time the beep sounded, he was angrier than a caged tiger. "Where the hell are you? If you're not home in ten fucking minutes, I'm going to call your kid and tell him you're out whoring around again. Ten minutes, Sandra. I mean it."

The last time Sandra had been this late getting home from work was three years ago. Except, as it turned out, she hadn't been late at all. The bitch had thought she could just pack up and leave him without saying a word. He'd gone after her. Found her and dragged her ass home.

His heart began to race.

She wouldn't dare try that again.

Or would she?

He got up again. This time he marched into their bedroom and went straight to the closet. His heart pounded as he reached for a hanger and pushed her blouses, one at a time, to the side.

Her clothes were there.

Scratching his chest, he tried to remember what she'd been wearing when she said goodbye and drove off today. He stared into the closet as he replayed the morning in his head. Something wasn't right. They shared the closet. Usually the clothes were stuffed in there so tight it was a struggle finding a shirt. But not anymore.

Think, Bruce. Think.

Her favorite blouse was a brown-and-black print with a V-neck and wraparound tie. He pushed the blouses to the other side, one at a time, slowly. The brown-and-black blouse was gone. He turned and went to the dresser.

Most of her undergarments were missing. *Fucking bitch.* She'd thought she could leave just enough clothing behind to fool him. He looked at the clock on the nightstand. He knew she'd been at work today because he'd called her at her office right before her lunch break.

His job as a highway-maintenance operative kept him busy until five o'clock. Thanks to the boys talking him into stopping at Archie's for a beer, he hadn't gotten home until six thirty, which would have left Sandra with little time to pack her things and run off. Unless she'd already packed and he just hadn't noticed until now.

Every muscle in his body quivered.

And then it hit him all at once like a fucking brick straight to his gut.

She would have gone to Caroline's place.

He yanked his phone from his pocket, then changed his mind and put it back. It would be stupid for him to call. Caroline would warn Sandra and then call the cops on him. He needed to be smart. He needed to jump in his car and drive to Caroline's place on Old Creek Road. Surprise them both. This time, he'd let Caroline watch and learn what happened to anyone who tried to mess with something that belonged to him.

He slipped on his shoes, then went to the kitchen to grab the keys to the Buick from a hook near the sink. That's when he saw Trudy Carriger peering through her kitchen window, looking right at him. Nosy old bitch was always asking for favors. Said her eyesight was bad. But that was a crock of shit. Every week, he took out *her* garbage to avoid having to talk to her. Because if he didn't pull her receptacle to the street, she would trudge over on her skinny little legs, wearing the same old scraggly brown robe she always wore, and knock on his door. She didn't just ask the favor and leave him alone either. That would have been way too easy. She had to comment on what he was wearing, or tell him he looked tired, or ask about his health as her bug eyes roamed over his stomach.

He grabbed the keys to the Buick and headed for the garage. The bottle of whiskey sitting near the toaster called to him, but he ignored it.

As the seconds ticked by, his vision became clouded with rage at the thought of Sandra leaving him. He pushed open the garage door and stepped onto the cracked cement floor.

A shadowy movement in the far corner of the semidark room caught his eye. His gaze settled there for a moment and then roamed over his workbench with its rows of jars filled with washers and screws. Anger continued to bubble up inside him. Made his nostrils flare and his breath quicken. He couldn't remember a time, not one damn moment, when he hadn't been angry.

His entire life had been a shit show from the very beginning. At four years old, he was left with a dog collar around his neck and the leash slipped over the spoke of an iron fence. People he told the story to didn't believe he could possibly remember anything that happened at such a young age. But he did, and he would never forget trying to reach high enough to pull the leash from around the spoke. He also tried to remove the collar from his neck, but the harder he tried, the tighter it got, so he gave up and just stood in the cold for hours and hours until someone finally found him.

His mom could have left him anywhere, but she chose to leave him at the far end of a cemetery where the only sound was the howling wind. If he closed his eyes, he could still hear it, sounding like the cries of dead people, all contorted bones trapped beneath a block of cold stone, whimpering and moaning. An old man with a crooked back and a long, pointed nose found him and brought him to the hospital to be checked out.

Nurses and doctors kept asking what his name was. He told them Buddy. That's what he'd always been called. They wanted to know his dad's and mom's names too, but he'd never met his dad, and his mom was just "Mom." His picture was put in the paper, but it didn't help. For a while they called him the invisible boy.

A crunching noise like someone stepping on a wrapper snapped him back to reality. "Who's there?"

He stepped that way, straining to listen.

Something shot out from beneath the Buick and grabbed hold of his leg. He looked down and saw a hand clasped around his ankle.

He screamed, but it came out sounding like a squeak of a mouse as he tried to shake loose. A hard yank brought him to the ground. Desperate to get loose, he tried to jab the hand with the pointy end of his key, but it was no use. His shoe and sock were pulled right off his foot, and then he saw a needle stab into the flesh between his toes. He let out a string of expletives, and just like that, the hand disappeared. Afraid he might get stuck with another needle, he scooted back away from the car.

Bruce pushed himself to his feet and squinted into the semidarkness. "Come out here where I can see you."

The intruder appeared, standing near the back of the garage. It was a woman. On the tall side, slender, and dressed in jeans and a baggy sweatshirt, she stood near the trunk of the car. Her hair was black, cut straight at the shoulders. She wore red lipstick.

Shaking off a sudden bout of dizziness, Bruce reached for the shovel leaning against the wall nearby and knocked over a jar filled with nuts and bolts. Broken glass and screws scattered across the floor. He held the shovel in the air like a weapon. "Get on out of here before I kick your ass."

"Go ahead and try," the intruder said.

Was that a smirk on her face? "I don't know who the fuck you think you are, but you picked the wrong time to—"

"The name is Cockroach, and today is the last day of your sorry life."

"Cockroach?" Between the ages of four and ten, Bruce went from one foster home to another. No one wanted to keep him. They didn't like when he caught a beetle or a butterfly and ripped it apart. It was just a bug. What was the big deal? Tossing the cat in the pool had been the last straw. He finally ended up in a home for troubled kids. By his sixth birthday, the anger within had begun to churn and wouldn't stop. By the time he hit puberty, he was enraged. Every time he was yelled at, slapped across the face, or whipped with a belt, he turned his anger on a smaller kid. A kid named Cockroach. "Why are you here?"

"Why do you think?"

"You can't hurt me, dipshit. I'm bigger and stronger, and I'll flatten you like I should have done years ago. And then I'll put a hammer to your ugly face."

"You're already dying. It doesn't take much fentanyl to kill someone. You'll go to sleep and never wake up. Not a big deal. It's not like you make the world a better place. Sandra won't shed a tear for you. Nobody will. And what do you think the stepson you treated like garbage will do when he learns of your death?" A pause. "I think he'll smile."

Bruce stumbled and dropped his keys. The shovel fell to the floor. He reached for his car to stop himself from falling. His other hand went to his throat. Every breath was a struggle. Wet foam dribbled from the corners of his mouth as his substantial weight caused his legs to give out. He dropped to his knees and then fell backward, his head cracking against the cement.

A few seconds later, he felt Cockroach pulling him by his feet, dragging his body toward the front of his car. His arms and legs were useless. Cockroach tried to lift him into the front seat, but his deadweight was too much. She gave up and dragged him toward the back, then turned his head so that his face was inches from the tailpipe.

Bruce closed his eyes for a moment. When he opened them, he could hear the familiar knocking of his Buick's engine as fumes spewed into his eyes and nose.

"Sandra should be back in a few days. I used your new credit card I found in your mailbox to send her flowers, along with a note to her office, letting her know that reservations had been made at the Spa Solage in Calistoga. She should be enjoying a deep muscle massage as we speak."

Footsteps sounded. The door leading to the kitchen opened and closed.

Sandra hadn't left him.

Bruce should have been glad to know the truth, but he wasn't. It only made him angrier.

He coughed, gagging on his saliva.

The bitch didn't deserve a day at the spa. If she had been home where she belonged, none of this would have happened.

Chapter Fifteen

After work, Aria drove to Stockton and parked next to a cemetery across the street from Christina Farro's apartment building. If she was one of the Black Wigs, maybe she would drive to a secret headquarters or meet with one of her team players for coffee.

While keeping an eye on the door to the apartment, hoping Farro would go somewhere so Aria could follow, she opened her laptop, figuring she could multitask. She wanted to search matchmaking sites to see if she could find the woman Brad Vicente had mentioned, a woman named Li.

Aria was glad to have something to keep her mind engaged because for some odd reason she couldn't stop thinking about Corey Moran.

It boggled the mind.

Not once since leaving her hometown of River Rock after being subjected to her uncle Theo's sick perversions had she ever imagined that she would develop any sort of relationship with a man, intimate or otherwise. But something about Corey Moran had flipped a switch inside her, made her want to get to know him better. It was the strangest thing that had ever happened to her.

Feeling the need to tell someone, she grabbed her cell phone and called Sawyer.

"Hey," Sawyer said.

"Hi. Is this a good time?"

"Derek is picking me up for dinner, but I have a few minutes. What's going on?"

"I met a guy. Average height, boyish, midthirties, I'm guessing."

"Okay . . . and—"

"And he found a dog on the street and brought it to the shelter. No pets are allowed where he's living, otherwise he probably would have kept the animal until someone posted a flyer."

"I'm not sure where you're going with this," Sawyer said.

"I have his name, address, and phone number. It's part of the procedure at the shelter when someone brings in an animal." She drew in a breath. "Do you think I should call him?"

"What?"

"Do you think I should give the guy a call?" Aria repeated.

"Why?"

"I thought maybe I'd ask him out for coffee."

"I thought you didn't like people?"

"I don't," Aria said. "But what am I supposed to do? They're everywhere."

Sawyer laughed.

"I can't explain this connection I felt, but I was definitely intrigued by him."

"I know exactly why he intrigued you," Sawyer said.

"You do?"

"Yes. He brought in a lost dog. You probably had an instant connection with the dog and therefore transferred that awareness to the man at the other end of the leash."

"Ha! Very funny."

"If you're serious about calling him, give me his name and address and let me check him out first."

"Check him out?"

"Yes. See if he's married or has a record," Sawyer said.

"I don't really think that's necessary," she said, then quickly thought better of it. "How long would that take?"

"Not long."

"Okay." She gave Sawyer all the information she had on Corey Moran, which wasn't much.

"I'll get back to you."

"How about on Sunday when you come to the house to take Lennon for a driving lesson?" Aria asked, inwardly scolding herself for being overly eager.

"Perfect. We'll talk then."

After Aria hung up, she realized she'd forgotten to tell Sawyer where she was or about her conversation with Mr. Panfili, the guy named Adam, and Nick's one friend, Felix Iverson.

She might have called her sister back if she hadn't glanced up and seen Christina Farro walking straight for her. Not really walking—marching. She wore jeans and a tank top. Aria saw well-defined arms, muscles flexing under the fading light. Her mouth was turned down. Her eyes slightly narrowed. There was no doubt she was angry, but what Aria wanted to know was how did the woman know she'd been watching her?

Aria didn't bother rolling up her window. The woman was intimidating to look at, bordering on scary, but dangerous?

Christina Farro leaned low and rested both elbows on the window frame so that their noses were only inches from touching. "What are you doing here?"

Aria's stomach rolled. She wished more than anything she had turned on the engine and taken off the second she saw the woman coming her way. But something told her Christina Farro would have jumped on top of her car and found a way to stop her. "Er, um, I was going to visit a grave—an old friend is buried here."

"What's your friend's name?"

"Um, Cyndi Lauper."

Christina Farro sighed. "The one who sings 'Girls Just Wanna Have Fun'?"

Sweat dripped down Aria's spine. Maybe she wasn't cut out for this line of work, after all.

"Let's start over," Christina Farro said. "Did your sister send you?"

"My sister?"

"Okay, I'm going to give it to you straight. Your sister, Sawyer Brooks, came to see me. I answered her questions, and I figured that would be the end of it. But then I see you, Aria Brooks, sitting in a car for the past thirty minutes, staring at the apartment building where I live. So I want to know why you're watching me."

"For the record," Aria said, "Sawyer doesn't know I'm here." The woman's anger, Aria noticed, seemed to simmer, coming off her in waves. If she was a part of the Black Wigs, there was no telling what she was capable of, and worse, what she would do to Aria if she said the wrong thing. Aria decided to tell her the truth. It felt like the safest route. "Brad Vicente said one of the Black Wigs had scars all over her body, mostly her neck—" Aria's gaze fixated on a scar above Christina's collarbone.

"Ah, so you came to . . . what? Ask me a few questions?"

"To follow you," Aria said. "If you were involved with the Black Wigs, I thought you might go to meet the others at a secret location."

"Like a bat cave?"

"Sort of," Aria said under her breath. If this woman didn't pull her out of the car and beat the shit out of her, Sawyer would do the honors when she found out what Aria had done.

Christina Farro unfolded herself from Aria's car window. She stood tall and raised her arms high over her head as if to get the kinks out. Then she was back in her face. "I know all about you and your sisters. I know about your dad and Uncle Theo and all the other creepers hiding out in the woods where you came from. I know you shot your own mother—"

Jesus. The woman knew more about Aria and her family than Aria knew about her. It was unsettling. "I had no choice," Aria said in her own defense. "My mom was going to kill my sister."

"I get it," Christina said. "Sometimes we do what we have to do to set things straight in the world, which is why I have to tell you, warn you, that if you and your sister don't stop snooping around, you're going to regret it."

"So you are a Black Wig?"

Christina Farro laughed. Not a tinkling sound, but low and menacing. "I'm just a girl who's trying to find her way through life. Just like you." She smiled. "Now get going, Aria, unless you want to take a little walk with me through the cemetery to see if we can find Cyndi."

She didn't need to be told twice. Aria turned on the engine. As soon as Christina Farro straightened and took a step back, she put on the gas and drove off. Every part of her was trembling. When she looked into the rearview mirror, Christina Farro was gone.

Nobody could convince Aria that Christina Farro wasn't a member of the vigilante group known as the Black Wigs. She might even be the leader. At such a close view, Aria had seen the woman's jaw clench and her face flush. Not only was she dangerous, she was lethal.

Chapter Sixteen

Sawyer and Derek sat at a table for two by a window overlooking Sixteenth Street. Mikuni's, a Japanese restaurant and sushi bar, was buzzing, servers running back and forth, trying to keep up. "No more talk about work," Sawyer said after they had both filled each other in on their day.

"All right. What do you want to talk about?"

"Sex."

His face flushed as he glanced at the couple sitting nearby.

"My therapist thought it would be a good idea for us to talk about it since it's been on my mind."

"You've been seeing a therapist?"

"After everything that happened over the past few months, I thought it would be a good idea to get it all out of my system. Talking to an unbiased third party is a good outlet for me. No judgment. I think of it as self-care for my mental health."

"No judgment here if you ever want to talk to me."

She angled her head. Derek's wife had been in a car accident three years ago. She'd died instantly. "The therapist said you might not be interested in taking our relationship to the next level because you could still be dealing with your loss—you know—trying to figure things out."

Their food was brought to the table.

"What do you think?" Sawyer asked after the server left.

"Did you talk to your therapist about my trauma, or yours?"

"Both, I guess. If we're a couple, that means they're sort of connected."

He unwrapped his chopsticks and then set them aside, keeping his gaze on hers.

"What?" she asked.

"I'm trying to wrap my mind around you talking to your therapist about our sex life."

Sawyer leaned forward, her voice low. "We don't have a sex life. That's the point." Sawyer mixed some wasabi and soy sauce in a tiny dish. "That particular session with the therapist did leave me with more questions than answers."

"About me?"

She nodded.

"Like?"

"Like what it might be like to lose a spouse, someone you loved and were fully committed to. It must be difficult to put yourself out there, knowing you'll never find someone quite like the woman you lost. No one you date will ever have the same characteristics or interests."

"I'm not trying to find anyone like Lisa," Derek said. "She's gone. I wish she wasn't, but those are the cards I've been dealt. You're not anything like Lisa. The opposite in many ways."

Sawyer wondered what that meant. She didn't know Lisa. Had never met her before the car accident.

"If it's okay with you," Derek said, "I'd rather discuss our nonexistent sex life." He picked up his chopsticks and used them to dip a bite of sushi into the sauce before popping it into his mouth.

She tried to do the same, but the chopsticks were not cooperating. Finally, she set them down and used her fingers.

"The truth is," Derek explained, "I'm not sure it's a good idea for us to rush things. Like you said, you've been through a lot recently. When we make love—"

She liked the sound of that.

"—we should be sure we're ready to take the next step."

"I agree," she said. "As long as there are no rules or guidelines—no sex until the third date. That sort of thing drives me nuts."

"I haven't been back in the game long enough to pretend to know anything about rules."

She chewed and swallowed. "Perfect. Because I'd prefer to go into this knowing there aren't any."

"Deal."

They continued to eat. Sawyer snuck glances at him. She liked his face. The color of his eyes, a cross between gray and blue, thick eyebrows, just the right amount of fashionable bristle on his jaw.

He looked up. Saw her staring. "What?"

"Nothing," she said with a shrug. "Just admiring my date."

He took a moment to do the same. Heat rose up her neck as his gaze settled on her mouth.

"Stop," she said, smiling.

"You're a beautiful woman, Sawyer Brooks."

"I'm a lot of things, but beautiful isn't one of them." As soon as the words escaped, she regretted them. She'd never been good at receiving compliments, but that was one of a list of things she was working on. She was prone to swat away compliments like gnats and yet hang tight to the one negative comment said to her years ago. A therapist, not Jane, once told her she had low self-esteem. *You think?* If she believed she sucked, how was she supposed to believe someone else when they told her she didn't? As she debated how to respond, Derek made it easy for her by simply letting it go.

"What do you think about coming with me to a family barbecue at my parents' house?" he asked, changing the subject like a pro. "The family is excited to meet you."

All the good tingly feels left her body.

"Too soon?" he asked.

"Why do you say that?"

"You're as white as my napkin."

She fidgeted in her seat. "It's just that I don't do well around large crowds. And in this case, we both know I would be the object of a lot of curiosity."

"I can't argue with that."

She shoved a piece of sushi roll into her mouth, chewed, and then washed it down with water. "Are they huggers?"

"My family? No."

Her eyes narrowed.

"Okay, maybe Mom would be considered a hugger, but Dad, not so much."

He offered her the last of a sushi roll and finished it off when she declined. "I can warn them off. Tell them you have poison oak or something so they don't touch you." He chuckled.

"God. No. I don't want them to think I'm a stressed-out woman whose anxiety is so off the charts that she can't even meet her boyfriend's family."

His gray eyes sparkled. "So I am your boyfriend."

Heat rushed to her cheeks.

He reached across the table for her hand. "It's been so damn long since I've had a girlfriend. I feel like I'm back in junior high and I should officially ask you to be my girl."

She laughed. "Is that how it worked way back then?"

"Hey," he said with a smile. "It wasn't that long ago. But, yeah, that's basically how it worked. I would ask a girl to be my girlfriend, she would say yes, and then two days later I would get a message on the computer at home, usually from her friend, telling me she liked someone else."

"How many girls did you ask?"

"Lots. Too many to count." His smile was infectious. "How about you? I bet the boys lined up to talk to you between classes."

She didn't want to think about what was going on in her life when she was thirteen or fourteen. "I was shy," she told him. "I kept to myself."

"Lucky you. Getting dumped over and over again is definitely not for the faint of heart."

She shook her head in wonder. "Who would ever dump you?"

"Mindy Waxer, Charlene Finnigan, Deb Shady . . . the list goes on."

She chuckled. "Sounds horrible. How does anyone ever know when they have found 'the one'?"

"Easy," he said without hesitation. "There are basically five stages to every relationship. It starts with attraction, you know, when all those endorphins are working overtime. And then reality hits, which means both people might see flaws in the other but they're on a high and so nothing seems so bad but they know the highs can't last forever, so it's worrisome. And then comes disappointment."

Sawyer frowned.

"The dreaded first argument. Conflict isn't fun, so you begin to doubt what the two of you share." He was still holding on to her hand, and he gave it a squeeze. "But if you can hang tight and make it through the disappointment stage, you can move on to stability. Stability can be a lot of hard work. But don't worry. It can also be fun. You just have to be willing to make the effort to spice things up."

"Hmm."

"Yeah, hmm. You might get bored because the chase is over. You no longer gaze at my face overly long because you've seen it a zillion times and it's the same face you saw yesterday and the day before that."

"So how do people get through the bored stage?"

"It's not easy. If there's still a spark, it's not easily ignited. The romance is gone. I might stop shaving or brushing my hair before you come over"—he shook his head—"that won't happen, but I'm just trying to throw out examples of what could happen."

"I see. Sounds horrible."

He smiled. "It is. But it's also wonderful because if you make it that far, something deeper awaits you. If you choose to be with this person, with all their flaws mingled together with all your flaws, communication is key. And compromise. It can't work without communication and compromise."

She thought of Harper and Nate. Her sister and brother-in-law had made being a loving couple look so easy and doable. But then everything seemed to have imploded—all at once, in the blink of an eye. "It doesn't sound like any fun at all."

"It's magnificent. Trust me."

She wanted to do just that. She wanted to trust him.

It was dark by the time Derek pulled up to the curb outside Sawyer's apartment, set on the bottom floor of the building. Raccoon sat on the windowsill, looking out at her, judging. Always judging.

They both got out of the car and walked hand in hand to her door. As she reached inside her purse for her key, she looked up at him. "I had a great time."

"Me too." He was looking at her again, giving her that jittery feeling in her stomach. It was an odd feeling, unfamiliar. She wasn't sure whether or not she liked it. Mostly because she didn't know what it meant. Not really. "When do I need to let you know about Sunday?"

"Not this Sunday," he said, "but next. You can let me know anytime. And don't worry, I won't let them cross-examine you."

She smiled, pretending she wasn't worried at all.

He leaned down to kiss her, his eyes intense, smoldering—or maybe she was imagining it—but his gaze was more of a caress than it was anything else. His lips touched hers. Warm, inviting lips that heated her insides and rushed through her body like a wildfire.

No sparks needed to set off this fire.

She wanted him. Every bit of him. Crazy that she'd never felt anything like it before. Not ever. She'd grown up wary and distrustful of the opposite sex. Her last boyfriend, Connor, had been nothing more than an experiment. She'd never felt even a flicker of what she was experiencing at the moment.

Derek was no experiment.

There was no putting out the wildfire consuming her. Her only thought was to get him inside so she could drag him to the bedroom and strip off his clothes. She liked to be in control, so she imagined him on the bed, climbing on top of him, and—

Honk.

She ignored it. They both did.

That quickly, the kiss had grown into much more than a kiss. With their bodies pressed close, his hand at the back of her head, keeping her steady, the kiss had become all-consuming, bordering on reckless.

She wanted more.

So did he. She could sense it. Hell, she could feel it.

Honk! Honk!

He pulled away first.

They both looked to the street, at the source of the blasting horn.

Sawyer narrowed her eyes. It was a white BMW. Lexi Holmes was at the wheel. The passenger window was rolled down, and Lexi was frantically waving her over. "A possible murder linked to the Black Wigs," Lexi said loud enough for the neighbors to hear. "We have to hurry."

Sawyer looked from Lexi to Derek.

"Go," he said, nudging her along.

"But—"

"No buts—we have all the time in the world."

How could he be sure? He knew better than most that the world didn't work that way. Hadn't past experiences taught Derek to grab on to the good and hold on tight?

Sawyer hopped into the passenger side of Lexi's car, buckled her belt, and hardly had a chance to wave at Derek before they drove off.

"You're seeing Derek Coleman?"

Sawyer looked at Lexi. "No, we just like making out every once in a while for fun."

Lexi's smile wasn't genuine; there was nothing in her eyes. It was a "You're cute" or "Nice try" sort of smile. "Good for you," she said into the silence.

"What do you mean?"

"After his wife died, there wasn't a female within a ten-mile radius of that man who didn't go after him. Baked goods left in his office, homemade dinners brought to his doorstep, pictures of women in negligees sent via email and text."

How would Lexi know what was sent over his cell phone? Sawyer wondered, but didn't ask.

"But Derek wasn't interested," Lexi said. "He didn't bat an eyelash. Just kept to himself. Put all his energy into his work. He was in robot mode, and he had blinders on. I should know. I was more patient than most. I waited a year before trying a few of my best moves on him. I also sent a text or two, along with a photo."

Sawyer lifted an eyebrow.

"I'm only six years older than him. Anyway, I wasn't offended by his noninterest. I used to be friends with his wife. So I understood."

"Understood what?"

"That the woman he'd lost was a natural phenomenon that doesn't come around often. You know, like fire rainbows—a painting in the sky that's not caused by fire or rain. Or the blood falls in Antarctica, or seventeen-year cicadas." She looked at Sawyer. "Google it. Anyway, you get my drift."

"I do. She was one of a kind," Sawyer said.

"Exactly. And she was beautiful, smart, and kind. But somehow you managed to catch his eye."

"He's just a man," Sawyer said, refusing to be offended. "He puts on his pants like every other male."

This time Lexi's laugh was real.

Sawyer looked her way. "Are you ever going to fill me in on where we're going, or are you more interested in my personal life?"

Chapter Seventeen

It took only twenty-four minutes to get to Fallview Way in El Dorado Hills. Sawyer figured it would have taken most people longer, but Lexi was an aggressive driver with a lead foot.

She pulled over a block away from the house where emergency vehicles with flashing red lights were parked. They climbed out of the car and walked together toward the one-story home with its low-maintenance landscape—a tiny square of lawn, a few decorative rocks, and a row of nondescript greenery. The garage was open. Yellow crime tape had yet to be secured around the scene. The reason could have something to do with what Lexi had told her on the drive from Sacramento. Apparently the first uniformed officer to arrive on the scene had called in a 10-56, a suicide. That was before an elderly neighbor told the officer about the person she saw wearing a black wig, leaving Bruce Ward's home. That bit of news changed everything, and a detective in the El Dorado Hills CSI Unit was called in.

Lexi gestured toward a man Sawyer didn't know or recognize. "That's John Hughes, detective with the El Dorado County Sheriff's Office," Lexi said. "I've known John for years. He's the reason we're here. He trusts me."

Standing next to John Hughes was Detective Perez. Sawyer was surprised to see him but knew she shouldn't be. Although El Dorado Hills wasn't his jurisdiction, it was in the detectives' best interests to work together and share information to see whether there was any connection to the Black Wigs.

Bruce Ward. The name sounded familiar. She wished she had her files with her. The past few days had been a whirlwind of activity, and her mind was spinning.

The detectives were standing just outside the open garage. It was dark now and outside lights were being set up. Inside the garage behind the two men, Sawyer could see an old Buick and a body near the tailpipe. A woman wearing a lab coat hovered close to the deceased.

Detective John Hughes, average in height and wearing a rumpled suit, was gray-haired and shaggy-faced. The smile that spread across his face when he saw Lexi lit up his eyes. Most detectives Sawyer had met since working at the *Sacramento Independent* had serious expressions permanently etched across their faces.

Introductions were made. Sawyer shook hands with Detective Hughes, then said hello to Detective Perez.

He tilted his chin in greeting but didn't look pleased to see her there.

Lexi stepped to her left to get a better view of the dead man. "Suicide or homicide?"

"Too soon to say," Detective Hughes said. "We certainly haven't ruled out the possibility of either."

"Is it true someone wearing a black wig was seen leaving the premises?" Lexi asked.

Detective Hughes nodded. "Correct. The witness lives across the street. She's getting up there in age, so I'm not sure how reliable she is." He looked at Sawyer. "I was told you've been working on the Black Wigs story for a while now. What are your thoughts?"

Caught off guard, it took Sawyer a second to pull herself together. "It's true. I have been researching and writing about the Black Wigs for months now. Something that stands out is that the vigilantes work as a team. Lexi and I interviewed Brad Vicente at the prison earlier today, and he confirmed this when he said four or five women were in his house for days. In the case of Myles Davenport, the man attending his ten-year reunion, the video shows multiple women wearing identical wigs as they take Myles Davenport captive."

Detective Hughes rocked back on his heels. "What about Nick Calderon's murder? Do you believe that was the work of the Black Wigs?"

"No," Sawyer said. "I don't. Just like this case, it seems only one person was seen coming and going on the security camera." She shrugged. "But I'm not a detective, and my opinion is based on what little I've been told."

"Anything else?" Detective Perez asked, sarcasm lining his voice.

His attitude grated on her nerves. "Yes," Sawyer said. "I guess there is something else. The Black Wigs abduct their targets and take them to a secret destination."

"Not true in the case of Brad Vicente," Lexi said smugly. "He was bound and tortured for days inside his own home."

"True," Sawyer said, wondering why Lexi would bring her along and then try to undermine her.

"Even the best-laid plans can go awry," Detective Hughes said.

Sawyer smiled at the detective. "Exactly. Instead of abducting Brad Vicente, something might have gone wrong, which set the Black Wigs' Plan B into motion."

Detective Hughes nodded. "The woman's teammates, or whatever you want to call them, could have been watching and waiting. They followed him home, rescued their friend, and decided it was too risky to move Brad Vicente from his residence."

"That's an interesting theory," Detective Perez said.

"All of this is just conjecture at this point," Lexi chimed in.

Detective Perez rubbed the back of his neck. "Maybe the Black Wigs are still tweaking their MO as they go along. Maybe they've decided it's more efficient to work independently."

Lexi nodded her agreement. "The only victim we know for sure who was actually abducted—as seen on video outside the high school—was Myles Davenport. Days later, he was found dead in the woods near Barrett Pass Road."

Sawyer stepped to the side to make room for a tech who was using barricade tape to establish the perimeter of the crime scene.

A young man in his twenties with a camera hanging around his neck called out to Detective Hughes, letting him know he was finished unless there were additional shots needed. Detective Hughes took the photographer to the side to discuss.

Once Detective Hughes walked away, Sawyer had a good view of the medical examiner hovering over the body lying on the cement floor next to the Buick's rusty tailpipe. She walked closer and watched the ME pull a plastic bag from her box of goodies and use a pair of tweezers to collect evidence from the man's pale, bloated face.

"Is that a strand of hair?" Sawyer asked.

Before the ME could say a word, Detective Perez came up to stand beside her and told her it was time for her and Lexi to leave.

Sawyer noticed broken glass, nuts and bolts, and a shovel on the ground near the path where someone might enter the garage from the house. There was also a shoe and a sock, tossed aside haphazardly. She glanced at the dead man's feet and saw that he wore only one shoe. Just like Nick Calderon. Her heart rate elevated. "Why is he wearing only one shoe?"

The detective followed her gaze. "Let's leave the questions to the examiner and investigators."

She looked at him then. Really looked at him. Although she'd proven time and time again that she was on his side, he didn't like her, and she really didn't understand why. Annoyed, she made sure to hold in her anger. "Whatever happened to Otto Radley?" she asked in a random moment of bravado.

"Nobody knows," he said. "He could be anywhere."

Not true, she thought. Then she straightened and said, "Before Sean Palmer was injured, he gave me a flash drive with a clip of home video taken outside an apartment at night. The images show a dark, shadowy man who looks a lot like Otto Radley approaching a woman sitting on a park bench. She could be wearing a wig. Before the video ends, another woman with the same short black hair appears, and they all appear to be wrestling on the ground."

"Where is the video now?"

"I brought it to a digital enhancement shop, hoping they could enhance the video."

Detective Perez did not look happy with her. She wasn't sure she cared, and yet she scolded herself for letting him get to her. *Two steps forward and ten steps backward,* Sawyer thought.

"How long have you had this video in your possession?"

"About as long as you've had it."

"I'm not following."

"I brought the original flash drive to the station ten days ago. You weren't there, so I left it with the person at the front desk." *There,* she thought. *Chew on that.* "I know you're busy, but if you do get a chance to look at it, you'll see the video appears to have been taken at night from an upper-story apartment in West Sacramento. It's grainy, shadowy, but when a big guy like Otto Radley makes an appearance, he's hard to miss."

Detective Hughes returned to tell Detective Perez he was heading inside the house.

Lexi had just finished talking to the ME when she asked Detective Hughes if it would be all right if they talked to a few neighbors before they took off.

"Absolutely," he said, prompting Detective Perez to release a heavy sigh. "I've already talked to the closest neighbors, including the witness, Trudy Carriger, across the street." Detective Hughes pointed at the blue-gray house with the white trim. "She's getting up there in age, most likely doesn't see well since she thought I looked like a shorter George Clooney, but she's all we've got. If it'll help you with your story, then have at it."

Both Detective Hughes and Perez headed for the front entry.

Sawyer watched them go. She liked Detective Hughes. He seemed reasonable and helpful and kind. Detective Perez, on the other hand, had a major chip on his shoulder. She was about to tell Lexi about the missing shoe and sock on both Nick Calderon and Bruce Ward, but decided against it when Lexi attacked her.

"What were you thinking back there?" Lexi asked as they walked to the end of the driveway. "When they ask for your opinion, they don't really want it. It's not professional."

Sawyer chuckled. "Detective Hughes asked me for my opinion, and I gave it to him. Nothing wrong with that."

"We're supposed to blend in with scenery, do our best to stay out of their way."

Sawyer stopped walking. "I don't appreciate being lectured. You and the others wanted nothing to do with this story, but I agreed to let you help out. If you don't like the way I interact with people, then we have a problem. Maybe it would be in your best interest to get out now before I bring you down with me."

Lexi drew in a long breath. "I'll take this side of the street," she said, pointing to her left. "You take the other side."

"Sure."

No sooner had Lexi walked off and Sawyer crossed the road than she heard someone hissing at her. It took Sawyer a second to see an elderly woman peeking her head through the front door of the blue-gray house with white trim. Trudy Carriger, the witness Detective Hughes had mentioned, used one frail hand to gesture for Sawyer to come her way.

"What can I help you with?" Sawyer asked.

"I've been watching you people from my kitchen window. Are you the journalist from Sacramento . . . The one who found that poor little girl?"

"Sawyer Brooks. Nice to meet you."

"Trudy Carriger," the woman said, offering a thin-skinned hand mottled with brown spots. "I'm the one who called the police to check on Bruce."

"How did you know to call?"

"Come on in out of the cold, and I'll warm you up with some tea and tell you what happened. Maybe you could mention my name in the paper."

Although it was a balmy night with clear skies and Sawyer wasn't cold, she said, "I would love some tea." Inside, the smell of cinnamon and apple pie wafted through the well-kept house.

Trudy Carriger ushered her to a couch with a blue floral design. Sawyer took a seat and hardly had time to absorb all the little knick-knacks spread across every tabletop before Trudy returned with a silver tray. Her hand shook, making the porcelain rattle as she handed Sawyer a vintage, teal-blue teacup and saucer.

"I hope you like hibiscus tea. I sprinkled a little ginger on top."

"Smells wonderful. If you don't mind, we'll need to get right down to business." Sawyer sipped her tea, told Trudy it was delicious, then pulled out a notebook and pen.

The woman sat in a simple straight-backed chair across from her and looked at Sawyer expectantly.

"Detective Hughes said he already talked to you. Are you sure this won't be too much in one day?"

"Not at all. I don't get many visitors."

Ah. The woman was lonely. "According to Detective Hughes, you witnessed someone leaving Bruce Ward's house. Do you remember the time?"

"Hmm. I know Bruce's wife, Sandra, came home a little before five p.m. About forty-five minutes later, she was walking out of the house carrying an overnight bag and her purse when she climbed into her car and drove off."

"Any chance you know where she was going?"

"No idea."

"Did you see the person with the wig arrive after that?"

"No. Bruce Ward was dropped off by a coworker at six thirty. Bruce is a highway maintenance operator. He and Sandra only have one dependable car, so his friends take turns driving Bruce around."

Writing as fast as she could, Sawyer wondered if the woman stared out her kitchen window all day long. "And then you saw someone wearing a wig leave Bruce Ward's house?"

"Not until seven fifteen. I was washing dishes when I saw someone push through the side gate."

"Can you describe this person?"

"He wore—"

"He?"

She nodded. "It was a man."

Sawyer's eyes widened and her heart skipped a beat. "Are you sure?"

"Well, I wouldn't bet my life on it." She entwined her fingers nervously. "He didn't walk like a woman."

Sawyer's tiny bubble of excitement burst. "How does a woman walk?"

"You know . . . with a sway in the hips."

Sawyer clamped down on her disappointment. The woman was clearly confused. Just as Detective Hughes had said, she was getting up there in age. No reason to press her. She could always revisit the gender later. People she interviewed usually tired of questions quickly, and she wanted to keep it moving. "How tall would you say the intruder was?"

Trudy pursed her lips and squinted her eyes as if that might help her remember. Sawyer stood and walked over to a bookshelf and pointed at the highest shelf. "That tall?"

"Shorter than that."

Sawyer pointed to the next lowest shelf. "How about this tall?"

Trudy shook her head. "I would say he was two shelves taller than you." She clicked her tongue. "Maybe only one shelf taller than you."

"Okay. Good. Somewhere between five foot eight inches and five foot ten." Sawyer returned to the couch. "Are you sure this person was wearing a wig?"

"Absolutely. It was crooked. I could see lighter hair sticking out from the sides."

"Blond or light-brown hair underneath?"

"Light brown . . . the color of wheat."

"Perfect."

"It looked to me like the wig was slipped on in a rush," Trudy went on. "My friend Helen wears a wig, and she never gets it on straight." Trudy used her hands to try to mimic how his hair looked. Finally, she picked up her napkin and placed it lopsided on her head.

Sawyer smiled. The old lady was cute and sweet and kind, like her grandmother. "Other than the walk, did you notice anything else unusual?"

Trudy seemed to ponder the question a moment before saying, "There was something—maybe a dragon—fire—there were flames on the front of his T-shirt."

"You think it was a dragon?" Sawyer made another note.

"I'm not sure about the dragon. But the design looked like reddish-orange flames."

"Okay. You're doing great. Did this person climb into a car and drive away?"

"No. He just came out of the gate and walked away, keeping to the sidewalk."

"And that's when you called the police?"

Wide-eyed, she said, "I wish I had. But I didn't. I figured he was a friend of Bruce's and maybe they were working on his old car that he won't let Sandra get rid of."

"So what made you call the police?"

"Tomorrow is garbage day."

"Tomorrow is Saturday," Sawyer pointed out.

"Tomorrow is a special garbage day when they pick up bulk trash. Stuff that won't fit into the regular bin. I knew Bruce had a lot of trash in his backyard, and I didn't want him to miss the opportunity to get rid of the old tires and mattress he has back there. Sandra is always trying to get him to clean up the place, so I went to knock on the door, but before I got that far I heard a loud noise coming from inside his garage. It was a car engine. I went through the side gate and tried opening the door to the garage, but it was locked. After that, I went and knocked on the front door. I even rang the bell, but nobody answered so I came back here and called the police. It was almost eight p.m. by then."

Trudy's face fell.

"It's okay. You did the right thing. Nobody could have saved him."

"Oh, I'm not worried about Bruce. Sandra will be glad he's gone. I was just thinking how I wish I could get someone to haul all that junk from his backyard to the street before it's too late."

Sawyer tried not to show her surprise since she wanted the woman to keep talking. "Sandra and Bruce don't get along?"

"He pushed her around once and bruised her good. She ran over here, and I called the police. That was a few years ago. She said she was going to leave him, but I think she was scared and had nowhere to go. I offered her a room, but she said it would only make things worse."

"Any chance Sandra could have been the one wearing the wig?"

"Not a chance. I may be old, but I'm not dead and I'm certainly not blind. I've known Sandra for years. I know what she looks like. Besides, Sandra is short. I'd be surprised if she hit five foot two."

"So you have Sandra's phone number?"

Trudy nodded.

After gathering Sandra's work and cell number along with Trudy's home phone number, Sawyer thanked her and headed outside just as Lexi was making her way back.

"Were you just at the witness's house?" Lexi asked.

Sawyer nodded. "She wanted to talk, so I let her. I'll give you a copy of my notes."

"No need. I'll get a full report from Detective Hughes."

"What is wrong with you?" Sawyer asked. "Have I offended you in some way?"

Lexi headed for her car.

Sawyer stayed close on her heels.

"You just do whatever you want, and somehow it always works out for you, doesn't it?"

"I follow my instincts, if that's what you mean."

After they climbed in and buckled up, Lexi said, "I didn't have to bring you along tonight, but I did."

"Thank you."

Lexi was a tough nut to crack. Passive aggressive at times. Helpful at times, and yet angry and resentful. The best thing Sawyer could do would be not to overreact. The drive home was spent in silence.

Chapter Eighteen

Early Saturday morning, Cleo paid the Lyft driver and then jumped out of the car and shut the door. As she made her way to the coffee shop on the corner, she found it strange that she wasn't feeling nervous. She'd waited so long for this day to come, and it was finally here. It was her turn. Today was the day she would make Eddie Carter beg for his life.

Cleo ordered a mocha with oat milk. Ten minutes later, she tossed out her empty Styrofoam cup, slipped her arms through the straps of her backpack, and walked two blocks to the twenty-four-hour gym. As she passed by the blue MINI Cooper parked on the side of the road, she saw Psycho behind the wheel, ready to go. She tipped her chin as she passed by. It was good to know she had backup in case anything went wrong.

Eddie Carter's charcoal-gray Ford Escape was parked beneath a tall oak with branches that spread out like a giant umbrella. With an abundance of confidence, she walked over to the vehicle and reached for the handle, surprised when the back door came right open. Nice. No need to use the nifty tools she'd bought to break in.

She climbed into the car, shut the door, then hunkered down behind the driver's seat. Her small size made it easy to get comfortable. She was wearing a baseball cap over the black wig and large polarized sunglasses instead of a mask. If Eddie decided to throw his gym bag in the back seat, she could have a problem. But she would deal with that when the time came.

Crouched low, her Glock 43X loaded, she was ready to go.

She'd thought about bringing Eddie to her apartment, where she could strap him to her husband's favorite chair and use him as a dartboard. Fifty points for hitting him square in the forehead, twenty-five points per eyeball. Ten points for everything else.

Her heart no longer galloped inside her chest. Her adrenaline should be off the charts, but it wasn't. Maybe because she no longer had anything to live for.

Her husband had finally gone through with his threat and taken the kids and left her. Understandable, considering the hell she'd put her family through. Most days, she couldn't find the energy to get out of bed. When her husband found her searching the internet for ways to end her life, she hadn't understood why he'd made such a big deal about it. She thought everybody googled that shit. Apparently not.

She'd spent a hot second thinking about reaching out to her therapist. But ultimately decided against it. She already knew the drill. Her therapist would tell her she had PTSD and was going through a major depressive episode, and reaching out meant she wanted to live.

That was the part that had Cleo stumped. Sort of.

Why wasn't she reaching out? Did she really want to die?

She could call her mother or father. No. They had been through way too much to be bothered. Let them live in peace. They had been outraged after Cleo's ordeal at the fraternity. They'd mortgaged their home to pay for an attorney and stood by her throughout the long process to get to trial. But after listening day after day to all those clean-cut boys in their perfectly fitted suits and ties, telling the jury outrageous lies about Cleo, she'd seen her parents age right before her eyes. Her parents had looked distressed and scared. They'd been emotionally exhausted by the time it was over.

The truth was, Cleo did like boys back then. But contrary to popular belief, when multiple boys at that fraternity house had raped her, she'd been a virgin. Her decision not to have sex prior to that time hadn't had anything to do with religion or her parents' teachings. It was a choice she'd made due to the fact that she'd always been a romantic, a happy, carefree romantic, who'd wanted to find that one special man and spend the rest of her life with him.

Eddie Carter and his friends had changed all that.

A part of her had died when Eddie Carter raped her. Every time another boy had climbed on top of her, she'd fought harder, screaming until her throat had been raw and her voice abandoned her.

There had been a crowd of people in the room. At least a dozen faces staring down at her and doing nothing to help.

Before she lost her voice, shock had turned to anger. She'd bitten and screamed and done everything she could to fight back. But it wasn't until she'd stopped fighting that the crowd began to disperse. They'd wanted to be entertained. Once her body had gone limp, they'd left. But not the boys who wanted a piece of her. Those boys had stayed and waited their turn. They didn't seem to mind that she'd stared into their eyes, their souls, while each had taken his turn.

The driver's door opened, sending a jolt through her and bringing her back to reality.

Stay calm. Stay silent. Don't move.

The back of the seat moved from the weight of him. The engine roared to life. Tires rolled over smooth pavement, and the vehicle dipped forward when he pulled out of the parking lot and merged onto the main street.

She didn't have much time. The second the car came to a stop, she pushed herself upward. Sitting on the edge of the back seat, she put the gun to the side of his head.

She could see his face in the rearview mirror. His eyes were round and overly bright.

"What's going on?" he asked. His body tensed. "What are you doing in my car?"

Afraid he might try to run, she pressed the gun hard against his skull and said, "When the light turns green make a left. If you stop the car again, I'll shoot you." Her hand trembled. She didn't like that. *Steady as she goes.*

"Take my wallet." His voice was suddenly high and squeaky. "I'll pull over and you can have my car. And all my money too."

"The light is green, asshole! Go!"

The Ford Escape jerked forward before smoothing out. He made a left as instructed, then started to pull to the side of the road.

She pressed the gun into the side of his head. Hard. "Stay on the road! Don't pull over. Don't stop. I have nothing to lose, so don't test me."

The car jerked to the left, back on course.

"What do you want with me?"

"I want you to keep your eyes on the road and follow my directions. Do as I say and you won't get hurt." She looked over her shoulder, glad to see Psycho's MINI Cooper a few cars back. When she turned around, her gaze met Eddie's. She could tell by the look on his face that he was up to something. Before she could do anything about it, he jerked the wheel to the right, throwing Cleo off balance. She used her hands to stop herself from crashing into the door.

He slammed on the brakes. This time Cleo's head smacked into the back of his seat.

He put the car in park and jumped out.

Her adrenaline was running a marathon now. Eddie ran into the street, waving his arms. A car honked and swerved around him.

Psycho pulled over to help the man. The second Cleo saw Eddie Carter climb into Psycho's car, she bolted from his Ford Escape, ran to catch up to the electric-blue MINI Cooper, and jumped into the back seat.

Eddie looked over his shoulder at Cleo, then at Psycho. "That's her!"

Psycho leaned toward Eddie and zapped him with a stun gun. His body twitched as she passed the stun gun to Cleo and hit the gas. "Take care of him, would you?"

Cleo set the gun on the floor, then removed her backpack and placed it behind Psycho's seat. She leaned to the far right and squeezed her hand between the car door and the front passenger seat. When she found a lever, she pulled hard. Eddie's seat came down.

He was drooling. His eyes appeared dazed.

"We're in the clear," Psycho said as she glanced in the rearview mirror. "His timing couldn't have been better. Now we won't need to worry about getting rid of his car."

Cleo examined the stun gun, then pressed the prongs to his shoulder and tased him again.

His muscles contracted and his body jerked.

"What did you do that for?" Psycho asked.

"He should have followed my orders."

"Put that away. I need to focus on driving." Psycho took a hand off the wheel and gestured toward the back of her car. "Inside a gray travel bag you'll find duct tape. There's also a thin blanket back there. Bind him to the seat and then cover him up, will you?"

Cleo worked fast. After Eddie was taped up and covered with the blanket, she took a breath. "Thanks for the help."

"You're welcome."

For the next ten minutes, they drove in silence until Psycho started talking. "Am I the only one who loses sleep at night, wondering where Bug went off to?"

Cleo rubbed some of the tension out of her neck. "I didn't sleep well before Bug left, so I can't say her disappearance has changed anything. I will say this, though: only a coward would run off like she did. We made a deal. She should have stuck around to finish what we all started." Cleo stared ahead at the road. "Malice should have told us right from the beginning what she knew about Bug's plans to take off."

"Yeah," Psycho agreed.

"I don't trust Malice," Cleo went on. "Which is why I've been keeping an eye on her sister."

"Sawyer Brooks, the one who works at the *Sacramento Independent*?"

"Yes. Do you know her?"

"She came to see me."

Cleo leaned forward. "She showed up at your apartment?"

"Yes. I told Malice about the visit, but I thought it was best to keep it from the rest of you since I didn't want anyone to panic." She shrugged. "It made sense that a journalist would want to talk to me after all the media exposure the Black Wigs has gotten, thanks to dickless wonder Brad Vicente." There was a short pause before Psycho added, "When Malice told us that she'd known all along Bug might leave the country, I began to realize how very little we know about one another. And then last night, another sister showed up."

Cleo gasped. "What? How many sisters are there?"

"Three. Malice, Sawyer, and Aria."

"Is she a journalist too?"

"No. As far as I know, she's Sawyer's little helper. I don't think we need to worry about them. They're just as fucked up as the rest of us."

Eddie moaned and wriggled beneath the blanket.

Cleo watched him closely, but her thoughts were on Malice's sisters. She didn't like the idea of Sawyer Brooks breathing down their necks, playing detective. And now Aria too. This information presented a new urgency to her plans and what lay ahead.

Psycho was right: they knew very little about one another. Malice, Psycho, and Bug weren't the only ones with secrets. Shit was going to get real.

Chapter Nineteen

The connection between Nick Calderon and Bruce Ward hit Sawyer in a flash, jolting her awake.

The Children's Home of Sacramento. The picture she'd seen on Nick's Facebook page. The one with two other boys in front of the home: Bruce and Felix. Bruce had to be Bruce Ward.

She sat up and looked at the time. It was nine o'clock on Saturday. She'd slept in. Sliding her feet over the edge of the bed, she went to the living room, where she'd left her backpack, and grabbed her files, something she'd been too tired to do last night before bed.

If the name "Bruce" referred to Bruce Ward, what were the odds that two men who spent years at the same school for troubled kids would both be killed by some random person wearing a black wig and lipstick?

She tapped her finger against the picture. There were two photos of Bruce. One was of him as a kid, standing in front of the Children's Home of Sacramento. The other was of three men, who were dressed in hunting gear. One of them was definitely the same Bruce she'd seen lying dead in his garage.

Coffee. She needed coffee.

Fifteen minutes later, Sawyer was chugging down the strong brew like it was water and thinking about Nick Calderon and Bruce Ward and how they died.

A person wearing a dark wig, the hair bluntly cut at the shoulders, was seen on a security camera at the time of Nick Calderon's murder. Trudy Carriger saw a person fitting a very similar description leaving Bruce Ward's house.

A dark, shoulder-length wig and red lipstick did not fit the description of the Black Wigs. According to Nick Calderon's ex-wife, Nick was gay. Relevant or not, why would a group of pissed-off women go after a gay man?

And what about the shoe and sock? Why would both Nick Calderon and Bruce Ward remove one shoe and not the other?

Unless someone else had removed their shoe. But why?

Sawyer searched the internet, plugging in random word combinations about murdered victims who were missing a shoe. All sorts of crazy headlines popped up. She kept clicking and skimming through story after story of murderers with shoe fetishes, which didn't fit in either of these cases since the shoe had been left behind.

Her search took her down many paths, including one article that talked about syringes being used beneath toenails and fingernails as a form of torture. Another story mentioned drug users shooting up in the crook of the elbow or between the toes to avoid track marks.

She made a note to find out whether or not Nick Calderon or Bruce Ward had drugs in their system when the autopsies were done. It seemed clear when she'd looked inside Bruce Ward's garage that there had been a struggle. Broken glass and tools covered the cement floor, which told her Bruce Ward had tried to fight off his attacker. Maybe the killer hadn't expected a fight and in his or her haste to leave forgot to put the sock and shoe back on the victim. The likelihood of that happening in both cases, though, was slim. It didn't make sense. Why go to all the bother to hide an injection site and then not take the time to put the shoe back on?

Sawyer spent the next few hours looking for information about The Slayers and other vigilante groups. Endless links quickly took her down a rabbit hole of information. She ended up on YouTube, where she noticed The Slayers already had over a million upvotes.

News headlines for the Black Wigs included Sacramento Vigilante Group the Black Wigs Grows in Popularity, Everyday Citizens Taking Law into Their Own Hands, and so on. It made sense that The Slayers wouldn't be the only people following the Black Wigs' lead.

She got up, stretched, and went to the bathroom. After she'd refilled her coffee cup, her phone buzzed, letting her know she had an incoming call. It was a number she didn't recognize. She picked up the call anyway. It was Nancy Lay, the eighty-nine-year-old woman who used to work at the Children's Home of Sacramento. Apparently she'd been a cook, and she was willing to talk. She lived at Oak View Retirement Center off Bell Road in Auburn.

Sawyer hung up, then rushed to get ready.

When she opened the door to leave ten minutes later, Aria was standing there. Sawyer gasped and put a hand to her chest. "You scared me!"

Aria's eyes widened. "*You* scared *me*!"

"What are you doing here?" Sawyer wanted to know.

"I need to talk to you."

Sawyer groaned. "The answer is no. I haven't had time to do a search on that guy."

"It's not about that. It's about Nick Calderon. I went to his work and talked to his boss."

"Great. Maybe we can meet up later and talk about what you learned."

"There's more."

"Okay," Sawyer said impatiently.

"Where are you off to?" Aria asked. "How about I join you and tell you in the car?"

"Fine," Sawyer said. "Come on, then. I'll explain where we're going after you tell me what this is all about."

Once they were on the road, Aria related her visit with Nick Calderon's boss and how he'd called in a guy named Adam and they'd made it perfectly clear that Nick had been nothing but trouble.

"What's really weird," Aria went on, "is that I have a feeling they were afraid to fire him."

"What do you mean?" Sawyer asked.

"I think they were worried he might come back with a gun."

"But you're just speculating, right?"

Aria nodded. "I am. Anyway, as I was leaving the building, a woman came running out and told me that Nick did have a friend named Felix Iverson. I haven't had time to do a thorough search yet, but it's something, right?"

Sawyer's pulse quickened. "Felix Iverson! There's a photo on Nick Calderon's Facebook page that shows three boys standing in front of the children's home. The names Nick, Bruce, and Felix are scribbled in the margin. It has to be the same guy." She could hardly stay still. "We finally have someone who might be able to shed some light on Nick Calderon."

"Don't get too excited," Aria warned.

"Why not?" Sawyer glanced at Aria before fixing her gaze on the road again. "What did you do?"

"I went to Stockton."

"Why Stockton?" Sawyer asked. And then it hit her. "You didn't go to see Christina Farro, did you? You didn't knock on her door, right?"

"I didn't have to. She found me in my car. I had been parked across the street for less than thirty minutes when suddenly I looked up and there she was, heading straight for me."

"Oh, God. What happened?"

"We talked for a little bit. Well, she talked. I was speechless. And then she gave us a warning."

"Us?"

"Yes. You and me. She said that if we didn't stop snooping around, we would regret it."

"And that was it?"

"Not exactly."

Sawyer groaned.

"I then asked Christina Farro flat out if she was a member of the Black Wigs," Aria said. "I figured I drove all that way to see her and there she was, so I might as well just ask."

Sawyer shook her head.

"That woman is scary," Aria continued. "She knows everything about us. Isn't that odd?"

"Yes," Sawyer said. "It's very odd. Please don't do that again."

"No problem. I think I'll stick to researching on the computer."

"That's a good idea."

Chapter Twenty

Harper paced back and forth inside the empty warehouse off Power Inn Road. It was beyond strange being back at the place where she'd killed a man. She stopped to stare at the metal piping where The Crew's victim, Otto Radley, had been fastened before he quietly broke free.

She had walked inside the warehouse just in time to see Otto sneaking up behind Psycho. She could almost feel the butt of the rifle against her shoulder as she'd taken aim and fired. The jolt had been explosive, sending her flying backward.

The bloodstain on the cement floor had since been bleached and scrubbed many times, but the outlined shadow was still there. The real evidence was buried in the dirt about twenty feet away from the entry door.

She had killed a man.

And she hadn't been the same since.

It didn't matter how many times she reminded herself that Otto Radley, a real-life monster, had deserved what he'd gotten. The guilt and shame would not go away. Talking to someone about what she had done might help, but she couldn't risk it. Her husband, Nate, would never understand. How could anyone understand something she hadn't yet come to terms with?

When she'd helped form The Crew, the thought of killing someone had never entered her mind. Not once. Their plan had sounded so simple. They would kidnap their targets, take them to an isolated spot, and hold them captive for a day or two. The men would be blindfolded and bound. For months she'd felt energized by the notion of showing rapists what it felt like to be overwhelmed, powerless, helpless.

She rubbed her belly, smiled when she felt a kick.

It bothered her now to realize that if she'd sought help and found a way to accept the brutal truth that nothing would ever change what happened to her when she was growing up, maybe she would have made better choices. After she'd escaped her hometown and the ongoing abuse, if she'd found a way to accept what had happened, then maybe she would have been able to process her emotions and move past it. Instead, she'd buried her feelings and allowed the trauma to fester, turning her into a control freak, micromanaging everything around her.

It was as if a light had suddenly been switched on and she could see everything so much clearer now. But was it too late?

A movement outside captured her attention.

It was Lily. Five foot six, blue eyes with blonde hair tucked beneath her wig, she was the reason they had gone after Brad Vicente. Like most of The Crew, besides wanting justice for being wronged, Harper and Lily had little in common. Lily had grown up hunting with her father. She worked at an outdoor adventure shop. Never having married, she lived alone.

"Hey there. Long time no see," Lily said with a smirk. "How are things?"

"Same-o, same-o," Harper said.

Lily's booted footfalls echoed off the walls as she walked to the far end of the warehouse. "It's weird, being back here."

"Agreed. Gives me the creeps." Harper glanced at her watch. "Shouldn't they be here by now?"

Before Lily could respond, gravel being spit up beneath a car's tires caught their attention.

Lily pulled her mask from her back pocket and slid it over her eyes as she headed for the exit. "Sounds like it's go-time."

Harper put on her mask too and followed at Lily's heels.

"Why are they in Psycho's car?" Lily asked.

"No idea." The only guarantee when it came to plotting and planning seemed to be that nothing ever went as expected.

Psycho and Cleo climbed out of the car and slid on their eye masks. Psycho stretched her arms high above her head, then bent over and touched her toes.

Just another rapist, different day. No big deal. That was the vibe Harper got from Psycho.

Cleo was another story. She looked pale. Sweat beaded on her forehead. Appearing restless and irritable, Cleo glanced Harper's way as she approached but didn't bother with a greeting as she walked around the car and opened the passenger door.

Harper peeked inside the driver door that Psycho had left open. The passenger seat had been adjusted so that their target was reclined.

Cleo grabbed the corner of the blanket and pulled it off the man. Then she ripped off the tape covering his eyes and mouth.

His face was drenched in sweat and saliva. He coughed and sputtered and then immediately yelled for help.

Cleo shoved the barrel of her gun into his temple. "How stupid are you? Do you think I would have removed the tape if there was anyone else around?" She shook her head.

His eyes met Harper's. "Help me."

His eyes were rimmed with red. Fresh haircut, newly shaved, red shirt and black shorts that matched his black sneakers and red shoelaces. This wasn't the only time she'd seen firsthand that no one should try to judge a book by its cover.

"Please," he said.

He blinked, focused on her wig, then looked past Harper, his gaze moving from Lily to Psycho. "The Black Wigs," he said. His head jerked back so he could see Cleo. "Lena," he said. "I'm sorry."

Cleo's eyes narrowed. "Say that name again and I'll shove the barrel of this gun right down your throat."

"I'm sorry for everything I did. A day hasn't gone by that I haven't thought of you. If I could turn back time, it never would have happened."

Cleo laughed. "Did you hear that, you guys? It was a mistake. An accident. He wants to turn back time and take it all back."

Silence.

"Let me go," he pleaded. "I beg of you."

"Begging, huh? Do you remember me crying out, begging for someone, anyone at all, to help me?"

He wouldn't or couldn't stop crying, and Harper found herself ping-ponging between feeling sorry for him and wanting to scream at him. Bottom line was that he had done this to himself. For every choice there was a consequence. "It would be nice to be able to stop and take a breath, wouldn't it?" Harper interrupted, her voice cutting.

His head jerked back Harper's way and shook up and down like one of those bobbleheads. "I feel sick to my stomach," he told her as if she might help him. "It's hard for me to believe I could have ever done what I did to Le—your friend."

"You're right. It is hard to believe," Harper said. "Being tied up and bound, trapped, unable to move your arms and legs, and having no control over your situation is difficult, isn't it? How does it make you feel?"

He couldn't stop crying long enough to answer.

"He's a fucking pansy-ass baby, who's only sorry because we caught him," Cleo said. "If he felt so bad about what he did to me, why didn't he try to find me and tell me how sorry he was?"

When Eddie Carter gained control of his emotions, he inhaled, his breath shaky. "I tried to find you."

Cleo laughed.

"I did. I swear."

"You swear?" Cleo repeated with much exaggeration. "Did everyone hear that? He tried to find me. He swears!"

"I'm married," he said between sniffles, his voice rough and raw. "I have two daughters who need me."

"Cry me a river," Cleo said. "It must be tough to know you might never see them again."

Harper swallowed a lump that had formed in her throat.

Cleo shoved her gun into her back pocket, then leaned over him to grab a bottle of water sitting between the front seats, unscrewed the cap, and gulped down every last drop. "Instead of thinking about your family, Eddie, I want you to stop and calm down for a moment."

He was hiccuping and couldn't seem to stop.

Cleo sighed. "I'll wait. We have plenty of time."

"Why are you doing this?" he asked.

"Seriously? Do you want me to start from the beginning?"

"No. No. Please. I'm sorry."

"Let's not think about you or your family," Cleo said. "Let's forget about poor Eddie Carter for a minute and go back all those years ago to that fateful night at the fraternity house."

He was whimpering again. Snot bubbled out of his nostrils.

Cleo's brows turned downward. "For God's sake." She marched to the back door, flung it open, and stretched across the back seat. She returned with a small oily towel that she tossed at his face. "Wipe your nose."

Harper glanced around and saw that Psycho had disappeared. Bored, Lily picked at her chipped dark-green nail polish.

Eddie Carter's wrists were duct-taped together, which made wiping his nose awkward.

"Better," Cleo snapped. "Close your eyes if you have to, and go back to that moment when you were hooting and hollering with the guys while you rode me like a Brahman bull."

He cringed.

Cleo pulled a knife from her bootstrap and used it to unfasten the tremendous amount of tape she'd used to fasten him to the car seat.

As she worked, Eddie Carter begged for Cleo to listen, telling her he'd had numerous shots of tequila that fateful night. He'd been hammered and almost blacked out.

Harper had never seen Cleo so angry. Nostrils flared, Cleo said, "Shut up, Eddie. Shut up and listen. You weren't drunk in the courtroom when you told everyone I was a slut."

When Cleo reached down and removed the rest of the duct tape, Eddie Carter took everyone by surprise. He pushed Cleo so hard she stumbled backward onto the ground. Then he took off, heading across the gravel drive before making a sharp left straight down a steep, rocky hill.

Before Harper could yell for help, or do anything at all for that matter, Psycho ran past the car in a blur. Eddie Carter appeared to be in good shape, and he was fast.

But Psycho was faster.

Lithe and long, when she got close enough, she lunged for him, brought him to the ground. They rolled a few feet farther down the hill, dirt clods and dust flying about until Cleo caught up to them.

As Harper drew closer to the action, she saw Cleo straddling the man just as she had straddled Myles Davenport weeks before. She used her fists to pummel him, her knuckles making contact with every bit of his face. It wasn't until Harper drew closer that she saw blood. Lots of blood.

Psycho stood, her chest heaving from exertion.

"Stop!" Harper cried out when she saw Cleo pull a knife from her bootstrap, raise it above her head, and stab the man.

Harper attempted to pull Cleo off Eddie Carter, but rage had made Cleo into the Hulk.

"Put the knife down!"

Cleo tossed the knife aside and instead used her fists to beat him again. "You fucker," she said over and over. "You deserve to die."

Harper clamped a hand around Cleo's shoulder. "That's enough."

Cleo's shoulders slumped forward before she looked from Harper to Psycho. "I was seventeen," she said. "I liked boys. But I was a virgin." Cleo placed her hands on both sides of Eddie's face, her thumbs flat against his eyelids. "You have no idea how many nights I dreamed of putting my hands on your face, digging my fingers into your sockets, and plucking out your eyes."

His eyes remained shut even after Cleo pulled her hands away.

"Open your eyes, god damn it!" Spittle flew from Cleo's mouth when she shouted.

He did as she said.

Lily walked toward them, stopping a few feet away.

"My parents and I never talked about the incident after you and your friends were released, free to go live your lives." Cleo was crying now. "I wanted to forget, and maybe I could have if I hadn't started showing. I was pregnant."

Harper's insides rolled.

Cleo's brows slanted inward. "How many boys fucked me that night? I have no idea, Eddie. Do you?"

He shook his head, his blood-smeared face a maze of horror.

Cleo jabbed a finger into his chest, her anger palpable. "I didn't know whose baby it was until she was born. My mother and I knew instantly who the daddy was. My little girl was the spittin' image of Eddie Carter. My baby's father was a rapist." There was a long pause before Cleo said, "I gave her up for adoption because I didn't want to look into her eyes every day for the rest of my life and relive what happened." She used her forearm to wipe tears from her face, then jabbed him with her finger again. "I thought I had done the right thing, but I was wrong. She was my baby. I gave away my own baby. You took everything from me."

"I'm so sorry," he blubbered. "I've spent my life regretting what I did to you. Every year, I give to organizations to help end sexual abuse. I will do anything I can to help you move on. Anything. Just ask."

"Typical," Cleo said, wiping the tears away. "You haven't changed a bit. Your parents paid for the best lawyers in the courtroom. And now you still think you can buy your way out of trouble. That's not how it works, Eddie. Not here. Not this time."

Cleo glanced Psycho's way, apparently a silent message that it was time to get him into the warehouse, since Psycho approached and hooked her arm around Eddie Carter's. Cleo grabbed a fistful of Eddie's shirt and the two of them dragged him up the hill.

As he was pulled along, Eddie attempted to get to his feet, but his leg gave out. It was clear to Harper that he couldn't walk. Besides being stabbed, Harper realized he must have hurt his leg on the way down the hill, or maybe when Psycho pounced. She wondered whether his leg was broken or he was bleeding internally.

Once they reached the top of the hill, he was pulled haphazardly across the rocky terrain and into the warehouse. They used zip ties to fasten his ankles to the same rusty pipe they had used when Otto Radley was here. Then they yanked his arms behind his back and zip-tied his wrists.

Restless and agitated, he grimaced.

Harper found a water bottle, unscrewed the lid, and brought it to him, told him to open his mouth. When he did, she let the water trickle steadily down his throat. She was checking his wounds when someone approached from behind.

"What are you doing?" Cleo asked.

"It's hot. He's thirsty."

Psycho approached with a roll of duct tape and the same oily cloth from before. She used the towel and the duct tape to blindfold him.

"There," Psycho said. "I need to take off this damn mask and wig."

"The stab wound in his hip needs to be cleaned, and his leg might be broken," Harper said.

Cleo snatched the water bottle out of Harper's grasp. "You need to mind your own business."

"He's all of our business," Harper argued.

"Nope. Just mine. You're not the leader of the pack, so stop trying to tell me or anyone else what to do." Cleo tossed the water bottle to the ground. "Oh, and that reminds me. There's something else I've been meaning to talk to you about." She jabbed a finger at Harper's face, just missing her nose. "You better keep your fucking sister away from me. If she ever comes knocking on my door like she did Psycho's, who knows what will become of her. You might want to give her a heads-up and tell her to mind her own business."

Her words sent a shiver up Harper's spine. "Are you threatening to harm my sister?"

"Call it whatever you want. If she digs too deep, we could all be exposed. And then what?"

Harper stiffened. Clearly something more was going on here. "You don't trust me?"

"Why should I? Why should any of us? First you failed to mention what you knew about Bug's plans to abandon the group, and now your sister is working on a story about us and you don't think to warn us?" She shook her head. "That's bullshit."

Harper reached for Cleo's arm, but she yanked it back so Harper wouldn't be able to touch her.

"Why don't we go outside and talk about this?"

"No. I'm done. I've said what I wanted to say. I'm staying right here. The rest of you should leave," Cleo said to everyone in the warehouse.

"Are you staying the night?" Lily asked.

"I might. What's it to you?"

Lily raised her hands and backed off. "Okay. Fine with me. I'm outta here."

At a loss as to what to do next, Harper watched Lily leave.

Psycho came up to Harper, put an arm around her, and walked with her until they were outside. Once they were out of earshot, she said, "You should go. I'll stay with Cleo until it gets dark."

"How long is she going to keep him here?"

Psycho shrugged. "I don't know, but it's up to her. Listen. I know you had a different vision for what The Crew was going to be and how things would go down. We all did. But what's done is done, and we're all seeing the chaos that comes from having too many captains on one ship. Not the best analogy, but you get my drift."

"Why did you tell her about Sawyer? I thought you decided it was best to keep it between you and me."

"After Bug left the group, I changed my mind. Too many secrets cause schisms that grow bigger and wider, and pretty soon no one trusts anyone else. We're too close to the finish line to mess everything up now. It's time for everyone to be truthful with one another."

"She threatened my sister."

Psycho exhaled. "Cleo's husband took their kids and left her. She's devastated and she's not all there right now."

"Then we should tell her to go home. I'll take care of Eddie Carter myself. We don't need another dead guy on our hands."

"His wound is superficial. He'll be fine."

"What if she decides to silence him since he knows her identity?"

"Go home," Psycho said, ushering her toward her car. "Go home and focus on your family. This will all be over soon."

Chapter Twenty-One

Sawyer and Aria listened as Nancy Lay, a tall woman with short white hair cropped around the ears and red-framed glasses that made her eyes look twice as big, took them back in time to when she was head cook at the children's home for troubled kids, boys and girls of all ages. Apparently the boys had lived on one side of the building, while the girls lived on the other.

Six kids to a room. They each had a bunk bed and a dresser drawer. No closet space.

"The problem was always money," Nancy said. "Times were tough back then. And the school always felt like the land of the forgotten children. Bad enough that many of these children had been left as infants in garbage bins or outside a church's door. For one reason or another, their foster parents didn't want them either, so they ended up at the Children's Home of Sacramento."

"How long did you work there?"

"From the day the place opened until the day it was burned to the ground."

"So you must have known the kids pretty well."

She nodded. "Most of them. Sadly, it was the worst ones who usually stood out."

"Do you have any idea at all where I might be able to find documents that would list all the names of the kids who lived at the home?"

Nancy shook her head. "The headmaster had an office in the basement. That's where all the records and files were kept. All of it was lost in the fire."

"I was afraid of that," Sawyer said. "What was the headmaster's name, if you don't mind?"

Her face soured. "Valerie Purcell."

"I take it you didn't think much of her?"

"Greedy to the core. She didn't care about the kids, which is why the home was dark, cold, overcrowded, and filthy. Many times the pantry was nearly empty and the children were only given one meal throughout the day."

"I guess it's safe to assume that the kids received little help in the way of therapy and emotional support?"

She snorted. "That would be correct."

"Do you remember the names Nick Calderon and Bruce Ward?"

Nancy's face visibly paled.

"You remember them?"

She nodded. "They were inseparable. They formed a boys' club."

"Boys' club?"

"In today's world their group would have been considered to be a gang."

Aria said, "How about Felix Iverson? Does that name ring a bell?"

Nancy gave a nod. "Yes. He was part of the club."

Sawyer and Aria exchanged a quick look. Felix Iverson was definitely Nick's pal and someone they needed to talk to.

"There were two or three other boys in the group whose names fail me," Nancy said. "Aston New . . . No, Aston Newell . . . Yes, that was it. Aston was also attached at the hip."

Sawyer wrote the name down. Every new name was like finding a new piece of the puzzle. They needed to follow every lead. "I take it the Boys' Club was trouble," she said.

"Worse than that. They were evil. They used to pick on one of the smallest boys in the house. A boy named Jimmy Crocket. I remember that name because Aston and the others would call him Jiminy Cricket and a slew of other names meant to be cruel."

"If the home was for troubled kids, why was Jimmy there?" Sawyer asked.

"Jimmy had a difficult time. He wet his bed most nights, and he cried a lot."

"That doesn't sound like a good reason for his foster parents to give him up."

"Sadly, there's more to it than that. He came to live there when he was ten. He was a cutter. I had no idea what that meant until he came into the kitchen covered in mud. I pulled off his T-shirt before he could stop me. My jaw dropped at the sight of him. His skinny, pale body was covered in scars, tiny thin lines all over his chest and arms. I asked him who did that to him." She drew in a breath. "He said cutting himself made him feel better. He used whatever he could find—a paper clip, sticks, a butter knife. I grabbed a shirt from somewhere and put it on him. We never talked about it again."

"What did Aston and the others do to Jimmy?"

"It's all too horrible to repeat. Whenever I caught the boys in action, though, I reported what I saw to the headmaster. Sadly, she wasn't any better than Nick or Aston or any of the others."

It was quiet for a moment before Nancy said, "I wanted to quit, but then I would think, 'Who's going to feed these poor kids if I leave?'"

"Any idea what happened to the headmaster after the fire?"

"I believe she moved to Elk Grove." Nancy shrugged. "She was about ten years younger than me, so that would put her in her midseventies." She tilted her head. "Why are you asking about these kids? What is your story about?"

"I'm here because Nick Calderon and Bruce Ward were found dead recently. Both deaths appeared to happen under suspicious circumstances. My research brought me to the Children's Home of Sacramento and ultimately here to see you."

Nancy nodded. "I should be sad that they're gone, but I'm not."

"I realize Jimmy was very young at the time," Sawyer said, "but would you say he was capable of murder?"

"No," Nancy said without hesitation. "Poor sweet boy never stood a chance, but he's no killer."

"Any idea what became of him?"

Nancy shook her head, then raised a crooked finger. "Emily Stiller might know. She was a bossy thing." Nancy smiled for the first time since Sawyer and Aria had taken a seat. "That girl knew how to put those boys in their place. She was Jimmy's savior for a while."

"What happened to her?"

"A few months before the fire, she ran away, and we never saw her again. Perhaps you can use your high-tech computers to find out what happened to her."

Sawyer smiled. "I think that's a great idea." She jotted down Emily's name. "Oh, I almost forgot. I printed off a few pictures I found on the internet." Sawyer pulled out the sheet of paper and handed it to Nancy.

Her face softened, and her eyes grew bright and watery. "There they are," she said. "Emily and Jimmy are sitting right there together. Oh, my," she said as she rested a hand over her heart.

"What is it?" Sawyer asked, then watched as Nancy Lay pointed a shaky finger at the kids. "In the background, sitting near the shade tree. That's Stanley Higgins."

Sawyer took a closer look at the kid she was pointing at. He had a mop of curly brown hair and a round face. "He looks so young," Sawyer said. "What was his story?"

"Stanley was also bullied. The poor thing did everything he could to become invisible. I remember looking out the window one afternoon and seeing Felix and Aston throwing rocks at him. Jimmy told Stanley to run. By the time I got out there, Jimmy had a cut above his right eye."

"So Jimmy had a little bit of Emily in him, didn't he?"

"Yes, he did. He looked out for Stanley. So sad," she said. "So long ago." She handed the paper back to Sawyer. "I hope you find the answers you're looking for."

"Thank you, Nancy. You've been very helpful."

Chapter Twenty-Two

That night, Harper tossed and turned in bed. The clock on her nightstand told her it was two in the morning. She couldn't stop thinking about Eddie Carter. He was the first of their targets to admit to wrongdoing. The Crew's mission was to teach abusers a lesson—show them what it felt like to have no control over a situation and what might happen to them. Eddie Carter was remorseful. His regret seemed genuine. Yes, he deserved to be punished. But it was the look she'd seen on Cleo's face that worried her and kept her awake. The clenched fists when she continuously pounded his chest. The kicking and yelling as her anger turned violent. It seemed to Harper that Cleo had PTSD. In that moment of rage, Cleo seemed to be reliving the horror of what had happened the night at the fraternity house. It was as if Cleo suddenly had been thrust into survival mode, determined to win at all costs.

Harper knew the effects firsthand, how childhood trauma liked to rear its head when least expected. There were times when the anger would turn quickly to rage, and she would feel the urge to scream and kick something.

She sucked in a breath and closed her eyes, determined to go to sleep and push all thoughts of Eddie Carter away. She could drive to the warehouse first thing in the morning and check on Cleo and Eddie then.

The next ten minutes ticked by slowly.

Too slowly.

She opened her eyes and eased her way quietly off the bed so as not to wake Nate. Blindly, she searched for clothes and a pair of shoes before exiting her bedroom. She stepped into her jeans, then put on the T-shirt and sneakers. She grabbed a sweater from the coat hook in the entryway, then headed for the kitchen, where she found her purse and snuck out the door.

Less than thirty minutes later, she pulled up next to the warehouse and sat in silence as she took in her surroundings, taking note that Cleo's car was gone.

It was in that moment that Harper realized she hadn't thought this through. What was her plan? On the drive here, she'd imagined talking to Cleo and making sure Eddie Carter was okay. Now she found herself wishing she'd brought food and water and bandages.

She continued to stare through the windshield into the dark.

Maybe she would do the unthinkable and let him go. The rest of The Crew would be furious with her. But only if they found out.

Her frustration mounted. What was she supposed to do? She couldn't simply let the man bleed to death.

You're a hypocrite, an inner voice murmured in her ear.

She disagreed. Psycho was the one who had cut off Brad Vicente's dick. Besides, the man was alive, in prison where he belonged. And Myles Davenport would have been set free eventually. Nobody knew he would suffer a heart attack and die. He was young. What were the odds? And then there was Otto Radley, whom Harper had shot in self-defense. Not exactly self-defense, but close. If Harper hadn't pulled the trigger, he would have killed Psycho.

The difference between all the other captives and Eddie Carter was that Eddie Carter was sorry for what he'd done to Cleo. Harper wouldn't be sitting here at all if she wasn't worried about him bleeding to death.

The point of The Crew teaming up had been to make sure their tormenters learned from their mistakes. They wanted their abusers to be taught a lesson.

Her decision was made. She grabbed a flashlight from the glove compartment and climbed out of the car. The air held a slight chill. The frogs stopped croaking as she followed the beam of light around the side of the building to the metal door. It was wide open.

The beat of her heart drummed faster.

She hurried inside. The smell of bleach struck her hard. "Cleo? Are you there?" She dragged the beam of light over the area where she'd last seen Eddie Carter.

He was gone. The place was empty.

Looking around, she found dark stains on the cracked cement that appeared to have been washed with a scouring brush. She knelt down, put a finger to the wet spot, and brought it to her nose. Definitely bleach.

On her feet again, she moved the light over every inch of the place until she was absolutely certain no one was there.

Filled with dread, she walked outside and continued her search. Every few feet, she stopped and listened.

The only sounds were of wildlife in the distance. As always, the night belonged to the owls and coyotes.

Time to go home.

All she could do now was pray that Cleo had done the right thing and let him go.

The moment Harper stepped through the side door into her house, she sensed something wasn't right.

A bright light flicked on suddenly, making her squint. Her husband stood a few feet away. "Nate," she said. "What are you doing awake?"

He crossed his arms. "Funny, I was going to ask you the same thing."

She locked the door behind her, then walked to the kitchen, where she set her purse on the counter. "It's late. I'm tired. We'll talk in the morning."

"We'll talk now."

"I'm not ready," she told him. They had already been over this, which was why Nate had taken a job in another state. He wanted answers. She knew that. But it was too early. She needed more time. They were so close to the finish line.

"Fine," he said. "One week. I'm going to give you one week, and then if you still aren't ready to talk to me, I'm going to file for divorce."

She knew him better than anyone. He meant it. Her chest ached for him to wrap his arms around her and tell her everything would be okay. But it wasn't okay. He'd had enough. "Please—"

He shook his head. "That's it. One week. There's a blanket and pillow on the couch for you."

She watched him walk away. She felt empty inside, hollow. No tears came. Nate was her life force, her everything. She couldn't let him go.

A lot could happen in one week.

One thing was certain. If she told him now, this minute, he wouldn't let her out of his sight. And she had more to do. She needed to find Cleo and, more importantly, Eddie Carter. She needed to talk with the others. She needed closure. When her time was up, though, she would tell him everything, and then the choice of where they went from here would be out of her hands.

Chapter Twenty-Three

Sunday morning, Sawyer arrived at Harper's house ten minutes earlier than her scheduled appointment with Lennon. The fifteen-year-old kid with a mop of shaggy, dirty-blond hair opened the door before she could knock. His feet were bare and he looked half-asleep.

"Hey," he said, rubbing his eyes. "You showed up?"

"Of course I did. Why wouldn't I?"

Ella, Sawyer's ten-year-old niece, peeked around her brother's tall frame. "Maybe because of all the other times you told him you would take him driving and never did."

"Funny girl," Sawyer said as she nudged her way inside. "Where's your mom?"

"I'm not being funny," Ella continued. "Just truthful. And Mom is still asleep."

"What about Dad?"

"Working."

"On a Sunday?"

"He always works," Ella provided.

Sawyer pointed at Lennon's bare feet. "Why don't you get your shoes on and we'll go for a ride. Did you eat breakfast?"

"He had cereal," Ella said.

Lennon walked off, leaving Sawyer alone with Ella. "So how is school going? Any big tests coming up?"

Ella frowned. "School is boring. My friends and I want to drop out and start a group like the Black Wigs."

"What did you say?" came a croaky voice from afar.

Ella and Sawyer watched Harper approach from the hallway, tightening the sash on her pink flannel robe. Her hair was flat on one side and sticking out like porcupine quills on the other.

"Good morning," Sawyer said.

Harper ignored her and instead wagged a finger at her daughter. "Did I hear you say you wanted to be a Black Wig?"

Ella looked slightly worried, but she nodded just the same. "They're not bad people. The bad people are the ones who don't keep their hands to themselves."

"She has a point," Sawyer said.

"Stay out of this," Harper ordered.

Aria came through the front door just then. She looked around at all the worried expressions. "What's going on?"

"Ella and her friends want to join the Black Wigs."

Ella wrinkled her nose at Sawyer. "We want to start our own group like The Slayers."

"No," Harper said.

"They're cool," Ella argued. "Those girls are scaring all the dumb boys who did bad things to them." She propped a hand on her hip. "You always lecture me about what to do if someone ever touches me inappropriately. If something happened to me or my friends, don't you think they should be punished for what they did?"

Sawyer watched as Harper grappled with what to say. Ella knew very little about her mom's past, which sort of put Harper between a rock and a hard place. How do you teach your daughter to stand up for herself without becoming a bully? It was especially difficult when every situation called for a different approach.

Harper lifted her daughter's chin. "If someone ever touches you, push them away and scream as loud as you possibly can."

"What if they won't stop?"

Harper placed her hands on Ella's shoulders. "Then you need to run. Run as fast as you can and don't stop until you find help."

"Ready to go," Lennon said when he reappeared. He stopped and looked around at all the somber faces. "What happened? What did I miss?"

"Nothing," Harper said before fixing her gaze on Sawyer and then Aria. "What are you two doing here?"

Sawyer spoke up first. "I'm here to take your son for a driving lesson. We'll only be an hour."

"And I'm going back to my place," Aria said. "I saw Sawyer's car and thought I'd just run over and say hello."

Harper waved them all away, then shut the door.

"What's wrong with her?" Sawyer asked Lennon.

"Mom and Dad aren't getting along."

"You were here when Nate returned home from his trip," Aria said.

Sawyer exhaled. "I guess I hoped they would have worked things out by now."

"Mom slept on the couch last night," Lennon said. "After Dad left for work, she moved to the bedroom."

"Everything will work out," Aria told Lennon. "You two should get going. Good luck!"

Sawyer's plan had been to drive to the high school a mile away and have Lennon drive around the parking lot, but he convinced her he was ready for the streets of Sacramento. Since there was less traffic on Sunday, Sawyer agreed.

Lennon buckled up. Sawyer was glad she didn't have to tell him to put on his blinker before merging onto the road. They drove for a couple of blocks before he was able to make a smooth stop. "Not bad," Sawyer said.

They drove to Midtown, where there were more pedestrians than cars and the lanes were narrow. When she shifted in her seat, she caught a glimpse of the same green car she'd seen outside her apartment and then at the prison.

"What's wrong?" Lennon asked.

"Nothing."

"You sound like my mom. Why can't you just tell me what the hell you're looking at?"

Sawyer lifted an eyebrow. She'd never heard Lennon curse before. The anger that had crept into his voice was also a surprise. And yet she understood. Harper had been keeping secrets from them all, and it was obviously getting to Lennon. "There's a green car, one of those tiny automobiles, two cars back. I think I've seen that same mint-green car before."

"Do you think someone's following you?"

"I do."

Lennon glanced in his rearview mirror. "I see it. It's a Kia Soul."

Sawyer gestured toward the road in front of them. "Just keep your eyes on the road ahead, please."

"Should I pull to the side of the road and see if the car passes?"

"If you find a convenient spot to pull into, go ahead. Otherwise, forget it."

He came to a stop at the light. Lennon peered into his mirror.

"Just don't look over your shoulder, okay?" Sawyer asked. "I don't want whoever is in the car to know we're onto them."

"Got it. The driver is the only one in the car. He or she is wearing a baseball cap and sunglasses."

"Can you see the license plate number?"

"No."

"Hair color? Facial hair?"

"It's too hard to see with the other car in the way."

The light turned green. Lennon put on the gas, then pulled into an empty spot up ahead.

The car behind them swept by, followed by the green Kia Soul.

"The license plate number started with 6T," Lennon said.

Sawyer added, "And it ended with the number three." While Sawyer made note of it on her phone, Lennon hit the gas and jerked the wheel to the left. Sawyer fell to her right.

The car behind them honked.

Sawyer grabbed on to the dashboard. "What are you doing?"

"Let's get the rest of the license number."

"I'm not even sure the car was following us."

"Well, let's find out."

Sawyer hoped they had lost the Kia Soul since Lennon didn't have his license yet. "Maybe I should drive."

"I have a permit and I'm a good driver. You said so yourself."

"Did I say that?"

He didn't answer, just kept his eyes focused on the road. "I see the car," Lennon said excitedly. "It's stopped at the next light." He pulled up as far as he could before stopping. "There are two cars and a truck between us."

"Okay. You can follow the Kia Soul, but no speeding."

"Got it."

When the light turned green, the truck in front of them turned left, leaving two vehicles between them and the Kia. One of the cars pulled into a Safeway parking lot. The other went straight. The Kia was in the left-hand turn lane.

As Lennon drew closer, the Kia jerked to the right, cutting off oncoming traffic, making more than a few vehicles swerve and honk.

Before Sawyer could catch her breath, Lennon jerked the wheel to the right and put on the gas.

"Slow down!"

"No way. The Kia is way ahead. We've got to catch up."

"Your mother would kill me if she saw us now. Pull over."

"There it is!"

The excitement in his voice reminded Sawyer of the time she'd taken Lennon to a Sacramento Kings' game. Every time his favorite player made a basket, he went berserk.

But he was right. The green Kia Soul was up ahead. The car made a left into an alleyway.

So did Lennon.

He slammed on the brakes. He had no choice. They watched the Kia speed through the narrowest alleyway she'd ever seen, one side lined with dumpsters, making it impossible for them to follow without destroying Sawyer's car.

"Looks like the Kia lost us," Lennon said excitedly. "At least now you know someone is definitely following you."

"Yeah," Sawyer said. "Looks that way." She just couldn't muster up the same excitement Lennon was clearly feeling.

She waited for Lennon to back up and get out of there, but he simply looked at her with a silly grin on his face. Was he waiting for a compliment? "You did great. Let's go home."

"I got it," he said, still smiling.

"Got what?"

"The number. It's 6TYV303."

CHAPTER TWENTY-FOUR

Sawyer dropped Lennon off at his house and was about to drive off when Aria ran out of the garage apartment where she lived.

Sawyer rolled down the passenger window.

Aria said, "I'm going to pick us up deli sandwiches on my way over to your place, so don't make lunch. I'll be right behind you."

"Sounds good," Sawyer said. There was a lot of work to do, and she needed all the help she could get. A second later, Harper exited the house and waved a hand to stop Sawyer from driving off. "I was wondering if you guys wanted to have lunch. I'm making grilled cheese sandwiches and green salad with pears."

"Thanks," Sawyer said, "but we're heading back to my place to get some work done."

Harper looked at Aria. "You're working on the Black Wigs story with Sawyer?"

Aria nodded. "It's fun. All I do really is use the internet to help her search for information."

Sawyer wondered if Harper was feeling left out. "You can join us if you'd like."

Harper's face reddened. "No thanks. In fact, I think you should drop the story altogether."

Sawyer frowned. "Why?"

"Because the whole thing is getting out of hand. Copycats are coming out of the woodwork. Maybe if everyone wasn't writing about the Black Wigs and making them into larger-than-life heroes, people would forget about them and kids would stop trying to emulate them."

"If anything," Aria chimed in, "Sawyer will dig deep, pull back the curtain, and find out who's behind the Black Wigs."

"I don't like it." Harper pursed her lips. "The vigilante craze has gotten way out of hand, and the press isn't helping matters." She gestured toward the house. "You heard Ella this morning. Your niece wants to be a part of this circus. I'm begging you to let the story go."

Surprised by her sister's passionate plea to let the story go, Sawyer said, "I'm not the one who makes those kinds of decisions. And even if I did, I wouldn't back away from the story. People are tired of molesters and rapists walking free. Society should be targeting these perpetrators and holding them accountable. Instead, women are blamed for being 'vulnerable.' According to RAINN, the Rape, Abuse and Incest National Network, out of a thousand sexual assaults, nine hundred and ninety five walk free. That's unacceptable. People, men and women, need to be aware of what's going on around them. So my answer is no. I will not walk away from this story. But I appreciate your concern."

"Are you talking to victims of sexual abuse?" Harper asked.

Sawyer sighed. "Yes. Of course."

Harper crossed her arms over her chest. "Who have you talked to?"

"What's wrong with you?" Aria asked. "When you're ready to tell us what you're doing at all hours of the day and night, then maybe Sawyer will tell you more. Until that time, it's really none of your business."

Without another word spoken, Harper turned around and stalked back to the house.

"Wow," Aria said after the door slammed shut. "She and Nate need to make up real quick before her head explodes."

Sawyer nodded but didn't say anything more. Something wasn't right. Harper was the last person she'd ever expect to tell her to back off from a story, especially one involving sexual-abuse survivors.

Back inside the house, Harper went straight to her bedroom and locked the door behind her. With laptop in hand, she sat on the bed, her back against the headboard, and waited for the computer to boot up.

She took in more than one long breath. She needed to calm down and stop her frustrations from getting the best of her.

She logged on to the private group. Since there was no prearranged meeting, she decided to put the question out there and see if any of the other members popped in.

MALICE: I went to the warehouse to see how things were going. Eddie Carter was gone. The place smelled like bleach. What's going on?

While she waited to see if anyone had information, she opened a new tab and checked out headline news. Right away she noticed the caption: ANOTHER BLACK WIG COPYCAT? Officers responded to a neighbor's call that an unknown person wearing a black wig and red lipstick was seen leaving the premises of Bruce Ward, a thirty-nine-year-old highway maintenance operative who was found dead in his garage. Detectives are investigating. This is a developing story.

A heavy feeling settled in her stomach. No. Not again.

When she checked back with The Crew, there were two responses to her question.

LILY: I haven't heard from anyone since I left the warehouse yesterday.

CLEO: I was going to take Eddie Carter to the hospital. When I cut him loose, he took off again. So I let him go. I then followed protocol from the last time we were at the warehouse and scrubbed the place clean.

LILY: What if he goes to the police?

CLEO: Before I cut his ties, he promised he wouldn't tell a soul. Relax.

Relax? Cleo was lying. Harper was sure of it.

MALICE: I'll check hospitals in the area and try to locate him.

CLEO: Maybe you should focus on keeping your sister out of our business and let me worry about Eddie Carter.

MALICE: Every newspaper in the county is writing about the Black Wigs. So fuck off and stay away from my sister.

CLEO: Or what will you do? Kill me with one of your long, boring lectures about violence not being the answer? You have been in denial since the beginning. This was never going to end well for any of these assholes. You need to pull your head out of the sand and wake up. Payback is a bitch.

LILY: Enough! What's next? I want to move on and put this all behind me.

CLEO: I'm glad all of you will simply be able to move on when this is over. I don't need any of your help. I'm done with all of you. Signing off for good. Peace out.

Harper counted to three. Her hands were shaking. Cleo had lost her mind.

MALICE: Are you still here, Lily?

LILY: I'm here. What do we do now?

MALICE: Check back in a day or two. In the meantime, I'm going to call a few hospitals to see if Eddie Carter was admitted.

LILY: Good luck. We'll talk later.

Chapter Twenty-Five

The first thing Sawyer did when she arrived back at her apartment was clear off the coffee table and boot up her laptop. Yesterday, after speaking with Nancy Lay, the woman who had been a cook at the children's home, Aria had gone to the shelter to work, and Sawyer had spent the rest of her day getting a smog check so that she could register her car. Then she'd run to the grocery store to get cat food and a few other items.

She was eager to get back to work. With two yellow, lined notepads in front of her, she titled one in large capital letters with the word COPYCAT, and the other with the words BLACK WIGS.

To help her stay organized and keep track of all the players involved, she wrote corresponding names underneath the headers in outline form.

Beneath the Copycat header, she wrote the names Nick Calderon and Bruce Ward, along with any notes she'd taken at the scene of the crime or tidbits she'd looked up previously. She also wrote Children's Home of Sacramento, and under that she jotted down Nancy Lay (cook), and a few other names.

Beneath the Black Wigs header she wrote the names Brad Vicente, Otto Radley, and Myles Davenport. In parentheses next to Otto

Radley's name, she wrote Christina Farro, the woman he'd held captive for three years.

She looked through her notes again and wrote Tracy Rutherford's name next to Myles Davenport's since Tracy and her parents had taken Myles Davenport, along with other members of her high school football team, to court ten years ago.

COPYCAT

- Nick Calderon (DEAD—person wearing black wig seen leaving)
- Bruce Ward (DEAD—person wearing black wig seen leaving)
- Children's Home of Sacramento
- Nancy Lay (cook)
- Jimmy Crocket (orphan)
- Emily Stiller (orphan)
- Stanley Higgins (orphan)
- Valerie Purcell (headmaster)
- Aston Newell (orphan/bully)
- Felix Iverson (orphan/bully)

BLACK WIGS

- Brad Vicente (in prison)
- Otto Radley (MISSING/Christina Farro)
- Myles Davenport (DEAD/heart attack/Tracy Rutherford)

Sawyer tapped the pen against her chin as she recalled what Brad Vicente had said about the woman with the markings. Christina Farro had to be involved in the Black Wigs. During Sawyer's visit with Christina a few weeks ago, the scars had been clearly visible. Sawyer still remembered her fixation with the markings, knowing that every scar on the woman's body had most likely been the work of a madman. And yet Christina Farro had come across as confident, determined not to let memories of her trauma define her.

But now Sawyer wondered if there was more to Christina Farro's emboldened attitude. Maybe her overconfidence had been a ploy to shake off Sawyer and convince her she was sniffing down the wrong trail, when in reality, she'd been dead on. It bummed her out that Aria had blown her cover because now Christina would definitely be on the lookout for them. Maybe they could rent a car, find a disguise?

Sawyer envisioned Otto Radley in a grave somewhere, a naked and very dead Myles Davenport in the woods, and finally Brad Vicente, screaming as his penis was cut off with pruning shears. She decided right then to take Christina Farro's warning seriously and stay away. For now.

Besides, there were plenty of other leads to follow.

She closed the file on the Black Wigs and focused on the copycat murders instead. Maybe she should concentrate on finding Emily Stiller, the girl who stood up to the bullies at the children's home. Emily must have been sixteen or so when she ran away. Where did she go? What did she do? Had she started the fire? Was Emily out for revenge against these bullies after all these years?

More tapping of her pen.

What about Stanley Higgins or Jimmy Crocket? Where did they end up after the fire?

She typed "Jimmy Crocket" into the search bar and came up with nothing. But when she did the same with Emily Stiller, several links popped up. Most of Emily's posts on social media had to do with nutrition and fitness, but she was able to garner Emily's birth date.

Sawyer decided to use a "no hit, no fee" database to do another search, using the birth date and name. Most people had no idea how easy and cheap it was to amass information on a person using the public domain. Like taking candy from a baby.

By the time Aria arrived with sandwiches, Sawyer knew a lot about Emily Stiller. No criminal record. Two speeding tickets. Divorced. No children. And she was currently a trainer at Lifetime Fitness in Roseville.

Perfect. Sawyer grabbed her cell and dialed Emily's work number.

Aria set the bag of sandwiches on the table in the kitchen nook, then hurried across the room and plopped down next to Sawyer on the couch. "Guess who I'm meeting later today for coffee?"

Sawyer was holding the phone to her ear when she held up a finger, asking Aria to give her a minute.

Aria sat quietly and waited.

Apparently the fastest way to get in touch with Emily was to make an appointment for a consultation at the gym. When Sawyer ended the call, she said, "I can't believe I just did that."

"What did you do?" Aria asked.

"I made an appointment at Lifetime Fitness for Monday. An hour with Emily Stiller, a trainer. I need to talk to her, but I really hope I don't have to do any sit-ups."

Aria laughed. "Well, it won't kill you." She flapped her hands in the air as if erasing that conversation for now. "You can tell me all about Emily Stiller after I tell you my exciting news."

Sawyer had a lot on her mind, but she did her best to give Aria her full attention. "Okay. Tell me your exciting news."

"Remember that guy I told you about?"

"Um, the one who brought a dog into the shelter?"

Aria nodded. "His name is Corey Moran, and he called me back!"

"I didn't realize you had even called him. I thought you were going to wait until I did a background check on him."

"Yeah, well," Aria said with a smile, "I couldn't wait."

"When did you call him?"

"Right after you told me you would see what you could find on him."

Sawyer chuckled. "Wow. He must have really made an impression on you."

Aria was glowing. Her eyes were bright. She'd never looked so happy.

"I was beginning to think he wasn't going to call me back. But as I stood in line for the sandwiches, he called. Don't worry," Aria said before Sawyer had a chance to worry. "We're meeting at the coffee shop where I used to work, so I'll be surrounded by people who know me."

"Do you still want me to enter his name into one of my databases?"

Aria appeared to think about it before saying, "I guess it wouldn't hurt."

It took less than five minutes for his name to pop up. "No judgments. No outstanding tickets. No criminal charges."

"Great."

"Should I keep searching?"

"No. Let's eat. I'm starved."

They both got up and went to sit at the table in the kitchen. Sawyer unwrapped her sandwich, a pastrami on rye, and took a bite. As she chewed and swallowed, she stared at her sister's face. When, she wondered, had Aria removed her nose ring?

Aria made a face. "What are you looking at?"

Sawyer gestured at her nose and then her eyebrow. "Your piercings. What happened to them?"

"I always thought they were just decorative, but I'm not so sure any longer."

"What do you mean?"

Aria lifted a shoulder. "Just that everything changed after we got back from River Rock."

Sawyer kept eating as she waited for her sister to explain.

"After Mom, Dad, and Uncle Theo died, I was worried that all that death and craziness would somehow mess me up even more than I already was. But instead, everything that happened back in River Rock gave it all a finality, which in turn gave me closure and made it easier for me to breathe. Suddenly I was able to see life differently—brighter, with more color, a life filled with possibilities."

Goose bumps sprouted all over Sawyer's arms. "That's wonderful."

"It's mind boggling," Aria said. "I thought the feeling and the emotions I was feeling after we returned to Sacramento might go away, but they haven't. If anything, the spark of hope inside me has grown."

Sawyer wondered why Aria's smile suddenly turned to a frown. "But?"

"But a part of me feels guilty that this newfound hope for a better life was triggered by their deaths. Doesn't that make me as bad as them?" Aria angled her head. "Don't you worry at times that Mom and Dad's DNA runs through our blood?"

"No," Sawyer blurted. "I don't worry about that at all. Mom and Dad made horrible choices. Each bad choice built upon the next until they had nowhere left to go but straight to hell. As long as we do our best to try and make good choices, I think we'll be fine."

Aria didn't look convinced.

Sawyer couldn't stand it. "Don't you dare spend one second feeling guilty about what happened to them. They were evil—Mom, Dad, Uncle Theo. They caused Harper, you, and me, and countless others, nothing but pain. In the end, they all got what they had coming to them. It's over. They're gone. Be happy."

"Thanks," Aria said. "I must not be feeling too guilty since I've been thinking about what I want to do with my share of the inheritance from the sale of Mom and Dad's house and business."

"What do you want to do?"

"There's been talk about the owners of the shelter selling their property. I think it would be a perfect sanctuary for animals that have been abused, neglected, or abandoned. I would call it Forever Sunshine. The animals would be protected for the remainder of their lives."

"Forever Sunshine," Sawyer repeated. "I like it."

When they were done eating, Sawyer went back to her seat on the couch in front of her laptop and said matter-of-factly, "I'm being followed."

"What? Seriously? By who?"

"All I know is that he or she drives a mint-green Kia Soul. We pulled to the side of the road in the hope of getting the license plate—"

"We?"

Sawyer wrinkled her nose. "Don't tell Harper, but the car was following Lennon and me when we were driving around Midtown earlier today. It was the third time I noticed the car, so we took chase."

"With Lennon at the wheel?"

Sawyer nodded sheepishly. "He's a natural."

"You didn't get a good look at the driver?" Aria asked. "How about a license plate number?"

"No and yes. I have the number on my phone."

"And you haven't bothered to look it up?"

"I've been busy. I'll probably need to pay a PI to get the information for me."

"Can't you just call the DMV?"

"No. Not since the Driver's Privacy Protection Act was passed."

Sawyer booted up her computer again. Just as she thought, she was unable to find out who the Kia Soul belonged to, so she left a message with a PI she'd used before.

Aria pulled out her laptop. "Okay," she said, "I've only got an hour before my coffee date with Corey Moran."

"You're meeting him today?"

"Yeah. Is that a problem?"

"No, of course not. It's just that it's all happening so fast."

Aria laughed. "It's just coffee, Sawyer. We're not getting married."

"Okay. Okay. Got it. Let's get to work."

"I'm already on it," Aria said.

Sawyer and Aria had talked about the different cases on their drive to see Nancy Lay, but she hadn't explained her theory about there being two separate cases going on. The Black Wigs and the Copycat. "Since you don't have a lot of time, let's concentrate on the Copycat Killer."

"Bruce Ward is a ghost on social media," Aria said.

Sawyer nodded. "If not for Bruce's neighbor, Trudy Carriger, his death would have been ruled a suicide."

"She's the witness who thought the person she saw was a man?"

"Yes," Sawyer said. "But I don't think her eyesight was very good."

For the next few minutes, the only sound was their fingers clicking away on the keyboards. "Whoa!" Aria said.

Sawyer looked up. "What did you find?"

"Did you know that Valerie Purcell, the headmaster at the children's home, was found dead inside her Fair Oaks home?"

Sawyer popped up and went to hover over Aria. The article was short. Apparently she'd fallen down a flight of stairs. Nothing about when she died or who found her. "She's the third person with a connection to the children's home who has been found dead," Sawyer said. "All three within days of one another."

"Crazy," Aria said. "And creepy. Who's next, I wonder?"

Sawyer was wondering the same thing as she made her way back to her notepad and computer. After a moment she said, "My gut tells me I should concentrate on locating Felix Iverson and Aston Newell."

"And what will you do if you find them?"

"I guess I would warn them, tell them what's happened and let them know there could very well be a target on their backs."

"But there are other members of the gang too." Aria anchored a strand of hair behind her ear. "Maybe Emily Stiller will remember their names."

"Possibly," Sawyer said.

"Speaking of Emily Stiller," Aria said. "I hate to say it, but if all these bullies are being killed, wouldn't the likely killer be Emily, Jimmy, or Stanley?"

"It's possible. But there were a lot of kids who lived at the home. The fire, unfortunately, wiped out any chance of finding a list of names of children who once lived there."

"Bummer," Aria said.

"Yes. It's really going to be a process of elimination at this point, which is why I'll be meeting with Emily Stiller tomorrow and hopefully get a feel for who she is and whether she might be capable of murder."

"I don't like it," Aria said. "You're already being followed. You really do need some protection. Maybe I should go get my gun from home."

"No," Sawyer said. "I'll be fine." Sawyer continued clicking away on the keys of her laptop, typing Felix Iverson's name into one of her search databases. More than one Felix Iverson appeared, but only one with an address in the area. She typed the address into another database that revealed his age. "This has to be the same guy. He lives in Sacramento, off El Camino Avenue."

Aria was also typing. She stopped and said, "Looks like Aston Newell works at an automotive shop in Midtown. That's not too far from here. He works Monday through Friday."

Sawyer wrote down Felix Iverson's address and then made note of Aston Newell's workplace. She then shut her laptop and got to her feet. "I can't just sit here. I'm going to drive to Felix Iverson's house right now."

"Wait a minute." More typing. "Did you look at Felix Iverson's Facebook page?"

"No need. I have his address."

"He looks pretty sketchy." Aria's mouth dropped open. "It says here that he attended Chico State University."

Sawyer went to stand over Aria again. Aria had clicked on a photo that showed him shirtless, holding a beer, and laughing. He was about five foot nine, his dark hair peppered with silver streaks. He had a bony chest and arms. Sawyer winced.

Aria scrolled through a few more pictures, each one worse than the last. Felix pointing a BB gun at the back of his friend's head. Felix guzzling wine from a box. Felix firmly clutching his balls as he looked directly into the lens of the camera.

"Okay. I'll bring my pepper spray and Taser, just in case."

"Guess I'll go to the coffee shop early." Aria shut down her laptop, gathered her things, and got to her feet. "Text me later so I know you made it home."

"I'll be fine. But okay. I'll text you. And good luck with Corey Moran."

Sawyer stared at her sister for a moment too long, prompting Aria to raise her hands and say, "What?"

"Just be careful."

Aria chuckled. "I'm meeting a guy for coffee, and you're telling *me* to be careful? You're the one traipsing off to see a possible killer."

"I don't think Felix Iverson is a killer. I think he could be in danger, and I need to warn him."

"Text me when you get home," Aria said before she walked out the door.

Chapter Twenty-Six

Cleo stood in front of a tall, rectangular mirror propped against the wall in her bedroom—the bedroom she used to share with her husband. It was hard to believe that she'd had a taste of normalcy—a kind, gentle man and two perfect children—and then threw it all away. Somehow, the people she loved most hadn't been enough to stop her from drowning in her past. Why hadn't she been able to reach out, just one more time, and grasp on to the lifeline her family had tossed her way?

She had no idea. But she did know it was a miracle she'd lasted this long and still walked among the living. And yet that didn't stop her from wondering when, exactly, she'd passed the point of no return.

Taking more care than usual to put on her wig, she flattened and prepped her long black hair, twisting and twirling before pulling on a black cap. Over the cap she placed the wig on her head, starting at the front. Using a wide-tooth comb, she brushed the shiny black hair into place. There. She was ready to go.

Next, she picked up the tube of lipstick and began to apply the color she'd seen on the slightly fuzzy image of the person leaving the home of a dead man. The photograph had been caught from a security camera, then leaked to the media. She found it humorous that she was copycatting a copycat.

What was his or her deal? she wondered. Did the Copycat Killer have a list of people to go after? Or were the victims random?

Starting at the center of the upper lip, she then moved the creamy red lipstick outward toward one corner of her mouth and then the other. After using a tissue to blot her lips, she gazed at her reflection. Exotic is what many called her. Her father was white. Her mother was Asian. Cleo was neither, yet both. Either way, the woman staring back at her didn't look anything like the horribly wretched woman she always saw in her mind's eye.

Once, a therapist had asked her how she envisioned herself, and Cleo had told the therapist that when she spoke, she heard a voice of thunder. And when she closed her eyes, she saw herself as a woman with flaming red eyes and clenched fists.

Nothing about her reflection hinted at the rampant madness that resided inside her. Even now the rage tossed and turned, bubbling over, creeping into every nook and cranny within. Anger had been building inside her for so long that it had become a limb, an organ, a part of her.

An uncontrollable tremor got her moving and set her on her way. She walked determinedly to the steel safe hidden away in the bedroom closet, used the key around her neck to open the small but heavy door. Reaching inside, she grabbed hold of the Zip Blade Tiny Knife and put it in her front pants pocket. She then guided the KA-BAR Becker hunting knife with the chromium vanadium drop point steel blade, full tang, into the leather sheath around her waist. Next came the Havalon Piranta Z skinning knife with its unassuming but extremely sharp blade. That went into her leather bag along with her Glock 43X.

A short time later she was in her car, her mind focused on one thing.

Don Fulton. Number two on her list.

She didn't need The Crew.

She had realized that after Psycho had left her alone in the warehouse with Eddie Carter. She'd lied about him running off. After cutting the zip ties, she'd dragged him to Otto Radley's burial site. When he tried to crawl away on all fours, she'd followed him deeper into the woods where the moonlight was blocked by fluttering leaves. She'd pulled out a knife from her ankle strap and slit his throat, severing his trachea. He had managed to rip the duct tape from his mouth and take a few giant, gasping breaths. He'd gargled blood and coughed. Within thirty seconds, he'd fallen unconscious. Died while she collected broken branches and piles of twigs to cover his body with. She'd considered burying him atop Otto Radley. The dirt had still been semisoft, but she needed to clean the warehouse and return to her apartment before dawn.

The trek back home had been a long one. Once she got as far as Sutterville Road, she'd called Lyft and gotten a ride to Treetop Apartments in West Sacramento.

Overall, getting rid of Eddie Carter had been surprisingly easy.

In fact, she should have taken care of Eddie, Don, and Felix a long time ago. Maybe then things would have turned out differently. Maybe she would be happily married, at home with her family. Maybe. Just maybe.

If only.

A few houses away from Don Fulton's house, she pulled to the side of the road. It was a nice house. A large house. Too big, in her opinion, for a single man without children. From the road, the home looked like a European country estate, stretched out on an acre of green grass and tall redwoods.

Before she could make a decision as to whether she would walk from here or pull closer, Don Fulton walked right out the front door. From where she sat, it looked as if he hadn't changed much over the years. He still had a full head of hair. He was wearing baseball pants and a jersey, and carrying a duffel bag.

He walked with confidence. At a good clip with shoulders upright, looking straight ahead. The lift gate on his Cayenne popped open, and he slung his bag inside and shut the trunk and then walked around the Porsche and climbed in behind the wheel.

She was glad she hadn't yet gotten out of her car. From where she sat, the acoustics coming from the Porsche sounded smooth, impressive. He didn't just drive off. He took off, leaving her in the dust.

Shit.

Thank God for speed bumps and stop signs because she might not have caught up to him without them. Her 1.6-liter engine didn't stand a chance against his Cayenne. Once they hit the main road, she was sure she'd lost him until she spotted his bright-red shiny Porsche in the gas station.

Back on the road, she lucked out when less than five miles from the gas station, he pulled into a baseball park. He had a choice of three different parking lots, none of which were paved. She followed him to the lot farthest from the baseball field. He found a spot in the shade. A lot of guys with expensive cars tried to stay away from other cars to avoid getting their car dinged by careless people. Whatever the reason, his parking choice made her job easier.

She pulled up next to him, not too close, not too far.

He looked over at her. His narrowed gaze made it clear he was not pleased with whoever had gone out of their way to park so close to his prized possession.

She made eye contact and smiled her most dazzling smile.

For a split second, she wondered if he'd recognize her from all those years ago. She would enjoy that. Another thought that suddenly struck her was that she had no plan. Zero. She thought about raising a hand and curling her finger, asking him to come to her.

Nah.

Instead, she watched him jump out of his Porsche and walk around to the back of his car without another glance her way.

She grabbed a handkerchief from the glove compartment and slipped it into her pocket. Then she opened the door and climbed out, pulled the Zip Blade Tiny Knife from her front pocket, and unfolded the blade. The knife was so small she knew he wouldn't be able to see the blade in her hand.

He had unzipped his duffel bag and was putting a pair of cleats inside when she walked up behind him. "Excuse me," she said.

"I'm in a hurry. What do you need?"

"I was just wondering if you remembered a girl named Lena Harris. I believe you two met at a fraternity house party."

He whipped around fast. Stared at her long and hard.

Hands at her sides, she kept a good solid grasp on the knife's handle. "You remember, don't you?"

The confused expression on his face made her happy. Mostly because she could tell by the slant of his brow and the intensity in his gaze that yes, he knew exactly who she was.

Just as quickly, he snapped out of his momentary lapse of bewilderment and played it cool by slipping on his baseball cap, then tugging it low over his forehead. This time when his eyes met hers, he smiled. "How have you been?"

"Not too good," she said, poking out her bottom lip in a "Poor me" pout.

"Well, you look good," he said, turning back to his precious car.

As he leaned into the trunk and set about casually zipping up his duffel bag, she covered the small area between them in two long strides, leaned into him from behind so she could reach her right arm around his neck. She knew the drill. With a thrusting motion, more stabbing than slicing, she severed the trachea, the carotid artery on both sides, and his jugular all in quick succession.

He slumped forward headfirst into the trunk of his car, body twitching and blood spurting.

She wiped the blade of her knife against the clean part of his pants to get the blood off, then put the knife away. She looked around. Nobody was there, so she leaned over, circled her arms around his legs, below the knees, and lifted him up and into the back of his nice car before shutting the lift gate. She then used the handkerchief to wipe away her fingerprints.

Calm as ever, she walked back to her car, climbed in, and started the engine. She took her time backing out, making sure she had plenty of room to maneuver her way smoothly out of the parking lot and onto the street.

Her heart didn't beat in earnest until the baseball field was out of sight. The adrenaline rush hit her full force, giving her a high like none other.

Control. She had it in spades. At this rate, there would be no stopping her. She wouldn't just go after three rapists, she'd round up the entire mob and take them out one at a time.

Yes. That's right, she thought happily. She would spend the rest of her life going after every guy she could find who had been at the fraternity house. Every male who had dared to touch her, or who had merely stood by and watched, would die.

Chapter Twenty-Seven

Sawyer was parked outside the trailer park, about to climb out of her car, when her phone buzzed. She picked up the call. "Hey, Geezer. What's going on?"

"Sorry to bother you on a weekend, but I just got a call from a friend at the morgue. Looks like Nick Calderon died of a fentanyl overdose."

Wow. "I'm glad you called. That's huge. Any marks from a syringe?"

"Funny you should ask. Remember I told you I had seen a shoe and a sock under the dining room table?"

"Yes."

"The examiner found an injection site in his toe," Geezer said.

"That's amazing—you know—that they were able to see that."

"I agree. Gotta go now. Just thought you would want to know."

"Thanks, Geezer."

They hung up, and Sawyer got out of the car and headed for Felix Iverson's trailer. Her immediate thought was that if the Black Wigs had been responsible for the recent deaths, then why wouldn't they have injected Brad Vicente or Myles Davenport? She felt confident she was on the right path and that Nick's and Bruce's deaths had nothing to do with the Black Wigs, but everything to do with a copycat.

Dirt and gravel crunched beneath Sawyer's shoes as she walked past a row of run-down trailers in a dilapidated mobile park. To her left was a trailer home with a roof that appeared to be made from sheets of plywood, then topped with old car parts, including scraps of metal and strips of rubber from old tires.

A rat scurried out from under the steps leading to the door and disappeared in the high weeds nearby.

The last trailer home, the one belonging to Felix Iverson, appeared to be the worst off, which was saying a lot. The metal roof sagged in the middle, as if a truck or a giant boulder had fallen from the sky and landed square in the center of his trailer before being hauled off. The grimy, rust-coated windows were covered from the inside with what looked like worn bedsheets.

Sawyer reached into her pocket to make sure her pepper spray canister was there if needed. The capsule could be unlocked with a flick of her thumb. After that it was simply a matter of pushing and spraying.

The three wooden stairs leading to Felix Iverson's trailer door were rotted. She tested her footing before putting weight on each step. Standing firmly at the landing, she knocked and waited.

No one came. She listened for any noise coming from within. No music. No appliances. No footfalls.

After a long pause, she knocked again.

The door snapped open, catching her off guard and giving her a start. Hand on her chest, she stepped backward and nearly toppled over.

Felix Iverson reached out and grabbed her arm, holding her steady. She jerked her arm back, prompting the man to raise his hands as if he were under arrest. "Just trying to help."

"I know. Sorry. You surprised me, that's all."

He was wearing a white tank top and torn-up jeans that hung low on his hips. He leaned a hand against the dented doorframe, his eyes checking her out from head to toe before his gaze met hers. "Funny that I surprised you so easily, when you're the one knocking on my door."

She forced a tight smile. "I'm Sawyer Brooks, reporter for the *Sacramento Independent*. I was hoping I could come inside and we could talk about the Children's Home of Sacramento."

His hair was much longer than it had been in the picture she'd seen. He flipped it back, out of his face. "It wasn't me."

Confused, she frowned. "I'm sorry?"

"I didn't burn the place down."

"Oh. I'm not here to talk about that. I wanted to talk to you about Nick Calderon and Bruce Ward." She looked over his shoulder, tried to get a peek inside, but with all the windows covered up, the place was dark.

"I haven't seen them in years, but sure, if you want to come inside for a drink, then by all means." He stepped aside and swept his hand through the air as if she were royalty, giving her room to enter.

The unmistakable scent of mold, along with cigarettes and stale beer, hit her all at once. She tried not to gag as he pulled out a plastic lawn chair for her to take a seat.

"Want a beer?"

"No, thanks."

He shrugged a bony shoulder, grabbed a beer for himself, and popped the tab. The amber liquid bubbled over the top of the can despite his best effort to quickly suck it up. The kitchen was small. Dirty dishes were piled high in the sink, threatening to topple.

Before taking a seat, he locked the door, sealing the place off from what meager bit of light and fresh air the opening had provided. When he saw her watching him, he said, "People come and go around here, in and out, as if they lived here. Better to keep this private."

She didn't trust him, kept her eyes on him as he pulled out another plastic chair and sat across from her.

"So what do you want to know?" he asked.

"Are you aware that Nick Calderon and Bruce Ward were murdered?"

"Heard about Nick," he said without emotion. "What happened to Bruce?"

"He's dead, and it appears the killer went out of their way to make it look like a suicide. It should be a day or two before investigators have autopsy and toxicology reports."

"They think he was poisoned?"

"It's a possibility." She decided to keep what she knew about the fentanyl found in Nick Calderon's system to herself.

"I was told that security cameras showed someone leaving his house."

"That's true," she said.

"So why are you here? It wasn't me."

His mannerism and defensive attitude bothered her, like a finger poking her in the ribs, telling her to say what she had to say and get out. "Nick Calderon engages a lot on social media, and there are quite a few pictures of you, Nick, and Bruce posted on Nick's Facebook page—"

"Okay, so we've hung out a few times. What about it?"

"Is there any reason you can think of that someone might want to kill two of your closest friends?"

He chuckled, then chugged his beer, finishing it off in a couple of long gulps. "I have no friends."

The thought that Felix might have killed Nick and Bruce floated through her head. But why? What would be his motivation? "Doesn't it worry you that whoever went after Nick and Bruce might come after you?"

This time he guffawed as if that was the funniest thing he'd ever heard in his life. He even slapped his bare knee that stuck out of a giant gaping hole in his jeans. Then he stood, and she watched him closely as he walked through the narrow kitchen and disappeared into a back room. When he returned, he was holding a machete with a sweeping curved steel blade that glinted in the semidarkness.

Sawyer's pulse quickened. She jumped to her feet and whipped out her pepper spray. Held it straight in front of her, thumb on the button.

That same throaty chuckle erupted. "Put that skunk spray away, darling. I'm not going to hurt you."

"You first," she said.

He held the machete in front of him. "It's a beauty, isn't it? It's a kukri. Almost fourteen inches of razor-sharp slicing power. If anyone comes to see me, I'll show them this." After admiring his weapon a moment longer, he finally set it on the one clean space left on the counter opposite the sink area.

Sawyer glanced at the door and wondered how fast she could unlock the bolt. How far she would get before he caught up to her with that blade of his.

He opened the refrigerator and popped open another beer.

A rodent, smaller than the rat outside, skittered across the floor and quickly squeezed its way under the stove, sending a shiver up her spine. She put the pepper spray away.

Felix returned to the plastic chair and took a seat.

"You want to know what I find amusing?"

"What?"

"The fact that you have gone out of your way to come see me." He raised his beer. "Look at you, sitting there all soft and sweet, warning me that my life might be in danger." He feigned a shiver and laughed some more. "That's funny shit."

"It's not a joke."

"Nobody ever gave one fuck about me or the boys. But here you are, telling me to be careful, and what? Stay alert to any unusual noises?"

Before she could ask him who "the boys" included, he started talking again.

“Nobody,” he said flatly, his fist hitting the table hard, making her jump, all the laughter gone from his voice. “Nobody checked to see if they were feeding us properly at that facility. Did anybody care that we were malnourished and sleeping in rat-infested beds?” This time when he stood, he placed both hands flat on the table so that he could keep his balance. He then leaned so far over the table that he was right up in her face.

Sawyer sucked in a breath and held it. The man was crazy.

“Did anyone give a rat’s ass about any of us?” He shook his head, then pushed away from the table and plopped back down into his chair.

Sawyer inhaled.

He took another long swig of beer before he said, “Now that I think about it, there were a few kids who might have wanted to see Nick and Bruce dead. But why wait all these years?”

Sawyer perked up a little. “Do you remember their names?”

“Nah. We gave them all special nicknames.”

“Boys or girls?”

“Both.”

“Would any of them have reason to come after you?”

He shrugged. “Don’t know. Don’t care. Let them come.”

“What about Emily Stiller, Jimmy Crocket, or Stanley Higgins?”

“Ahh, is that her name? Emily. She was a bitch, but I liked her spirit.” He nodded as if agreeing with his own statement. “I could see her making the rounds. Yeah. I can see that.” He looked over his shoulder at his machete. “If she comes here, though, I’ll be ready.”

“What about Jimmy Crocket or Stanley Higgins? Could they be a threat?”

He chuckled. “Jiminy Cricket was a beanpole, and Stupid Stanley peed in his pants if you looked at him cross-eyed.” Felix looked blankly at the wall as if he might be reliving a few moments from his past. “Stupid Stanley thought if he stayed quiet enough, people would leave him alone. But that’s not how it worked at the home.”

"Do you have any regrets about that time in your life?"

"No way. We were kids. Kids do crazy shit."

Sawyer saw it differently. Adults did crazy shit to kids, but she wasn't here to have a debate. "Do you remember the names of any of the adults who were in charge at the time?"

Instead of looking at the wall, he looked upward this time and then shook his head.

"What about the others in your club? Could you give me their names?"

"Don't waste your time, sweetie."

"It's my job. It's what I do."

"Well, I can't help you there."

"Because you don't recall their names?"

"Because I don't think they would want you coming to see them. No offense, honey."

Sawyer pushed herself to her feet and thanked him for his time.

"Aww. Leaving already?" He frowned. "I was just starting to think this might be the beginning of a beautiful friendship between you and me."

Sawyer walked to the door. As she attempted to turn the lock, she panicked when she heard the legs of the chair scrape against the floor.

Haste makes waste, she thought as she tried the lock again. She could feel his warm breath on her neck. The lock wouldn't budge.

He leaned into her, his bony chest brushing against her back as he reached over her shoulder and undid the bolt. "There you go, honey pie."

She opened the door and jumped over the dilapidated steps, landing on the ground with both feet.

"Come back real soon, will you?"

Trying to take even breaths, she kept walking.

"A bit of advice, Sawyer Brooks. You might want to get a real weapon before you come around these parts, because if I wanted a piece of your ass, that itty-bitty thing in your pocket wouldn't stop me from getting what I want."

Sawyer didn't look back. She never should have come to the trailer park alone. She should have waited for Aria to join her and let her sister bring her gun along for the ride.

Chapter Twenty-Eight

It was Monday. Another sunny day. Ten minutes after arriving at the gym where Emily Stiller worked, Sawyer regretted coming. Nancy Lay and Felix were right about Emily. She was no pushover. The young woman with the beautiful red hair and sea-green eyes meant business. Before Sawyer could protest, Emily dragged her upstairs to a massive equipment room where dozens of people were running on treadmills or lifting weights. Every time Sawyer tried to start a conversation about why she was there, Emily cut in, spouting off all the great reasons to exercise and eat right.

"Come on," Emily said, leading her across the room. "It's time for a little fun with the kettlebells."

"Now?" Sawyer asked.

"Yes. Now. Stand with your feet shoulder-width apart. Grasp one kettlebell in each hand, palms facing out, like this."

Emily demonstrated, resting a kettlebell on each shoulder. "Now bend your knees just a few inches and as you stand back up I want you to press the weights straight up overhead."

Sawyer went ahead and played along. It wasn't too bad.

"Bring the weights back to your shoulders," Emily told her. "Yes, like that. Now bend your knees, that's right, into a semisquat, and stand back up."

After fifteen or twenty more of those, Sawyer was eyeing the exits.

"You look like you're in decent shape. I want to show you some of the equipment next. Maybe we could start out with three days a week and then work up from there."

"If you could just answer a few questions I have about Stanley Higgins and Jimmy Crocket—"

She eyed Sawyer suspiciously. "Is that why you're here?"

"Yes. I'm a reporter for the *Sacramento Independent*, and I just had a couple of questions."

"Why didn't you say so?"

"The people at the front desk told me the only way I could talk to you was if I agreed to a consultation."

Emily anchored her hands on her hips and shook her head. "Come on. Let's go to my office."

Relieved, Sawyer did as she said.

Once they were seated in a tiny room with a glass wall, Sawyer reached into her bag and handed Emily the same sheet of paper with the black-and-white photos. "I showed these to Nancy Lay. She talked very highly of you."

"She's still alive?"

Sawyer nodded.

Emily's gaze roamed over the pictures. "Talk about a blast from the past."

Sawyer quickly filled her in on everything going on. Emily had heard about both Nick's and Bruce's recent demises and, like Felix Iverson, she showed no emotion.

Emily's head shot up. Her green eyes fixated on Sawyer's. "You don't think Jimmy or Stanley had anything to do with their deaths, do you?"

Sawyer drew in a breath. "Well, they were both bullied by these guys."

Emily's hand covered her mouth. Her eyes widened. "You think I had something to do with their deaths?"

"Of course not," Sawyer said, which was a lie, since Jimmy, Stanley, and Emily had all been bullied and it made sense that they might want revenge. "I'm just talking to people who knew Nick Calderon and Bruce Ward. I'm doing what journalists do—dotting the *i*'s and crossing the *t*'s."

For a second Sawyer wasn't sure whether Emily was crying or giggling. It turned out to be the latter. Thankfully it wasn't the sort of giggling a madwoman might not be able to hold back, but more of a what-the-fuck-is-going-on sort of laugh.

"I have five minutes before I have to take someone else on a tour of this place, so I'll make this quick and easy for you. Do you have pen and paper in that bag of yours?"

"I'll use my phone," Sawyer said.

"The Boys' Club consisted of five boys," Emily said. "Nick Calderon, Bruce Ward, Chuck Zimmer, Aston Newell, and Felix Iverson are all monsters who deserve to have their eyes plucked from their sockets. Chuck Zimmer died in a car accident a few years after the children's home burned to the ground, so three out of five are dead. Not bad."

Sawyer visibly stiffened at her callous tone.

She heard the sound of voices as people walked by Emily's office. Then Emily said, "If you had seen what I saw, you would be glad they were dead too. If I had wanted to kick their asses, I could have. But I'm no killer. Neither is Jimmy."

"What about Stanley Higgins?"

She shrugged. "I never really knew Stanley. He never said much."

"Do you know what became of Jimmy or Stanley?"

"No idea where Stanley is, but I know that Jimmy lives and works right here in Sacramento at Midtown Design Studio. I run into him every once in a while, but it's usually, 'Hey there. How are you doing?' That sort of thing."

"He's not on social media, and I couldn't find anything about him on the internet."

"Jimmy is smart that way. He doesn't like people. Understandable. Who does?"

Sawyer found herself giving a noncommittal nod.

"Oh, look," Emily said as she waved at the person on the other side of the glass wall waiting outside her door.

Emily came to her feet, and Sawyer couldn't help but quickly size the woman up—five foot eight, muscular, as in strong enough shape to kick some serious ass.

"If you decide to come in for a real workout, let me know." Emily patted her own well-defined abs and said, "Looks like you're getting a little pooch. Your arms look weak too, and your skin is on the pale side. Probably need some vitamin D."

CHAPTER TWENTY-NINE

Sawyer was already sore from doing kettlebell squats when she climbed out of the car at her next destination only a few blocks away from the gym. Aston Newell, one of the alleged bullies at the children's home, worked at an auto shop near the tracks. She'd always appreciated the freight trains that passed by. The railroad tracks were part of the original line from the 1850s. She'd read somewhere that the freight trains running through Midtown carried more freight these days than ever before in US history.

The sound of an electric drill and a loud radio playing heavy metal music poured out of the large open garage. She saw the shadowy figures of the mechanics working on the cars lifted high on hydraulics inside.

A UPS truck pulled up in front of the office, prompting a man in blue oil-stained coveralls to step out of the garage to collect the package.

"Excuse me," Sawyer shouted over the din, but no one heard her. In her haste to get the mechanic's attention, she tripped in a pothole, but managed to catch herself before doing a face-plant. Weaving her way around the UPS truck, she followed the man in coveralls into a small office. A vending machine and two plastic chairs were pushed up against a window overlooking the outside area. A large oscillating fan blew a welcome blast of air over her as she waited for him to do whatever he was doing with the package. His fingernails were rimmed with black grease. She wondered how difficult it would be to get the grime out of his nails. When he finally looked up, his eyes bore into hers.

"Ahh," he said. "You must be the chick Felix called me about." He shook his head. "You're wasting your time, trying to warn the Boys' Club. Whatever bullying took place happened a long time ago. People have moved on. Nick's and Bruce's deaths are nothing but a coincidence, a one-off, a once-in-a-million happening. Nobody on this planet is going to be able to take me out, or Felix, for that matter."

"Maybe you can tell me about the other guys in your club?"

He smiled. "Not going to happen. Sorry, lady." He tipped his head toward the side door leading to the garage. "I've got work to do. Good luck with your search."

Thanks to Emily, she had all the names she needed. But she'd wanted to test Aston. See if he would cooperate. She raised a hand as a goodbye before turning back toward the exit. She walked past two mechanics yelling at each other, trying to be heard over idling engines and hydraulic equipment.

Before she climbed into her car, she felt the ground rumble beneath her feet. She stood still, waiting for the train she knew was coming. The blast of the horn made her smile. She didn't know why. When the train passed by, she watched in awe as the powerful machine took her mind off everything else, at least for a few minutes.

Back at work in her cubicle, Sawyer had just hung up the phone and was looking at her notes when a noise from behind prompted her to swivel around in her chair. "Hey," she said.

Derek smiled. He had on a blue button-down shirt and nicely cut trousers. Casual dress looked good on him. When she first started working at the *Sacramento Independent*, Derek had often worn a suit and tie. The shift away from formal wear for men seemed to be happening much slower than it did for women's fashion. This newer, more relaxed dress code suited Derek well.

"Good thing we work in the same building," he said, "because otherwise we'd hardly ever see each other."

"Why don't you come over for dinner this week? I'll make you my famous tacos."

"I thought you said you didn't cook."

"Did I say that?"

"Pretty sure."

She batted her eyelashes in an exaggerated attempt to play coy. "I guess I don't like to play all my cards right up front."

He laughed, and then Lexi showed up and ruined the moment. A common occurrence of late.

Lexi crossed her arms. "You two lovebirds just can't get enough of each other, can you?"

"It's true," Derek said. "We can't." Before he walked away, he glanced at Sawyer and said, "I'll call you later."

Sawyer fixed her gaze on Lexi and waited for her to speak. It didn't take long.

"I just got off the phone with John Hughes. He wouldn't confirm, but he did suggest that Bruce Ward's wife, Sandra, is a suspect."

Sawyer was dumbfounded. "That would mean they believe Sandra is the person Trudy Carriger saw wearing a black wig and red lipstick leaving the scene of the crime." She shook her head. "Trudy knows Sandra. They're neighbors. She would have recognized Sandra."

Lexi crossed her arms. "Sandra lied to the police. She didn't go to the spa like she originally told them."

"Interesting, but still not enough, in my opinion, to make her a suspect."

"According to Sandra's son, Bruce's stepson, his mom and stepdad never got along. In his words, 'Everyone hates Bruce.'"

Sawyer grimaced. "So where did Sandra go if she didn't go to the spa?"

"To a hotel, where she met up with her boss, a well-to-do older man, who also happens to be married."

"Well, there you go," Sawyer said. "If she met up with her boss, then she has an alibi, right?"

Lexi shrugged. "Sandra is at the police station as we speak, and the police are doing a search at her house, most likely hoping to find a wig or two."

"It's not Sandra," Sawyer said with a shake of her head.

"Oh, okay." Lexi crossed her arms. "Why don't you call Detective Hughes and let him know. It could save him and his team a lot of time."

"The witness—"

"Trudy Carriger, the hundred-year-old woman?" Lexi asked.

"Yes. Trudy Carriger. She's probably in her eighties, and she's a very with-it older woman. She can see just fine. The person wearing the wig and seen leaving Bruce Ward's house was at least five foot eight, and Sandra is shorter than me."

"It's really just a process of elimination at this point," Lexi said.

"If resources and budgets are so damn tight, I just think their time would be better spent focusing on what the witness saw. Besides, if Sandra killed Bruce, then who killed Nick Calderon?"

Lexi had stopped listening, but she lit up when she saw Sawyer's notes. "Tracy Rutherford. She's the one who took Myles Davenport to court ten years ago."

"That's right. I've been meaning to enter her name in the database, but I keep getting sidetracked."

"I looked her up," Lexi said. "She used to work for Antiva, an anti-virus computer company. I talked to the head guy at the company, and he said Tracy was one of their best employees."

"That's great," Sawyer said. "I need to talk to her."

"She's gone. Disappeared a few days before Myles Davenport was found dead."

Sawyer frowned. "How do you know for sure?"

"I talked to her landlord. Her apartment was month to month. She had paid in full and left a note saying she wouldn't be back. Friends and family haven't seen or heard from her in over a week. Nothing on social media. It's almost as if she never existed."

"Well, that's odd," Sawyer said, making a note next to Tracy's name, wondering if she was part of the Black Wigs, along with Christina Farro and a woman named Li.

"Earth to Sawyer," Lexi said. "What are you thinking?"

"Nothing, really." Sawyer checked the time. "I made reservations at the Blue Fox for lunch at twelve thirty. Want to come along?"

"That's the restaurant Brad Vicente mentioned, correct?"

Sawyer nodded.

"Great. I'll drive. Meet me in the parking lot in fifteen minutes."

Chapter Thirty

Sawyer and Lexi were seated at a small table in the center of the main dining room. No privacy and little elbow room. Lexi snapped her fingers, though, and complained just enough to get them moved to a coveted booth.

Sawyer had never been to the steakhouse before. The Blue Fox was touted as being a high-class and memorable experience. But a quick look at the menu told Sawyer it was, first and foremost, hideously expensive.

"If Brad Vicente brought his dates here," Lexi said, "he has very nice taste."

"Have you been here before?"

"Many times."

Sawyer didn't know much about Lexi. Now seemed like a good time to ask a few questions. "Are you married?"

"No. No children either."

Sawyer moved aside the napkin covering the basket of warm bread, grabbed a slice of sourdough, and slathered on the garlic butter.

"Like you, I had an abusive parent."

Sawyer knew never to assume anything about anyone. Everybody had a story. But Lexi? The question floating through her mind should have been, why *not* Lexi? "I'm sorry."

"Don't be. My father left my mom and his three children at a young age. I didn't blame him. My mother was abusive, verbally and physically. I had two younger brothers, which made for a loud and angry household. I can't remember a time when my mother wasn't screaming and yelling at us. She was always calling me names, telling me I was worthless, throwing shoes at me, or smacking me with a serving spoon, whatever was closest." Lexi sipped her water. "If Mother announced suddenly that she was going to the store, that meant we were all supposed to join her. If I didn't have my shoes on—wasn't ready to go—she'd slap me, hard. If I hurried to the car without shoes, she'd slap me, hard. It was always a lose-lose situation."

The server brought their food, setting the lobster bisque in front of Sawyer. Lexi got the salmon with asparagus.

When the server walked away, Lexi continued her sad story. "My psychiatrist has taught me that it wasn't about me. It was about my mother's inability to express her anger and frustration. If I had found help sooner, my youngest brother might not have taken his own life. And I might not have turned to drugs and alcohol." She smiled. "Thankfully, I got help. I have been in and out of therapy and on and off medication for years. Instead of drinking and drugs, I take antidepressants and antianxiety medication. Every day is a struggle with self-esteem. Every day, I look in the mirror and tell myself I am a good person."

Sawyer was no longer hungry. She had no words. Not of comfort or sympathy or anything at all.

"There's a reason I'm telling you all of this."

Sawyer waited.

"When I first heard about you and your sisters, I tried to find out more about you. I paid attention. And I saw how brave you were."

"I'm not brave."

Lexi blew air out of her mouth, almost a whistle but not quite. "You are. You just don't realize it yet. I'm not saying that you're not afraid. But your determination and resolve seem to take over, and I believe it's those qualities that enabled you to find that missing girl last month." She pointed a finger at Sawyer. "You know what needs to be done, and you go after it. You're not afraid to take risks or ask for help. That's bravery."

"I'll tell you what I'm not good at," Sawyer said.

Lexi arched an eyebrow.

"Compliments. They make my palms sweat. I think my inability to receive any sort of praise without cringing is a sure sign of low self-esteem."

"Sounds like this is something you've thought about."

Sawyer nodded and then picked up her spoon and tasted her soup. It was divine.

They talked and ate, and when the waitress brought their check, Sawyer showed the woman a picture of Brad Vicente and asked if he'd ever eaten at the establishment. The young woman wrinkled her nose. "Unfortunately, yes. He was a regular before—you know—"

"Before he was arrested," Lexi provided.

"Yes." The waitress looked around as if to make sure no one was listening. "He was good friends with Ian Farley. Ian mostly worked on weekends since he was taking classes at California State University Sacramento. He used to be a popular server here at the Blue Fox. But he quit the same day Brad Vicente was arrested. Rumors floated around for weeks about Ian helping Brad Vicente spike his victims' drinks."

Sawyer exchanged a what-the-hell look with Lexi.

The waitress visibly stiffened. "I said too much."

"No," Lexi told her in a gentle voice. "Brad Vicente is appealing the court's decision. If he finds a way to get out of jail, he could ruin the lives of many more women. Nothing you've told us will be repeated after we leave."

"Thank you," the server said. "You might want to talk to Tina on your way out." She pointed to the woman standing behind a podium near the entrance. "She's the hostess who was working the last time Brad Vicente was here."

"Thank you," Sawyer said. "You've been a big help." Since it had been Sawyer's idea to go to the Blue Fox for lunch, it seemed only fair that she pay the bill. Sawyer reached inside her purse for her wallet and pulled out the only credit card that wasn't maxed out and put it on the tray. After the bill was paid, they stopped to chat with the hostess.

"All I know," Tina said, "is that the woman with Brad Vicente appeared to be tipsy. She was wobbling as she made her exit. I kept watching because I thought for sure she was going to fall over. She was about to get into her car when I saw her date—Brad Vicente—help her walk to his car instead. To tell you the truth, I was sort of relieved that he wasn't going to let her drive. Later, though, when I heard what happened, I couldn't help but wonder if that woman had a black wig shoved inside her purse." Her eyes got wide. "Maybe she was faking the whole tipsy thing, you know?"

"Are there security cameras in the parking lot?" Sawyer asked.

"No. But management has talked about having them installed."

"You wouldn't happen to recall what kind of car the woman was driving, would you?"

"It was small and mint green. That's all I know."

Sawyer instantly thought of the car that had been following her for days now. There was no way it could be a coincidence. No point in saying anything to Lexi until she had more information.

An older couple walked in, cutting their talk short. Sawyer thanked Tina before she and Lexi headed out to the parking lot. A few minutes later, they were climbing into Lexi's car.

"I wonder if the woman was faking it?" Sawyer asked. "Maybe she planned the whole thing and wanted to get into Brad Vicente's car. All her friends in black wigs could have been waiting at the house."

"Anything's possible." Lexi buckled her seatbelt and then looked at Sawyer for longer than was necessary or comfortable.

"What?"

"We're not investigators. It's not our job to investigate a crime, examine the scene, interview witnesses, and pursue suspects. It's up to law enforcement to piece it all together. You do realize that, don't you?"

Sawyer groaned. "You sound like Palmer."

"Thank you."

Sawyer rolled her eyes. "My job as a crime reporter is to talk to police, detectives, criminals, and victims and then keep the public informed about what's happening in their neighborhood, all the while being sure to remain unbiased." She sighed. "I get that. But what I don't understand is how I am supposed to separate all the information I've gleaned and do nothing with it. If it turns out that A, B, and C means that D might be a suspect, then I'm going to make sure somebody with authority knows it."

"Whatever you're doing seems to be working in your favor, so who am I to argue?"

After Lexi started the engine, she thanked Sawyer for lunch.

"My pleasure," Sawyer said. And that was the truth. Never mind that Sawyer could have paid her utility bill with the money spent. She'd learned a lot about her new partner in crime, and she respected Lexi more than she had just hours before. Not because Lexi had been abused or because they shared traumatic childhood stories, but because Lexi had trusted Sawyer enough to open up.

"Where to?" Lexi asked.

"Ian Farley's." Sawyer held up her phone. "I have an address for our server in West Sacramento. According to Zillow, it's a rental house."

Sawyer read off the address.

Lexi punched it into her navigation system, and they were off.

Chapter Thirty-One

Harper logged on to her computer to see if any other members of The Crew had signed on to their private group.

Once she saw that no one had commented since Cleo left, she exited out of the group site and simply sat quietly for a minute or two. Was she the only one who was worried about Eddie Carter?

She typed his name into the search bar. The most relevant pages popped up.

Eddie Carter and his wife, Trisha, donated half their salaries every year to charity, saying that they had more than they needed and there were too many people who didn't.

Harper rubbed her stomach as she clicked various links and skimmed through content. Eddie Carter and his wife seemed too good to be true. They used a charity evaluator to help figure out where their money would benefit the most people.

It was the next page header that stopped Harper cold:

Eddie Carter Missing Since Sunday

The suspicious disappearance of a father and husband last seen at Maximum Workout has sparked worry in the community. A search is underway . . .

Her heart raced as she logged back on to the private group and began to type.

MALICE: Is anyone there?

Nobody. Just a stupid blinking cursor.

MALICE: It's official. Eddie Carter is missing and a search is underway.

Harper's eyes watered as she stared at the screen, hoping one of the crew members would log on and talk her down from the cliff's edge. How had it come to this? She felt lost and alone. She rested her head on folded arms and let the tears come, taking in gulps of air as giant sobs consumed her. Five minutes later, maybe longer, she sat up and straightened her spine. Lily and Psycho had logged on.

LILY: I know you're having a difficult time and I'm sorry, but you need to find a way to move on. When was the last time you talked to a therapist or psychiatrist?

PSYCHO: This slow breakdown you're dealing with at the moment all stems from the trauma you suffered in the past. This is exactly the reason these assholes we went after got what they deserved. If not for them, we wouldn't be talking to you right now.

LILY: Malice. You never told us who your perpetrator was. I never asked because it seemed obvious to me that it was too painful for you to talk about.

She was right. It was too painful. Even now. But it was time.

MALICE: My father was my abuser. When he first started coming to my room, he would lavish attention on me, and he made me feel as if I were the special sibling. He would buy me treats and sneak them to me when my sisters were out of sight. Always praising me for silly things I did throughout the day. When he hugged me overly long, I didn't mind. But hugging soon became rubbing. And then he began to come into my room at night, creeping onto my bed and lying next to me. I pretended to be asleep. It did no good. My father soon became my worst nightmare. He's dead now, but that hasn't changed anything. I still can't sleep. I still haven't found a way to move on.

LILY: Did you tell anyone at the time?

MALICE: When I had finally gathered the courage to tell my mother, I saw her peeking through the door, watching, before quietly walking away.

A long stretch of nothing but a blinking cursor.

PSYCHO: And now he's dead and buried. Let it go.

MALICE: I'm trying. We're all trying.

Psycho had to know better than most that it wasn't that easy. But she wasn't here to argue, so Harper quickly changed the subject.

MALICE: Do you think Cleo will go after Felix Iverson?

LILY: If she does, I doubt she'll stop there.

PSYCHO: If she asked for help, I wouldn't hesitate. I have no regrets.

LILY: Although I don't feel any closure after everything that has happened, I would do it all again.

That surprised Harper. Maybe because Harper saw Lily as the most put together of The Crew members. But who knew what lay within any one of them? Overall, their differing reactions to revenge merely proved that not everyone had the same response to vengeance. For Harper, it was finally clear that no jolt of pleasure or satisfaction would be forthcoming. Revenge simply had no cathartic effect on her.

PSYCHO: For what it's worth, that someone you loved and trusted did that to you is seriously fucked up. Your father was a piece of shit and doesn't deserve another thought. At least Otto Radley spent some time locked in a cell before he took the fast train to hell.

LILY: Maybe the best revenge will be having another happy, healthy baby and living your best life.

Harper knew that Lily was right. Without The Crew she might not have realized that she was taking her family for granted. Maybe there was hope, and she could somehow find a way to move on from her troubled past. But first, she had one more enemy to deal with.

MALICE: What about guilt?

PSYCHO: What about it? Would you rather have let those guys go on with their lives without retribution? If society and the law had taken care of them in the first place, we never would have had to do the things we did. Fuck guilt. We're all just trying to make things right within ourselves.

LILY: Agree. How guilty would you feel if Otto Radley had found another victim that night?

So true, Harper thought.

PSYCHO: Before we shut down, Malice, you should know that only days ago your sister Aria was parked outside my apartment building. I confronted her and gave her a warning. She asked me point blank if I was involved with the Black Wigs.

Harper was stunned. A heavy feeling settled in her stomach. What was Aria thinking?

MALICE: I had no idea. Thanks for the heads-up. I'll take care of it.

PSYCHO: If you don't, your sisters might end up on Cleo's list.

A shiver crawled down Harper's spine.

MALICE: Our work here is done. If anyone hears from Cleo, please sign in to let me know.

PSYCHO: Will do. Take care.

LILY: Thank you both. Goodbye for now.

The screen darkened. Harper wiped her eyes and signed off. It was over.

Almost.

Chapter Thirty-Two

The address for Ian Farley took Sawyer and Lexi to a one-story blue house with white trim on Thirty-Fourth Street. It was a prime location for a CSUS student. The university was five minutes away by car and fifteen by bicycle. There were plenty of restaurants, gyms, and coffee shops.

Sawyer and Lexi walked to the front door. Lexi rang the doorbell, and right away, footfalls sounded from inside. The kid who answered the door wore sweatpants and a T-shirt. His hair was short on the sides and longer on top.

"I am Sawyer Brooks and this is Lexi Holmes. We're with the *Sacramento Independent*, and we have a few questions for Ian Farley. Is he home?"

Before the young man could answer, there was a commotion in the other room, and another boy with a crew cut and a nose ring walked up from behind the guy who had answered the door. "Ian isn't here."

Sawyer tilted her head. "Listen, we just have a few questions for him, and then we'll leave."

One of the boys started to shut the door, but Lexi lodged her foot between the door and the frame. "If he doesn't talk to us," she said in a firm voice, "we're going to call the police and tell them we have reason to believe that Ian Farley helped Brad Vicente drug his victims."

"That's bullshit," the boy with the nose ring said.

Lexi angled her head. "Not according to the people we talked to at the Blue Fox."

So much for the promise she made to their server today, Sawyer thought.

But it worked.

A third young man approached. "I'll take care of this."

The other boys walked off. "I'm Ian." He stepped outside and shut the door behind them.

"Do you have ID?" Lexi asked.

His hands visibly shook as he pulled his wallet from his back pocket and showed them his license. "What do you need to know?"

"When was the last time you saw Brad Vicente?"

He looked at his sneakers. "I don't remember."

"You really might want to figure it out," Lexi told him, "because when the police pick you up and take you to the station, they'll sit you in a little room without windows and leave you there alone for hours with nothing to eat or drink until you do remember."

"Okay. Okay. It was two or three days before I heard on the news that he was arrested. He brought a date to the restaurant. She was about five foot nine with her three-inch heels. She was hot—I mean nice looking. Perfect body. Long blonde hair, but I think it was a wig."

"Why do you think that?" Sawyer asked.

"Because my mom had cancer and she wore wigs. This woman's hair didn't match the cap you have to put over your real hair before you put on the wig."

"Did you talk to the woman?" Lexi asked.

He shrugged. "She might have had a question about the wine."

"Did you put something in her wine?"

"No," he said.

Sawyer could tell he was lying. The kid was in trouble. Big trouble. "Were you friends with Brad Vicente?"

His gaze was fixated on his feet again. But this time his shoulders began to shake. Ian Farley was crying.

"Did you ever go to his house?" Sawyer asked.

He didn't look up, but he nodded just the same.

Sawyer had a million questions ready to go. "Was the blonde woman you met at the Blue Fox at Brad's house?"

Another nod.

"Was she wearing a wig?"

"No, but the other women were."

"How many other women?"

"At least three. Maybe four."

"Describe the wigs they were wearing."

"Short black hair."

"How short?"

He gestured just below his ear. "They also wore masks that covered their eyes and part of their noses."

"Anything else?"

"The one who had been at the Blue Fox put the blade of a knife to my throat and threatened to kill me."

"I wonder why?" Lexi asked, her sarcasm clear.

"Do you know why she wanted to kill you?" Sawyer asked.

"No," he cried. "I only went to the house because Brad invited me to come over and play video games."

"Tell me about the other women," Sawyer said firmly.

"One of them wore a tank top. She had scars everywhere . . . on her neck, arms, and chest."

Christina Farro's image flashed through Sawyer's head. When Sawyer had met Christina, she hadn't been able to look away from all the scars. Christina had told her she didn't bother trying to hide her "mutilations," as she called them, because they were a part of her. She'd also claimed she didn't care what had happened to Otto Radley after his release. Something about the way she'd said it hadn't rung true to Sawyer, which begged the question: Was she a part of the Black Wigs?

"How did you get away?"

He shook his head. "It's all a blur. I don't remember. I've told you everything I know."

Ian Farley turned around and disappeared through the door without another word spoken, slamming it shut behind him.

Lexi looked at Sawyer. "There's no way he doesn't remember how he got away."

"Obviously."

"What are you thinking?" Lexi asked.

"One of the women he described, the one with scars all over her arms, could be Christina Farro."

"The woman held captive by Otto Radley," Lexi said under her breath.

Sawyer nodded. "What if she is part of the Black Wigs?"

Lexi took hold of Sawyer's arm and nudged her down the path and to the car. "It makes sense, doesn't it? If anyone would want revenge on a person, it would be her. The things that man did to her are unspeakable. And now he's missing."

Sawyer agreed. After she climbed in and put on her seatbelt, she looked back at the house being rented by Ian and his friends.

Lexi started the engine. "What are we going to do about Ian Farley?"

"I'm going to talk to Palmer."

After they had been on the road for a couple of minutes and the trees swept by in a blur, Sawyer looked over at Lexi. "You were brilliant back there. I didn't think there was any way we were going to get to talk to Ian." Sawyer shook her head. "And you called me the brave one?"

Lexi grunted. "They're just little boys. Nothing brave about that."

Chapter Thirty-Three

After Lexi dropped her off at her car, Sawyer drove straight to Palmer's house. Greeted at the door by his wife, Debbie, she asked Sawyer to wait in the parlor. Although the term was outdated, the large room where she now stood was exactly how she would have envisioned a parlor to look. The walls were painted canary yellow, and the thick curtains were lined in green velvet. A gold-gilded-frame picture hanging over the hearth was of a man from the eighteenth century. He wore a red velvet jacket and looked off to the side as if to make sure the artist captured his best profile.

Thanks to her parents' obsession with antiques, she recognized the Empire sofa, Chippendale upholstered armchairs, and Queen Anne table. Before she could examine the room further, Palmer entered using a cane.

Sawyer beamed. "I had no idea you were up and about. I thought Debbie might be straightening your bedsheets before she led me to your room."

"Second day on my feet," he stated proudly.

Sawyer stayed by his side as he made his way over to the Empire sofa and took a seat.

He patted the seat next to him, and she sat down. It made her happy to see color in his face. "I never would have pegged you for a fancy parlor man."

He chuckled. "It's an old, historic house, and we're doing our part to preserve history."

She could hear people talking in the other room. "You have visitors. Debbie should have told me. I could have come back another time."

His eyes sparkled. "My son is here."

"And your granddaughter?" Sawyer asked, happy for Palmer. He had mentioned his son before, said they'd had a falling-out of sorts. For that reason he hadn't seen his granddaughter in years.

"And my granddaughter," he said. "They'll be staying for a few weeks, so there was no need to send you off. How are things at the office?"

Sawyer smiled. "It's not the same without you."

He angled his head. "How are you and Lexi getting along?"

"I think I'm beginning to actually like her."

Palmer's laughter turned to a cough. He pulled a handkerchief from his pocket, and once he collected himself, he said, "You two have more in common than you know."

Sawyer said nothing.

"So what's on your mind?"

"The Black Wigs. And now we have two more homicides that I believe are the work of a copycat, but the investigators have different ideas." Not wanting to keep Palmer away from his son for too long, she told him everything that was going on, ending with her and Lexi's lunch at the Blue Fox and all about their chat with Ian Farley, the server who quit soon after Brad Vicente was arrested.

When Sawyer was finished, she recognized the expression on Palmer's face immediately. They both knew what she needed to do.

"You know what I'm going to say."

She drew in a breath. "I need to talk to Perez."

"Yes."

"The man can hardly stand the sight of me."

"He'll come around. You're bullheaded and stubborn. And so is he. You'll be fine. You always are."

"And if he doesn't come around? What then?"

"Just do what you always do, Sawyer. Be you. Do you. Believe in yourself. Your instincts haven't failed you yet."

She smiled. "This is why I need you at the office."

"To pump you up and remind you to trust yourself?"

"Exactly."

His face grew suddenly somber. "Now it's my turn."

"For what?"

"To tell you what's going on with me."

Her heart pounded. Was he sicker than she thought?

"I've had a lot of time to think lately, and I realized that I've never taken the time to tell you how much you mean to me." He lifted a hand to stop her from protesting. "Not just because you saved my life—"

"I didn't—"

"You did. But that's not what I'm getting at. I'm sure you know that I saw something inside you the very first time we met. Something special. Something that told me, 'That girl means business and she's going places.'"

Sawyer smiled, her insides filling with warmth. Maybe she liked receiving praise more than she'd thought.

"When we first met in class and I told you that the baggage you were carrying within would weigh you down and stop you from becoming a decent reporter, I knew then what I know now. You've got the determination and perseverance that it takes to be a good crime reporter. You've also got what many reporters don't. You have a big heart." He sat up taller as if trying to get comfortable. "I don't think you have any idea how much you mean to me. I think of you as a daughter."

And this was exactly why she'd come to see him. Deep down, she'd realized it the second he walked into the overdecorated parlor. He'd always been her mentor, but he'd quickly become so much more. Other than Harper and Aria, he was the only person in the world she trusted wholeheartedly.

Sawyer reached for his hand and gave it a squeeze, but worry settled over her when she noticed a change in his expression. He had more to say. "What is it? You're getting better, right?"

"My doctor assured me I'm going to be just fine."

Her shoulders relaxed.

"But I've decided to retire."

Her heart dropped to her stomach.

"I want to read and spend time in the garden with Debbie. Maybe even take a trip to Paris."

"Wow," Sawyer said, pulling her hand away and using it to push loose strands of hair out of her face. "I'm going to miss you."

"I'll be right here. Stop by anytime."

"You know I will."

Chapter Thirty-Four

Aria had just finished sending a text to Sawyer when Corey Moran walked through the door to the shelter. Weird timing, considering the text she'd just sent her sister included a picture of Corey she had taken through the window of the coffee shop yesterday when she saw him walking across the street toward the café.

Her insides did somersaults.

Their visit at the coffee shop had been cut super short when he'd gotten a call and had to rush off. She'd told him she would be working all week at the shelter if he wanted to stop by and visit Duke. That was the name she had given the dog he'd found on the street and brought in the day they met.

She had no idea whether he would come. But here he was, looking better than ever in light-washed jeans and the same chunky boots he'd worn the first time they met. He also had a newly shaved jaw, which made him look younger. The only thing different about him was the man bun. It looked good on him.

"Is Duke around?" he asked.

"Duke? Oh, yeah, Duke." She laughed. Just the sight of him had her completely discombobulated.

He laughed too.

"So how much time do you have?" she asked.

"As much time as you need."

Okay, then. "I'll walk Chompers and let you take Duke."

"Sounds good. Just tell me what to do."

She grabbed a leash and took Corey to Duke's cage. While he worked on rounding up Duke, Aria went to get Chompers, an old dog and the shelter's longest resident. The poor dog was a slow walker, but Chompers loved being outdoors.

The moment they stepped outside, Aria drew in a breath. It was a beautiful day. She kept sneaking glances at Corey. And her day kept getting better by the minute.

"You love what you do, don't you?" he asked.

"I do. I love being with animals, and I love this place." Aria looked around, admiring the view. "Whenever I walk the trails, I feel like I'm in another world."

Aria unlatched the gate leading to the trails. She was glad he had come since they hadn't had time to get to know one another at the coffee shop. They walked quietly, Corey working hard to keep Duke from running too far ahead while Aria tried to nudge Chompers onward.

"I'm glad I came," he said when the path widened and they were able to walk side by side.

"Me too."

"Sorry about running off so quickly yesterday."

"No worries. So what do you do?" she asked. "Don't answer that if you don't want to. I'm being nosy."

"I'm fine with nosy. I am a graphic designer. I specialize in layout design and editorial illustration. I work with local clients mostly, but I do have a few clients across the country."

"Cool." Feeling a bit tongue-tied and awkward, she kept her head down as she walked.

"Are you okay?"

"I'm fine. I'm just not good at this."

"At what? Talking?"

She laughed. "Exactly. For the past sixteen years I've lived alone. Well, not exactly alone. I have Mr. Baguette, a cockatiel." She smiled, hoping she didn't sound too pathetic. "I also have two sisters and a brother-in-law and a niece and nephew, but overall, besides work, I really don't get out much."

He smiled, nodded.

"I used to work part time as a barista, and you can't really work in a place like that without talking to people. I've also been helping my younger sister a lot lately, so I guess I'm getting better at this talking thing."

"What does your sister do?"

"She's a crime reporter for the *Sacramento Independent*. Right now, she's working on the Black Wigs story."

"And you're helping her with that?"

"Yes. I mostly help her with research. Every once in a while, I will go with her to conduct an interview. For instance, the other day we met with Nancy Lay. She used to be a cook at the Children's Home of Sacramento, a place for troubled kids that was burned to the ground." Aria looked at him. "You're frowning."

"Just trying to figure out the connection between the Black Wigs and Nancy Lay."

She laughed. "Here I am telling you I don't talk much, and I'm babbling on about my sister's job."

"You're not babbling. I find the whole vigilante story fascinating. But I do have one question."

"Yes?"

"What is your name?"

She felt heat rise to her face. "I never told you my name?"

"Afraid not."

"No, that can't be true," she said. "I must have told you when I called you to meet at the coffee shop."

He shook his head. "You said something like . . . this is the girl at the shelter where you brought the dog. His name is Duke now, and I was wondering if you would like to meet for coffee." His smile grew bigger. "I was going to ask you at the coffee shop, but after getting a call from a client saying they needed something right away, it slipped my mind."

"And yet you still came here today," she said sheepishly.

"You're way too hard on yourself. If it makes you feel any better, I've never been a people person myself. In fact, I had a tough time as a youngster. I was bullied, and I'm still working on having normal conversations with people."

He stopped to unwind the leash from around Duke's back leg. When he stood straight again, their gazes met.

When she realized she was staring, she looked away and gave Chompers a pat on the head.

"Two crushed souls meet at a shelter filled with neglected and abused animals that just want to be loved," he said.

She nudged Chompers along and found herself asking, "I wonder how someone goes about fixing a crushed spirit?"

"They start by waking up each morning, looking in the mirror, and telling themselves they are beautiful and they are worthy."

"I like that. Once a day?"

"Yep. Only once." He rubbed his hands over Duke's back, giving her and Chompers a chance to catch up.

"What about meditation and eating right?"

"All good," he said, "but there's one more important thing a person with a crushed soul must do."

Aria arched a questioning brow.

"They must forgive themselves."

"Forgive themselves for what?"

"For every bad choice they've ever made," he said. "For eating the whole pie, when one slice would have done the trick. For not holding the elevator for a stranger, or for shutting the door in the face of a door-to-door salesman."

"Do salesmen still go door to door?"

"Trust me. They do. But I have forgiven myself for that one."

She laughed. "I wouldn't know where to start. I have never eaten an entire pie."

"I doubt you have anything to forgive yourself for. Just look at all the good you do for these animals." His gaze settled on Chompers, who had plopped down on the ground, too exhausted to take another step.

"Looks like I wore her out."

"We better get her back for some water." He handed the end of Duke's leash to Aria, then bent down and scooped up Chompers into his arms and headed back the way they'd come.

Aria followed close behind, thinking Corey Moran was too good to be true. The fact that he was sweet, funny, and nice was a little disconcerting. But he was also damaged goods. Even before he'd said what he said about being bullied, she'd recognized him as a lost soul. Scarred, and a little messed up.

It took one to know one.

Chapter Thirty-Five

Aston Newell made sure all the tools in the shop were in the cart before he rolled it to the side of the garage. He then grabbed the handle on the hinged panels of steel and rolled the garage door closed. Once he clicked the padlock in place, he stood tall, hands on his hips, and took one last look. The air was tinged with motor oil, grease, and sweat. Just as it should be.

He was proud of his shop. He'd worked hard to get where he was today. Just last month he'd hired two more mechanics, and yet he still couldn't seem to get home at a decent hour. The sound of the front door opening and closing caught his attention.

"Sorry. We're closed!"

He stood still and listened. The only sound was the whirring of the oscillating fan in the office. He took a step that way, then noticed someone standing within the doorframe. If not for the long black hair and crimson lipstick, he might have thought it was a man.

"Can I help you?"

He or she smiled, and something about those eyes . . .

It struck him then. He knew exactly who it was. He couldn't help but laugh as he stepped over to the cart he'd just rolled to the side and picked up a crowbar. Then he turned back to Cockroach and said, "A woman—Sawyer Brooks from the local newspaper—came by today to warn me that you might be paying me a visit."

Aston held the crowbar in his right hand and tapped one end to the open palm of his left hand. He did this again and again as he tried to process what was going on and what his next move would be if Cockroach came at him or pulled out a gun.

One thing was for sure, Aston thought. No way was he going to let Cockroach take his life for something that happened years ago. "Why are you here? Nick and Bruce were the instigators, the leaders of the pack. I only hung out with them because I wanted to survive."

"And you stood by and watched," Cockroach said.

Aston nodded. "That's right. I didn't touch you. Not once."

"You always were the loudest and biggest liar. It wasn't you who defecated in my bed and then shoved my face in it and held my head down so that I couldn't scream?"

"Come on. We were kids. Kids do stupid shit all the time."

"Have you ever had your face shoved in someone else's shit and held there until you passed out?"

"No, but you weren't the only one it happened to."

"Ah. So that makes it all okay," Cockroach said without emotion.

Aston's heart was racing now. Cockroach meant business. He should have listened to the journalist. If he had, he could have at least been prepared. He had two pistols locked up in a safe at home. This was crazy. "I'm sorry. Is that what you want to hear?"

"It would be a good start."

"You need to leave. Get out of here before I call the police."

The corners of Cockroach's mouth turned upward.

"What do you want?" Aston asked. "Is it money you need?"

"Get on your knees and beg forgiveness."

Wrong answer. Adrenaline rushed through Aston's body as he cracked his neck from side to side. Like a linebacker going for a sack, he rushed headfirst into Cockroach's chest.

Cockroach grunted and fell backward into the counter.

Aston's eye stung. He thought maybe he had slammed into Cockroach's zipper or the sharp edge of a button until he raised a hand to his face to see if he was bleeding and felt an object poking out of his left socket. He yanked it out, surprised to see that he was holding a syringe. He tossed it aside. "What the fuck did you do?"

Aston headed for the office phone to call the police, but fell to the floor before he reached the door. His breathing was erratic. He felt dizzy. What the hell was happening to him? He clutched his throat.

Cockroach walked over and hovered, staring down at him with the same fascination Aston had when he was just a kid watching Nick and Bruce do their worst.

Why hadn't he stopped them, he wondered? He could have run for help. He hadn't thought of Cockroach in years, if ever. Not until the journalist had come to see him. He wasn't a bad guy, he told himself.

He wanted to live, wanted to beg for his life. He was ready to do that, but when he opened his mouth, nothing came forth. He couldn't speak. Opening and closing his mouth like a fish, he tried to push the words out. It was no use.

There was nothing he could do to stop Cockroach from taking hold of his ankles and dragging him across the garage floor. Aston felt the upper half of his body being lifted onto a creeper that was then rolled under a car held up by a jack. How many times had he told his guys not to use the old car jacks? But nobody listened.

"Remember what you said to me after Nick and Bruce tied me to a tree?" Cockroach asked.

Even if he had remembered, what good would it do? Would Cockroach leave him alone?

"You said, stop your blubbering, kid, it will all be over soon. You were wrong." Cockroach stood up, then grunted and groaned while pushing hard on the side of the Hyundai Genesis, but nothing happened.

Maybe, just maybe, Aston thought, he might live to see another sunrise.

Then Cockroach smiled, and that's when Aston knew all that groaning and moaning and pushing of the car was just for show, to build tension and give Aston false hope.

Aston knew all that because of the smile. It was a fuck-you smile that said, "Look at me, I'm all grown up now, and I'm getting the last laugh."

Cockroach then moseyed on over to where the jack was and gave it a good hard kick.

It was dark when Sawyer parked in front of the auto shop where Aston Newell worked. It had been a very long day. After working late, she'd picked up the flash drive at Purple House Digital. The video had been lightened and brightened, leaving no doubt that Otto Radley was the man who had approached a woman sitting on a bench in the park wearing a short black wig.

She would show the newly enhanced video to Detective Perez in the morning. Right now, though, she had one more question for Aston Newell. She wanted the names of the boys who had been bullied. Boys who had grown into men and who might be motivated to seek revenge. Hoping to bribe him, she'd stopped at the grocery store to buy cookies. She would come by the auto shop every day and every night until she wore him down and he gave her the names. Someone out there, someone Aston probably knew, was killing his friends. She needed to make him see that this was truly a matter of life and death.

There was a light on in his office, and she assumed Aston Newell would be the one to close down the shop since he owned the place. With cookies in hand, she climbed out of the car and shut the door. As she approached the office door, she heard a loud crash come from inside the garage. The noise rattled her and she hurried inside, set the cookies on the counter, and went straight to the garage where she saw a man wedged beneath a car.

"Aston!"

The overhead lights flicked off.

She couldn't see a thing. Her heart pounded against her ribs.

Tools crashed to the ground. A tire flew through the air, hitting her upper body and flinging her to the ground. Next came a metal tool that bounced off her head, but not before leaving a gash near her hairline. Her fingers went to her head where she felt blood.

A shadowy figure ran past her, footfalls pounding against the floor as the person ran through the office.

She jumped to her feet and followed, sweeping a pair of scissors off the desk in the office on her way out, just in time to see the person round the corner and make their way through a parking lot behind the auto shop.

Thankful to be wearing flats, she rushed after the person, running through the parking lot and over an expanse of dead grass and weeds until she realized she was on the train tracks. She was gaining ground, getting closer. There was no way she was giving up now. She ran between the two solid steel rails, concentrating on the railroad ties so she wouldn't trip and fall.

The person was less than twenty feet ahead of her when she felt the earth rumble beneath her feet. A train was coming. She could see lights in the not-too-far distance, coming straight for her. The freight trains were faster than they seemed, and she jumped to the side, then watched the person she'd been chasing look over their shoulder and jump to the opposite side right before the train passed by, horn blaring.

She leaned over and sucked air into her lungs. *Fuck.* Whoever it was would be long gone by the time the train passed. She hurried back the way she came. Her cell phone was in the car. She grabbed it and called for help as she made her way back through the office to the garage. Flicking on the light, she went to where Aston lay, unmoving. One of his arms lay still beside his body. She felt his wrist for a pulse. He was gone.

Sawyer sat in the back of an ambulance as an EMT cleaned her up. She had two cuts, one on the side of her face close to her ear and the other at the hairline. He used butterfly strips to close her up, then told her she might need stitches.

Detective Kevin Grumley was on the scene. Sawyer had never met him before. He held a notebook and pen, something Detective Perez never did, and he asked Sawyer why she was there. She told him everything, starting with the write-up she was doing on the Black Wigs and how she believed the recent killings were the work of a copycat.

"The person you ran after," he said. "Male or female?"

"I have no idea." She thought of Trudy and what she'd said about the person being a man, but really, there was nothing about the way the person ran that would help Sawyer distinguish male from female. "I would guess the height to be five foot eight, maybe nine. Light-brown hair. I didn't see the person's face because the lights were shut off before I realized I wasn't alone. Once the person took off, I gave chase, and you know the rest." Sawyer rubbed a chill from her arms. "If we're finished here, I'd like to go home."

"Go ahead," the detective said. "I know where to find you if I have further questions."

It was well past midnight by the time Sawyer got back to her apartment. She had called Derek on her way home. Despite his concern, she turned down his offer to come to her apartment. She needed time alone to think. Her head was pounding, and she wanted to take a shower and then go straight to bed.

She fed Raccoon, rubbing his fur and apologizing for never being around. Raccoon didn't seem to mind. He looked nothing like the cat she'd found half starving only months ago. Raccoon was content.

Once she climbed into bed, she flipped through text messages, deleting the one from Derek asking where she was and the one from Purple House Digital since she'd already picked up the flash drive. She looked at the texts from Aria, smiled when she saw that her sister had sent a picture of Corey Moran walking toward the coffee shop. Man, she thought, her sister had fallen fast and hard, it seemed. The next text from Aria was a long one telling Sawyer all about how he had come to the shelter to help her walk the dogs.

Sawyer scrolled back to the man's image. He had a happy-go-lucky sort of face. Cute. He had a lanky physique and untamed sandy hair. Corey Moran. The name didn't ring any bells. She had already put his name through a database and nothing popped up. But still, who was he, really? Was he kind and caring? Or was he a womanizer, a "love 'em and leave 'em" kind of guy? She loved Aria and didn't want to see her get hurt.

Before shutting down her phone, she remembered the other name Emily had given her: Stanley Higgins. If she had thought about it earlier, she would have asked Aria to look him up.

She typed his name into the search bar. There were six guys with the same name in Sacramento. If he was close to Emily's age, that would put him somewhere between thirty-six and forty.

Bingo.

Only one guy fit the bill. The good news was, he didn't own an auto shop. The bad news was, he was a taxidermist in Citrus Heights, about twenty minutes away.

She would go see Stanley Higgins right after she met with Detective Perez. She would use the enhanced video to get in to see the detective and then tell him what she and Lexi had learned about Ian Farley, the server at the Blue Fox restaurant.

Unable to keep her eyes open for another moment, she shut down her phone, connected it to the charger on the nightstand, then turned off the light.

Chapter Thirty-Six

Early the next morning Sawyer was on her way to see Detective Perez when she drove her car into the parking lot outside Aston Newell's auto shop and turned off the engine. Crime tape had been wrapped around the office door.

Sawyer climbed out and headed for the train tracks. She sucked in a breath of fresh air, trying to wake up all her senses. Her sleep had been fitful. Every time she closed her eyes, she saw the person running from her. She'd been so close.

As she followed the steel rails, walking farther than she intended, she stopped when she came across fresh shoe prints to the left where the person would have jumped to avoid being hit by the train.

Bending close, she noticed that the soles looked different from your standard sneaker. This was a boot. She stood and placed her foot next to the print in the soil. Men. Size ten, at the very least. The person running from her was a man.

Thirty minutes after seeing the footprint, Sawyer sat just inside the doorway of the police station, doing her best to ignore the horrible throbbing of her head, inside and out. The minute Detective Perez walked through the door, she jumped to her feet.

He looked right at her and released a low growl.

"Just two minutes," she said. "That's all I'm asking."

"In my office," he said. "Two minutes."

They wove their way through mostly empty cubicles. It was still early, still quiet. She could smell coffee as they passed a tiny lunchroom with a refrigerator and sink.

Once they were inside his office and Detective Perez shut the door behind them, she told him everything she'd told Palmer about the interview with Brad Vicente, what she had learned at the Blue Fox, and finally about Ian Farley's possible involvement and his alleged attack by at least three women wearing wigs after he'd shown up at Brad Vicente's house.

It wasn't until she fell quiet that she realized he didn't appear to be paying attention. After shutting the door, he had slipped his jacket onto a hook on the iron coatrack standing in the corner of the room. He'd then unlocked a couple of desk drawers. Now he was straightening the top of his desk, organizing files, and sifting through a pile of papers he'd grabbed from his in-box. Finally, he looked up at her. "Is that it?"

"No." She reached into her bag and pulled out the flash drive and set it on his desk in front of him. As she did so, she told him about Ian's description of the woman with scars all over her arms and how she had instantly thought of Christina Farro, the woman held captive by Otto Radley.

The look on his face was borderline disgust. Clearly he didn't give a shit about anything she had told him.

"That's it," she said. "Although you already have the original flash drive, I thought you might want to take a look at the newly enhanced version. It's much clearer." She took a breath. "I also thought you would be interested to know what Ian Farley had to say. Maybe you can get more information out of him, and it will help you solve the Black Wigs case."

Elbows planted on his desk, fingers entwined, he set his gaze on hers. "What, exactly, are you trying to prove?"

She didn't understand the question. "I'm not trying to prove anything. I just want to help in any way I can."

"Detective Grumley called me last night, told me about you chasing after a killer and nearly being run over by a freight train. Do you think you are some sort of superhero?"

She stared at him, unblinking, her blood pressure rising.

"What were you thinking?"

She felt a rolling heat in her belly. She could not believe his arrogance and complete lack of professionalism when it came to hearing what she had to say. "I was thinking wouldn't it be great if I could stop this person from killing someone else."

"Did you have a gun on you?"

"No."

"So what were you going to do if you caught this person?"

She said nothing.

"What were you doing at an auto shop late at night?"

She told him about Nick Calderon and Bruce Ward's connection to the Children's Home of Sacramento and how that had led her to Aston Newell. She intended to ask about Calderon and Ward wearing only one shoe at the crime scene, but it was clear Perez wasn't interested in hearing what she had to say.

He gestured to his right, to the large paneled glass window. The blinds were open, and she could see the rows of cubicles she'd passed on her way to his office. "We've got plenty of hardworking women and men in blue who give up time with their families to hit the streets every day to keep the citizens of Sacramento safe."

"I realize that. And I, for one, appreciate everything they do."

His gaze was like a steel-pointed laser, burning right through her eyes. "I don't think you do appreciate what we do here. From the beginning I think you've been dead set on making the department look bad."

Her stomach roiled. "There's nothing further from the truth."

"Here's some advice, advice I don't hand out often. Quit your little reporter job and become a police officer. When you put on your uniform, you'll see that everything changes as you mentally prepare for the day. You strap on your ballistic vest and make sure your utility belt is on good and snug. You kiss your kids and spouse goodbye, never quite sure if you'll see them again."

"I was only trying to help, Detective."

"You've helped us enough. Stick to your newspaper stories. I've only put up with you out of respect for Palmer. He's a softie. Right out of the gate, you lucked out on a case or two and made him believe you were a gifted investigator, a shining star." He waggled a finger at her. "I think you're good at one thing and that's manipulating people."

Stunned into silence, it took Sawyer a few seconds to find the strength of mind to come up for air. More than angry, she was saddened, frustrated, and disappointed. The man cared more about his ego than solving a case. Her phone buzzed. It was a text message from the PI she had contacted about the license plate number. Call me.

"I guess this is it, then," Sawyer said, pushing herself to her feet. "Thank you for your time."

She turned and looked at him, watched him sort through his mail, thinking she should tell him about the footprints she'd seen near the train track, how she was now certain the killer was a man, when he said, "Shut the door behind you on your way out."

She left his office and the building knowing that she would never set foot inside that place again. What had happened to the detective to make him so damn bitter and resentful? She'd recently helped locate a missing girl and had really believed that the two of them had turned a corner and come to respect each other. But that was far from the truth. Without a "Thank you for your help" or a "Goodbye," she'd been excused. She wondered if he would even bother to look at the flash drive.

There were good guys and there were bad guys. Sawyer decided that Detective Perez fell somewhere in between.

Once she was back inside her car, Sawyer did her best to put it all behind her. Then she gave the private investigator, Mimi Fletcher, a call, hoping she'd finally solve the mystery of who drove a green Kia Soul.

"Oh, good. Glad it's you," Mimi said first thing. "I don't have long. I stepped outside for a smoke break so I could call you and let you know I have the information you asked for, but I have to get back soon. Infidelity business is booming. Everyone wants their spouse followed these days. Anyway, it'll cost you a hundred dollars."

Her price had doubled since they last talked. They were acquaintances more than they were friends. Using an app on her phone, Sawyer sent her the money. "Okay. The money has been transferred to your account. What do you have for me?"

Sawyer would have preferred it if Mimi texted the information to her, but that's not how she did business. Mimi rattled off the name Lena Harris, followed by an address at Treetop Apartments in West Sacramento.

"Thank you, Mimi."

"No problem. Got to go."

Still sitting in her car parked outside the police station, Sawyer used her phone to do a quick internet search on Lena Harris. There were a few people with the same name, but one Lena Harris stood out: Lena Harris, thirty-six, was gang-raped at a fraternity in Chico. Lena had gone to court, naming three males. After a short trial, all three defendants were found not guilty.

Sawyer tried different search engines and specific keywords, but she couldn't find any of the defendants' names. Finally, she called Lexi, who answered on the first ring.

"Where are you?" Lexi asked.

"I'm sitting in my car outside the Sacramento Police Department."

"Is it true that you were at that auto shop last night where the owner was killed?"

"It's true," Sawyer said.

"What were you doing there, and why the hell did you chase after a killer?"

All the fight had been sucked right out of her. "I wasn't thinking," Sawyer said flatly, wanting to get on with why she'd called her in the first place.

"You need to slow down and stop pretending you're a one-man police force, or you're going to end up dead."

"You sound like Detective Perez."

"Speaking of Detective Perez, what did he say about Ian Farley?"

"In a nutshell he told me to mind my own business."

"Oh," Lexi said. "He seemed fine with us being at the crime scene the other day."

"It was all an act. I'm telling you . . . if looks could kill, I'd be dead."

"Okay. So what now?"

"I'm interested in finding out more about a woman by the name of Lena Harris. She's thirty-six now, but she was eighteen or nineteen when she was gang-raped at a fraternity party in Chico. I read that there were multiple males named as defendants. A jury found them not guilty, but I'm curious to learn their names." Sawyer could hear the clacking of a keyboard in the background. "If you're at your desk, I thought maybe you could use PACER or another electronic records service to see if the defendants are listed anywhere."

"Got it."

Before Sawyer could say, "Got what?" Lexi named all three defendants: Eddie Carter, Don Fulton, and Felix Iverson.

"Felix Iverson? Are you sure?"

"I'm sure. His name is listed right here in front of me. Why? What's going on, Sawyer?"

"I've got to go," Sawyer said. "I'll update you later." Sawyer hung up, then drew in a breath.

Not only had Felix Iverson been a bully at the Children's Home of Sacramento, he had also attended Chico State University long enough to go to a frat party and end up named as one of three defendants at a rape trial.

Sawyer turned on the car's engine so she could run the air conditioner and cool off. She tapped her fingers against the steering wheel as her mind spun.

Lena Harris had to be a part of the Black Wigs group. But who was the Copycat Killer? The size-ten footprint told her it was a man. That left Jimmy Crocket and Stanley Higgins.

Sawyer grabbed her laptop from her carrying bag and looked up Lena Harris. She had two parents who had supported her throughout her courtroom ordeal, so she wasn't an orphan and therefore had no connection that Sawyer could see to the children's home. Lena's connection to Felix Iverson had to be solely because of the events that took place at the fraternity house.

The bigger question was why had Lena Harris been following her?

Her phone buzzed. It was Aria. Sawyer told her about everything that happened at the auto shop when she went to talk to Aston Newell.

"He's dead?"

"Yes. I was too late." Sawyer then explained that she knew the name of the driver of the Kia. "I'm going to her apartment now to confront her."

"I think I should go with you," Aria said.

"Not this time. I need you to drive to Citrus Heights to see a guy named Stanley Higgins."

"That was the boy sitting by the tree who Nancy Lay, the cook at the children's home, noticed in the picture," Aria said.

"That's right. That's the one. Like Emily and Jimmy, he was also bullied, so you need to be careful. I'm pretty sure the killer is a man, which puts Emily Stiller in the clear." She went on to explain the footprints she'd found by the train track.

"I'll bring my gun with me," Aria told her. "I'll be fine."

"Good," Sawyer said. "But there's one more thing I need to tell you about Stanley Higgins."

"Spit it out," Aria said. "It can't be worse than possibly being a killer, can it?"

"Well, it depends on who I'm talking to. Stanley Higgins is a taxidermist."

"Oh."

"If you can't do it, I understand. Just text me if you change your mind, and I'll take care of it later. I need to get going."

"I'll do it," Aria said. "I won't like it, but I'll do it."

Chapter Thirty-Seven

Treetop Apartments off Fruitridge Road was a three-story building, nice and neat with perfect rectangles of newly cut grass out front. There was available parking since most people were probably at work.

Sawyer parked, climbed out of her car, and walked up three flights of stairs, made a right and found 313C at the very end. She knocked and waited. Knocked again.

The door flew open. So fast it took Sawyer by surprise and prompted her to take a step back.

"What do you want?"

Lena Harris looked just like the young woman she'd seen in the article. She couldn't possibly be as tall as the story claimed. Five foot three inches was Sawyer's guess. Lena had long black hair and flawless skin. She wore black jeans and a T-shirt. Flip-flops on her feet. Even with the menacing scowl, it was easy to see that she was drop-dead gorgeous.

"Don't make me ask again," Lena said, "because I don't like repeating myself."

Lena's aggressive posture and defiant look made Sawyer nervous. She might not be the Copycat Killer or part of the Black Wigs, but she definitely looked dangerous. "I want to know why you've been following me."

Lena looked over Sawyer's shoulder toward the parking lot and said, "If you really want to know, you're going to have to come inside."

Her flesh tingled, but Sawyer refused to be intimidated, especially after dealing with Detective Perez. Sawyer stepped through the door, holding her head high. Lena Harris had some explaining to do.

The woman was married with two kids, but the place was quiet. The apartment was all muted colors and sparsely decorated with hardly any furniture.

At the sound of the door being locked behind her, Sawyer turned around in time to see Lena's expression change from annoyed to full outrage. Her hair flew back from her face as she lunged for Sawyer, catching her completely off guard and taking her to the ground. The back of her head hit the floor. Her teeth clamped down on her tongue. She tasted blood.

Before she could get to her feet, Lena was on top of her.

Sawyer wasn't a fighter. She'd never been in a brawl, but this woman with her flashing eyes and permanent frown meant business.

Sawyer yelped as the sharp tips of Lena's fingernails swept down the length of Sawyer's jaw and neck. Lena was sitting on Sawyer's stomach, straddling her, holding her down.

Out of the corner of her eye, Sawyer caught sight of a gold cylindrical glass vase on the end table next to the couch. With a burst of adrenaline, Sawyer used her legs and core and pushed Lena off her, bolted upright onto her feet, and ran to the tabletop. She grabbed hold of the vase, and held it in front of her like a shield.

Lena stood a few feet away in a wide-legged stance, her chest rising and falling. They were both breathing hard.

Sawyer thought it might be over, but then Lena reached for one of four high-back chairs surrounding a square dining room table and charged at Sawyer, ramming into her, using the chair and her weight to send Sawyer toppling backward over the sofa. The vase crashed onto the tiles where the carpet ended and the tile floor started.

Sawyer got back to her feet, then ducked when a chair flew through the air, smashing into the wall. Splinters of wood rained down around her.

Sawyer ran to the kitchen and grabbed the broom leaning against the wall. When Lena rushed around the corner, Sawyer jabbed the bristles of the broom into Lena's chest, stomach, and throat. Determined to get out of the apartment alive, Sawyer jabbed harder each time, forcing Lena to take backward steps. The look on the woman was crazed. Her lip was curled, her eyes narrowed.

"I told your sister I was going to kill you if you showed up, and I meant it." She plucked a butcher knife from a wooden knife block on the kitchen counter.

Aria? Harper? What the hell? Keeping the bristly end of the broom aimed at the woman as if it were a gun, she asked, "What are you talking about?"

Lena swung the knife through the air in front of her as if testing her footing and the weight of the blade. "You really do need to learn to mind your own business."

Sawyer made the mistake of glancing over her shoulder to see if there was an escape route she might have missed. Big mistake.

Lena sprang forward, but Sawyer was pumped up, and she whipped back around in time to make Lena take a quick half step back.

With a good firm hold on the broom handle, Sawyer swung at the hand with the knife and struck gold. The steel blade flew across the kitchen and hit the stove with a clank.

Sawyer dropped the broom and made a run for it. She almost made it to the door, but wasn't fast enough. Lena had leaped for Sawyer and now had hold of Sawyer's ankle. She yanked hard enough to pull Sawyer to the floor.

There was no question that Lena Harris had gone mad. She was angry and determined to take out Sawyer at any cost. They rolled into a decorative table that was pushed against the wall in the small front entry. Framed pictures crashed to the ground around them.

Sawyer tried to claw her way to the door, but Lena kept pulling her back.

After all she'd been through, Sawyer thought, this was how she was going out? Sawyer didn't even know why the woman had it out for her. A feeling of slow motion took over as Lena twisted Sawyer onto her back, as easily as if she was a rag doll, then jabbed an elbow into Sawyer's side, making her grimace in pain.

"Why are you doing this?" Sawyer asked.

But Lena didn't answer. Her attention had suddenly fixated on something else. Sawyer watched Lena slide off her and scoop up what looked like a family picture that had fallen when they knocked into the table.

Lena's crazed expression softened. Pushing herself to her feet, she looked as if all the air had been sucked out of her. With the picture grasped in her hand, she said, "Get the fuck out of here before I kill you. If you want answers, talk to Malice."

"Malice?"

"Also known as Harper—a bigger pain in the ass than you. When you talk to your sister, you might want to ask her what happened to Otto Radley." Her jaw tightened. "Get out. Now!"

Chapter Thirty-Eight

Sawyer's hands shook as she unlatched the lock from Lena's apartment door, hoping, praying she wouldn't feel the pain of a steel blade slicing through flesh and muscle before she could escape. Relief flooded through her as she pushed the door open and ran outside. She didn't scream for help or even think about calling the police. There was only one thought in her mind.

Harper.

What had her sister gotten herself into?

Her legs wobbled as she made her way down endless stairs. She held on to the railing for support and then ran for her car, jumped inside, and started the engine. Her hands trembled as she tightened her grip around the steering wheel and drove away. Her thoughts were a jumble, circling around in her head, knocking into other thoughts and making it impossible to think clearly.

Her head throbbed. Her heart pounded against her ribs.

I told your sister I was going to kill you if you showed up, and I meant it. If you want answers, talk to Malice.

Malice?

Also known as Harper. When you talk to your sister, you might want to ask her what happened to Otto Radley.

Nothing Lena Harris had said made any sense.

Harper had been acting strange for a while now. It was time for the two of them to have a chat.

It wasn't long before Sawyer pulled up in front of Harper's house. She shut off the car, then jumped out and headed for the door. She'd always knocked before, but not today. She needed answers.

When she opened the door, she found herself face to face with Nate.

"Sawyer," he said, surprised. "What happened to you?"

If she looked anything like she felt, it had to be pretty bad. "It's a long story," she told him. "What are you doing home in the middle of the day?"

"Got off early." He grimaced. "Is that blood? Come inside. Let's get you cleaned up."

Once she was inside, he examined her closer. "You've been banged up good." He shut the door and led her into the bathroom down the hall, grabbed a couple of clean washrags, and handed them to her. "Here. Clean that blood off so we can see how bad those wounds are. I'll grab some ointment and bandages."

By the time Nate returned, she had found seven cuts, some deeper than others. Some of the cuts on her face and arms were from the glass vase after it broke. She had multiple bruises all over her body from falling and thrashing around on the ground. Four claw marks traveling from her face to her collarbone were from Lena's fingernails.

Nate took a closer look at the cut on her arm. "It's deep, but I think a couple of those Steri-Strips will do the trick. Unless you'd rather I take you to the hospital?"

"No. I'm good. Is Harper home?"

He shook his head. "Fix yourself up, then we'll talk. I'll be in the kitchen when you're done."

It didn't take her long to clean up. Nate was where he said he'd be. "Do you know where Harper is?"

"No idea. Your guess is as good as mine."

He had bread, lunch meats, pickles, and mustard lined up on the island.

"Hungry?" Nate asked.

"No, thanks."

As he made a sandwich for himself, he used his chin to gesture her way. "So what happened to you? Or would you rather keep it to yourself like your sister tends to do?"

Sawyer understood his frustration. He wasn't the only one tired of Harper's secretive ways. Bruised, battered, and pissed off, Sawyer was way past the stage of keeping secrets. If Harper was in any way involved with Lena Harris, then Nate needed to know about it because as far as Sawyer was concerned, his entire family could be in danger.

And yet she hadn't called the police because something told her that her sister might be in more trouble than danger.

Slipping onto a stool overlooking the island where Nate worked, Sawyer started talking. She told him all about the Kia Soul that had been following her, how she'd tracked the car down, and how the driver had turned out to be a dark-haired, petite female. "Harmless, right?" she asked Nate. "Wrong. When I asked her why she was following me, she invited me into her apartment, then shut the door and lunged, said she wanted to kill me."

Nate stopped what he was doing. "What the hell?"

"She was terrifying. I thought I was going to die right there in her apartment."

Nate grabbed a towel, wiped his hands, and pulled out his phone. "Did you call the police yet?"

She shook her head. "We can't call the police."

"Why not?"

"Because the woman told me to talk to Harper if I wanted answers."

Nate exhaled and simultaneously raked his fingers through his hair. He came around the counter and took a seat on the stool next to Sawyer. "Listen," he said. "I don't know what Harper is up to, but I know it can't be good. On Sunday, somewhere around two in the morning, Harper got out of bed. Quiet as a mouse, she walked through the house, gathering her purse and the keys to her car. What she doesn't know is that I followed her."

Sawyer said nothing. Just listened.

"There weren't too many cars on the road, so I had to stay far enough back not to be seen. She drove all the way to Power Inn Road and took a dirt driveway up to an abandoned warehouse. The only reason I know that much is because I returned the next day. The place was empty. I didn't stay long." He shook his head. "Why would she go to an abandoned warehouse in the middle of the night?"

"I don't know," Sawyer said.

"Every time I ask her what's going on, she tells me more lies."

"Like what?"

"Weeks ago, she told me she was writing a book and meeting with other aspiring authors to exchange pages. There is no book," he said. "She told me she was taking classes at Sac State. I went to the main office at the university and discovered she had never registered. They had no record of any Harper Pohler or Harper Brooks." He exhaled. "Whenever she's on her computer, she shuts it down if I walk into the room." He drew in an unsteady breath. "I was the last one to find out she was pregnant."

Sawyer thought about Lena Harris and what she'd said about asking Harper about Otto Radley. She wasn't sure why she kept that part to herself, but she did. "I'm sorry."

"Yeah, me too. When Harper returned from her middle-of-the-night outing, I was standing right over there, waiting." He pointed.

"What did she say?"

"Her lips were sealed. She wouldn't tell me anything. I told her she had one week, and if she didn't talk to me by then, tell me everything that was going on, then I was filing for divorce."

Sawyer's heart sank. "She loves you. This family means everything to her." She had to find a way to help her. Harper had always been the most caring, loving person. She was a good mother and a good wife. Her sister had to have gotten involved in something dark, something so horribly bad that she just couldn't seem to find a way out. Sawyer needed to go to the warehouse, their only clue.

Sawyer came to her feet. "Do you have an address for the warehouse on Power Inn Road?"

"I do. Are you sure you want to go there? You're in bad shape, Sawyer. I really think you should go to the emergency room and get checked out. That cut by your eye might need stitches."

"I'll be fine."

"Maybe I should go with you."

"The kids will be home soon," Sawyer said. "Stay here. They need you."

He didn't look happy about it, but he knew she was right. "If you learn anything about what's going on, anything at all, will you call me?"

"I will. I promise."

Chapter Thirty-Nine

Aria took a right off Old Auburn Road in Citrus Heights. The road was pitted with holes. Pebbles and gravel rolled and pinged against the undercarriage. She felt as if she were driving to a house in the woods instead of a business. She exhaled when she saw a sign for SH's Taxidermy.

The parking lot was empty, so she took the spot up front. She got out of her car, made sure her gun was locked tight in the holster around her waist. Above the wooden entry door was the head of a deer with beautiful antlers. It was enough to make her want to turn around. After being confronted by Christina Farro, she had thought she could handle anything, but now she wasn't so sure.

You can do this, she told herself. *Don't be a wimp.*

She pushed open the door and stepped inside. The rich tones of a single cello rolled over her at once. It was beautiful and somewhat eerie. The place reminded her of a museum with rows of glass-covered displays. There were six aisles. She chose to walk down the middle aisle, trying not to look to her left or right so as not to see the displays of raccoons, squirrels, and birds in flight, all frozen in time. She made the mistake of looking up and seeing stuffed bats hanging from wires hooked to the ceiling. Her stomach clenched. "Hello?"

Just as she took her last step out of the aisle and into an open space in the room, she saw a lone man standing over a workbench. He wore goggles with magnifying glasses attached like something she might see on a heart surgeon. As she drew nearer she saw that he was using a sharp dental tool to clean the area around the eye of a rabbit.

She was about to turn around and head back to the car when he looked up. He lifted his brows in surprise, then set down his tool, took off his goggles, and turned down the music. "Hello. How can I help you?"

Suddenly speechless, she said, "Um, I called earlier and left a message."

"I haven't checked my messages. Sorry."

His voice was monotone and so quiet she could hardly hear him. "I can come back later, if that would work better for you?"

"Now is fine."

"Okay. I am helping Sawyer Brooks, a journalist with the *Sacramento Independent*, on a story about the deaths of Nick Calderon, Bruce Ward, and Aston Newell."

His mannerisms and facial expression remained the same. He gave nothing away. She noticed a bowl of white powder on the table and thought maybe if she showed interest in his work, she might get him talking. "What's that powder for?"

"It is a chemical called borax. It is used to draw out moisture and dry the flesh. It also keeps insects away."

"Oh. What about that?" She pointed at a waxy figure.

"We call those mannequins."

The whole thing was disgusting. And trying to get this man to open up was like pulling teeth. It wasn't happening. But she was here and she wasn't coming back, so there was no reason to beat around the bush. "Is there anything you can tell me about Jimmy Crocket or Emily Stiller?"

"Like what?"

Come on, mister, she thought. *Throw me a bone. No, never mind. Don't throw me a bone. Gross.* "Did either of them strike you as the type of person who might want revenge?"

"Ah." He wagged a finger her way. "I know why you're here. I'm not a killer." He spread his arms wide. "I'm an artist. I make it possible for these animals to live forever!"

"Yes. I can see that."

"But do you really?"

She offered a watery smile, glad to be standing a safe distance away from him. She guessed his height to be at least six feet until he stepped off a stool behind the table, making him closer to five foot nine. His hair was pulled back into a ponytail. His eyes were squinty.

"I get the impression you're offended by my work."

She couldn't lie. "It's just not my thing."

He shrugged and said, "If I had killed any of those bullies you mentioned, they would be displayed on my wall in the back room."

His thin-lipped smile did nothing to settle her nerves. *God,* she thought. There was more in the back?

"Come with me. I'll show you." He turned and walked toward the back. She took a tentative step that way, thought about declining his offer, but something drove her to follow him down a semidark hallway, at the end of which was a closed door.

She reached under the light jacket she'd put on to conceal her weapon and felt better with the gun grasped within her palm.

He opened the door, then waited for her to step inside.

"After you," she said.

He stepped into the room. When there was a good distance between them, she walked inside and felt all the blood drain from her face.

"Isn't it wonderful?" he asked.

There were lions and tigers and bears. Literally. All with human faces made of wax. It was beyond crazy. Dizzy, she could hardly breathe. "What is this place?"

"People pay money to see this room."

There were chairs made of three-headed sheep and squirrels with doll heads where their face should be. Dozens of frogs, one on top of the other, forming a pyramid.

And much more. So much more.

She was going to be sick. She turned around, and this time, she did run. She could hear him calling out to her, telling her to come back anytime.

CHAPTER FORTY

Sawyer used the navigation system to get to the address Nate had given her. She knew she was at her destination the moment she saw the long line of police vehicles with swirling lights. After pulling into a dirt area off to the side of the road, she shut off the engine and called Harper. It went straight to voicemail. "It's Sawyer. Please call me right away."

She climbed out. Ingress and egress was being controlled by security. She showed the uniformed officer her badge, and he let her through. The crime scene tape stopped her from being able to see inside the warehouse. Pictures were being taken, sketches were being made.

Detective Perez talked to the ME who had just arrived, then raised a hand and called out for one of his men to show her the way. Detective Perez then walked over to where Sawyer stood with other media personnel. "You looked bad enough this morning," Detective Perez told Sawyer. "What did you do now?"

"Just another day on the job as a reporter."

"How did you get here so quick?" His head tilted. "Don't tell me. You carry a police scanner like the rest of these hacks?"

"No scanner needed," she told him. "Mind telling me what you found?"

"I do mind. I thought I made that clear. You might want to take a ride to the hospital. Whoever tried to scratch your eyes out might have caused an infection. It doesn't look good."

She watched him walk away. "What an ass," she said under her breath.

The woman standing next to her with a lanyard hanging around her neck said, "No shit. I've been working the beat for over a decade, and he doesn't even know who I am. So I guess that makes you special."

Sawyer looked at her. "Any idea what's going on?"

"Oh. You really don't have a scanner, do you?"

Sawyer shook her head.

"Dead man. Throat was cut. Whoever killed him covered him up with leaves and debris."

"Is the body inside the warehouse?"

"No." She pointed farther into the wooded area.

"Do we have a name?" Sawyer asked.

"We do." The woman smiled. "Eddie Carter."

"Eddie Carter," Sawyer repeated. A cold lump formed in her throat. Eddie Carter, Don Fulton, and Felix Iverson. Those were the names Lexi had repeated over the phone. All three of them were named as defendants when Lena Harris took them to court.

"Married man with two children," the woman was saying. "He was reported missing three days ago."

Sawyer's phone buzzed. It was Lexi. She'd forgotten all about their meeting. Sawyer thanked the woman and excused herself to go find a quiet spot out of earshot. "What's going on?"

"Looks like we're going to have to reschedule our meeting for another time," Lexi said. "I just got a call about a guy found dead in the trunk of his Porsche Cayenne."

What the hell was going on? Sawyer wondered. Dead guys were coming out of the woodwork. "Where?"

"At a baseball park, of all places. My source said it appears he's been in the trunk for at least a few days."

"How did he die?"

"Somebody sliced his throat wide open. And you'll never believe who it was."

Eddie Carter was dead, his body only a few yards away. And Felix Iverson didn't drive a Porsche. That left Don Fulton. "Tell me," Sawyer said.

"Don Fulton. Isn't that crazy? You were just asking me about that case with the three defendants all those years ago, and suddenly up pops his name. And now he's dead."

"I've got to go," Sawyer said, cutting her off. She shoved her phone into her pocket, then turned around. Through the canopy of trees she could see Eddie Carter's body being slipped into a body bag. She thought of Christina Farro with all the scars from her time spent with Otto Radley. She thought of Lena Harris, raped by multiple men at a fraternity party. There was also Tracy Rutherford, the woman who had taken a squad of high school football players to court for sexual assault and then watched them walk free. Lastly, she thought of Harper, her own sister, and how she was raped by their father, night after night, nobody to save her.

Sawyer swallowed hard as she filed away the names of the Black Wigs in her memory: Christina Farro, Tracy Rutherford, Lena Harris, and Harper Pohler.

Had her own sister been a part of the Black Wigs all along?

Where was she?

As she watched the body bag being lifted onto a gurney, her mind snapped back to Felix Iverson.

Eddie Carter and Don Fulton were dead.

Shit! If she didn't hurry, Felix would be next.

She took off running for her car.

Chapter Forty-One

Hidden beneath an old rusted Ford truck with the back end propped up on an even older washing machine, Cleo watched and waited for Felix Iverson to head out. For the last two days, she'd watched him leave his trailer around this same time and walk over a mile to a roadside diner, where he ordered a breakfast burrito.

After Harper's sister had left her apartment, she'd cleaned up the mess and then continued with her plans as if nothing had happened. If a rookie crime reporter was closing in on her and the other crew members, then it wouldn't be long before the men in blue started coming around and asking questions too.

The clock was ticking.

Cleo let out a grunt as she maneuvered her body in the tight space so that all her weight wasn't on her right hip. She'd already been lying beneath the truck for thirty minutes. She could hear more than one rodent scurrying around inside the old clunker above her head, but she couldn't see them. A friend's rat had bitten her when she was ten years old. Rodents freaked her out. If a rat scurried too close, she might scream. And she wasn't a screamer. Snakes, no problem. Spiders, fine. Rodents—no thank you.

The creaky metal door leading into the trailer opened.

Felix Iverson clomped down the stairs as he pulled a T-shirt over his head, tugging it over his rail-thin body as he walked past the truck where she lay hidden. Farther on down the gravel road, he passed by another half dozen trailers, all tilting and sagging, all surrounded by heaping piles of garbage and filth.

When Cleo could no longer see him, she crept out from under the truck. Briskly but quietly, she walked to his trailer and made her way up the stairs, careful not to fall straight through the rotted wood.

The door was unlocked. She walked inside. The disgusting smell hit her like a punch to the gut, but it didn't stop her. She knew what she had to do. She closed the door and made her way through the narrow kitchen to the back end of his trailer. His bedroom consisted of a thin mattress and a couple of worn blankets. She looked around for a place to hunker down until he returned. Since he didn't have a bed frame, she couldn't slip underneath the mattress. There was a closet, but the slider doors were gone.

That left the bathroom. She stepped inside, stood near the toilet with her back to the wall. She pinched her nose. There wasn't a spot on the toilet, bathtub, or the walls that wasn't splattered with urine. Dirty rags and trash covered most of the floor. No signs of toothpaste or toothbrush on the sink. Just dirt and grime. How did anyone live in such filth?

Felix Iverson had been the most vocal of the group of boys in the room where she'd been held down and raped. She could still see his face as if it had all happened last week. His hair hadn't been as long as it was now, but long enough that she remembered he'd pulled it back with a rubber band. She'd done her research, and she knew he'd attended California State University Chico but didn't last long.

She'd learned the hard way that frat parties had a way of drawing in some sketchy dudes. If you found yourself at the wrong sort of party, and you didn't stay close to a friend and refrain from drinking, there was a good chance you might become a target. First-year girls were herded into frat parties, while guys were often turned away. That right there should have set off alarm bells.

But it hadn't.

And she'd paid the price.

But the boys who had done the most damage would finally be punished. She wasn't sure what would come next. How many more rapists would she take down after Felix? There were others who had participated and whose names she'd learned since all the courtroom drama.

She was on a roll. Why stop now? The world had nothing left to offer her.

The smell in the bathroom finally proved to be too much. She stepped out and breathed in stale smoke and old socks instead. With some time on her hands, she considered which weapon she should use on him when he returned. Hunting knife or Glock? She pulled out her knife, admired its newly sharpened blade, and decided to go with that. It was quiet, and just as lethal.

Chapter Forty-Two

Wig and lipstick in place, Cockroach watched from afar as Felix Iverson approached his trailer, gravel crunching beneath his feet. The door creaked open and then slammed, prompting Cockroach to unfold from his crouched position and blindly touch the leather pouch around his waist. Inside was everything he needed.

After burning down the Children's Home of Sacramento, he'd spent the next five years in a foster home with two adults and two children. Although they hadn't kept in touch, more his fault then theirs, they had treated him well. And yet every night when he lay in bed, praying sleep would take him far, far away, he instead fantasized about getting revenge on every person at the children's home who had treated him badly. At the time, he'd been disheartened to learn that Valerie Purcell had not died in the fire, especially after he'd patiently waited for her to go to her office. As it turned out, someone had smelled smoke and gotten her out in time.

When he turned eighteen, he applied for grants and student loans, found an affordable apartment. He focused his attention on getting degrees in graphic design and fine arts, and one by one, he found clients who appreciated his work. Mostly, he stayed inside his apartment or perched on an uncomfortable wooden chair in his tiny office at a studio where he also worked and kept to himself.

And then the Black Wigs hit the media by storm, and those fearless vigilantes had stirred the sleeping embers within. He'd followed the ladies closely, watched the video of them kidnapping the guy in the parking lot over and over. He also watched hours of The Slayers on YouTube as they went after the people who had hurt them. Youngsters everywhere began to follow suit, letting the world know that justice would be served, one way or another.

And it all made so much sense.

He wouldn't be free until every person who had harmed him was obliterated. They had to go. In a way, the Black Wigs had started a movement. Justice could prevail. And in his case, justice *would* prevail.

And so it had begun.

Despite his newfound determination, he'd worried at first that he might not be able to follow through. Would he be able to take a life, no matter how miserable and wretched?

The answer had been a resounding yes. There had been no denying that after he'd taken care of Nick Calderon, he'd had his first good night of sleep in decades.

Next came Bruce Ward. When that was done, he'd found he had a crazy new spring in his step. He felt lighter. Happier.

He would not stop.

He could not stop.

And that was a problem because he realized somewhere in the middle of it all that he didn't want to get caught, which was why he took a bit more time planning Valerie Purcell's and Aston Newell's deaths. Valerie's fall down the stairs had gone exactly as planned. If not for that woman coming to the auto shop after hours, Aston Newell's death would have also been ruled an accident.

Better luck next time.

As he approached Felix Iverson's trailer, his insides vibrated with life. He felt different. Like a new man. Confident.

He took quiet, careful steps toward the dilapidated trailer. He held his breath as the palm of his hand settled around the doorknob. When it turned, he knew this was it. Felix Iverson would be dealt with once and for all.

He pushed open the door.

Felix stood in the kitchen area, his mouth stuffed with whatever he'd brought back to eat. Felix had hardly aged. His disregard of others and his lack of empathy and morality appeared to be serving him well. He was still dirty and scraggly, like the rats running around the trailer park, but there were no bags or dark circles under his eyes from lack of sleep. No lines in his face from undue stress. Hell, the guy didn't even look surprised to see him. Not a care in the world. If anything, Felix Iverson looked amused.

Did Felix know he was about to die?

He must have heard about the passing of all his friends. Maybe he didn't care, which made sense considering Felix's life, after all, had started out badly and tumbled downhill from there. Cockroach had read about Felix Iverson, back when Lena Harris had taken him and others to court. Of course, all those rowdy bad boys walked free, leaving a trail of tears and broken lives behind them.

"Cockroach, is that you?" Felix asked.

He said nothing.

Felix didn't bother swallowing, merely chewed while he spoke. "I was told you might be coming for me."

"Really? Who told you?"

"A journalist," Felix said with a shrug. "I don't remember her name, but she went out of her way to find me and warn me about you."

Cockroach unzipped the tiny bag around his waist and would have readied the syringe had he not seen movement behind Felix. A person, a woman, in fact, stepped out of the shadows and into the kitchen.

He could hardly believe what he was seeing. She was wearing a wig. A short black wig almost identical to his. How had she gotten inside without him seeing?

"Felix is mine," she said.

The voice coming from behind him must have caught Felix by surprise, because his eyes widened and he pivoted on his feet. "You've got to be kidding me," he said. Felix chuckled, but it was forced. Clearly, he was nervous. And rightly so. The odds were not in his favor.

"I'm going to ask nicely," Felix said, "before things get out of hand, for both of you to leave."

"Nice try," he said. "I'm not leaving until I've seen you take your last breath."

Felix scratched his chest through his shirt. "Hey, Cockroach. Did you really kill Nick and Bruce?" he asked as if the woman had not appeared out of nowhere.

"I have a name," he said.

Felix laughed. "Cockroach suits you just fine."

"Yes," he said. "I killed them both. And Valerie Purcell and Aston too. Once you're gone," he told Felix, "maybe I'll be able to find a way to be whole."

"You'll never be whole," Felix said. "People like you are too sensitive. Shit happens. Get over it."

"Enough small talk," the woman said.

Felix laughed. "So who are you, anyway? I was told Cockroach might be coming for me, but who the fuck are you?" He scratched his chin. "You must be part of that Black Wigs group everyone is talking about."

She said nothing.

Cockroach and Felix watched her pull a hunting knife from a sheath around her waist. She began spinning the blade by switching her index and middle fingers. Without looking at what she was doing, she flicked the knife inward into a spin, and stopped it with the blade pointing at herself. She did it again, balanced the knife in the palm of her hand, then set the knife into a spin, starting and stopping, twirling and spinning, and then stopped. This time the blade was pointed at Felix.

Again, she did a single revolution, followed by a double spin, and then stopped all motion with the heel of her palm.

Felix clapped.

As the woman raised her arm high in the air, as if readying to do one more final twirl and flip before digging the blade into Felix's chest, Felix took a quick backward step toward the counter behind him, reached blindly under a pile of trash, and pulled out a machete, which he swung in full glory, his hair swinging with his body as he pivoted around, finding his mark as if he'd been practicing for this very moment his entire life.

Cockroach felt trapped, paralyzed with fear. Just as he'd been so many times at the home.

Blood sprayed on the cabinets and counter space.

The woman stood there for a moment. Shocked. Dazed.

It was then Cockroach noticed that she'd been sliced open.

She sort of folded neatly to the ground. The hunting knife dropped from her hands, clinked and clanked against the dirty floor, and landed somewhere between him and Felix.

Adrenaline rushed through Cockroach's body, reminding him he was no longer that helpless little boy.

They both lunged for each other at the same time.

He had his syringe. Felix had his machete.

Felix swung first, the rage flowing through his veins seemingly keeping him steady.

Cockroach knew what was coming, and he ducked. His heart raced and his palms were sweating. Holding tight to the syringe, keeping it in front of him, he ignored the tremors shooting through his middle.

"You plan to kill me with that, Cockroach?"

He ignored Felix. If he couldn't use the syringe to inject him with fentanyl, he'd use his bare hands to kill him.

The next few minutes were like a boxing match, the contenders sizing each other up, unsure who would be making the next move.

When Cockroach looked at Felix, it was as if he were again a small boy. The laughing, sneering, demented face of someone who never should have been born smiled at him, sending a jolt of electricity through him. He sprang, alarmed when Felix too easily kicked the syringe from his grasp.

Stunned, he watched in horror, thinking this might be it as Felix drew back to take another swing. Instead, Felix slipped on the woman's blood, nearly losing his footing, giving Cockroach one more chance to get it right. He grabbed the hunting knife from the floor, then pounced, the blade landing squarely in the middle of Felix's chest, cutting through muscle and tendons and hopefully an organ or two before they fell to the ground.

Cockroach's head had hit a cabinet on the way down. He remained motionless, dazed. It took another second for his head to clear. When it did, he came to his feet.

Felix's eyes were wide open, the hunting knife sticking straight out of his chest. Looking around for his syringe, Cockroach found it near the kitchen sink and placed it inside his pouch.

Someone moaned. At first he thought it was Felix, but it was the woman. She moved her arm, and he went to her.

Her bloodied hand reached into her pants pocket, where she found her phone. Her breathing was shallow and raspy. "Is he dead?"

Cockroach lifted Felix's limp hand. There was no pulse and he told her as much.

"Go!" she said in a powerful voice that made it sound as if she hadn't been split open.

He stood there. She was a Black Wig. An inspiration to him and so many others. He didn't want to leave her.

"I'm calling for help," she said. "Go. Please. Now!"

He finally did as she said, removing the bloodied wig and then using his forearm to wipe the lipstick from his mouth on his way out.

Chapter Forty-Three

As Sawyer took a right into the trailer park, she noticed a man walking away. A clump of wet weeds or maybe rope—it was hard to tell—hung from one of his hands. His shirt was dirty, and he wore a fanny pack around his waist.

He looked her way.

She continued on, trying not to call attention to herself. As she pulled up close to Felix Iverson's trailer, she considered turning around and following the man she'd just seen.

The door to the trailer hung open, leaning downward as if one of the hinges had come loose. Sawyer turned off the engine, grabbed her pepper spray from the glove compartment, and got out.

She looked around.

It was quiet. Too quiet, she thought as she headed up the wood steps. "Felix? It's me, Sawyer Brooks from the *Sacramento Independent*. Are you home?"

No answer.

She stepped inside, looked toward the kitchen, and saw blood. Everywhere. Smeared across the floor and dripping off cabinets.

It wasn't until she drew closer that she saw two people.

Her stomach quivered. Felix was on his back, looking straight up at the ceiling, a knife protruding from his chest.

Next to him was a woman wearing a black wig. Lena Harris.

She reached for Lena's wrist to feel for a pulse.

Lena's eyes popped open, and she sucked in a breath of air.

Sawyer held back a gasp.

"My phone," Lena said in such a quiet voice, Sawyer had to lean down close to hear her.

"I dropped my phone," she said as her fingers made a trail through puddles of blood.

Sawyer pulled her own phone from her back pocket and was about to call for help.

"Not you," Lena said. "You need to go."

"I can't just let you die."

"I'm going to die. If you want"—she took a breath—"to help your sister and the rest of The Crew, go to my place."

Sawyer was about to tell her to forget it, but then Lena's eyes closed. Sawyer thought it might be over, but she was wrong. Lena was determined to have her say.

"You must get my laptop before the police do. The password"—her voice faltered, then returned—"Cheerios."

"I can't do that," Sawyer said. No way could she leave this woman to die alone, never mind leaving the scene of a crime and then hiding potential evidence. But then she thought of Harper, and she knew she had no choice. She had to go to the apartment.

"Key is in the geranium. Password. Cheerios," she said again, grimacing in pain.

Lena had managed to grasp her phone. "I already called 9-1-1. They'll be coming soon. Go." She hit the camera logo and then the video button and began talking. "My name is Lena Harris." She drew in a breath. "Tell my husband and my children I'm sorry. I never meant for things to get out of hand. Most of you would never understand. I was young and I was raped. I didn't deserve it. But in the end, nobody cared. I killed Otto Radley, buried him in the woods near an abandoned warehouse off Power Inn Road. Eddie Carter's body is there too. Don Fulton is dead too. His body is in the trunk of his Porsche. I cut off Brad Vicente's dick. He said there was more than one woman, but he's a liar. He couldn't handle being taken down by one tiny female, so he made up a big, elaborate story." Her voice softened as if she were about to go to sleep, but then she came to and brought strength to her voice. "Myles Davenport died of a heart attack. But if he hadn't, I would have killed him too. I killed them all. Every single one of them."

She gurgled, coughed, waved Sawyer off without looking her way.

Sawyer could hear sirens in the distance.

She thought of Harper. She had no idea if Harper was involved, but she knew she couldn't let her sister spend the rest of her life in jail. As she walked toward the door, she heard the last of Lena's confession.

"I wouldn't change a thing," Lena said. "And to all you fuckers out there who think you can go around sexually assaulting whomever you please, this is a warning. There are more people like me just waiting for you to make a move so they can take you out. You won't win. One way or another, justice will be served."

Chapter Forty-Four

Sawyer's heart was pounding like a jackhammer as she sped away from the trailer park.

What was she doing?

Her insides quivered as she raced to Lena Harris's apartment building in West Sacramento. It was closing in on four p.m. when she arrived. She got out of the car but didn't look around because she didn't want to seem suspicious.

She was in robot mode, knowing that if she thought too hard about what she was about to do, she would never be able to continue on. She needed to keep moving, make it quick, and stay focused.

The geranium was in a terra-cotta pot to the right of Lena's apartment door. She dug around until her fingers touched metal. She brushed off the key and made her way inside. The place had been cleaned up. No broken glass. The chairs back in place. Nothing that might reveal what had happened here only hours ago.

She shut the door and moved quickly to the kitchen.

Breathe, Sawyer, breathe.

Under the sink, she found a pair of rubber gloves and put them on. She found the laptop in the master bedroom, unplugged the charger, and brought it all to the dining room table.

She opened it, tried to log on using the password "Cheerios" and then "Cheerio." Maybe Lena hadn't said "Cheerios" at all.

No. That was definitely the word Lena had said. Twice, in fact. So much had happened, though. Sawyer was having a difficult time thinking straight. She could feel her nerves getting the best of her.

Her hands started to shake.

No. Take a breath. You can do this.

Cheerios. Cheerios. People had Cheerios for breakfast. She left the laptop and walked back to the kitchen, moving fast, knowing she was running out of time.

She began quietly opening and closing cupboards. Above the coffee cups was a row of cereal boxes. She pulled out the Cap'n Crunch and the Froot Loops. There it was! A box of Cheerios in the back. She had to put a knee on the counter to push herself up high enough so that she could reach it. She brought the cereal to the counter, pulled open the waxy paper, and looked inside. The box was full and didn't look as if it had been disturbed. She took off a glove and shoved her hand inside. Nothing.

Glove back on, she opened more cupboards, found a large bowl, and poured the cereal into it. The last thing to topple out was a neatly folded piece of paper. She almost cried from happiness. She unfolded the paper, saw the login and password, then drew in a long, shuddering breath. Thank God. Everything she needed was there. She folded the piece of paper and shoved it into her back pocket.

The clock was ticking. *Get out. Get out.* Her time was up.

She left the cereal in the bowl, put the gloves back where she'd found them, grabbed the laptop and charger, and headed out. She was halfway down the stairs when she remembered the key. It was in her pocket. She looked back toward the apartment. It was too risky. *Forget about returning the key,* she told herself.

It wasn't until she was behind the wheel of her car and halfway home that she could truly breathe. When no other cars were around, she rolled down the window and tossed the key to Lena's apartment, watching in the rearview mirror as it bounced off the pavement and onto the grassy center divide.

At home, she locked her door, fastened the chain, drew the curtains closed, and then placed the computer and charger on her table. She pulled the folded paper from her back pocket and put it on the table too. She then went to her bedroom and stripped off her clothes. She had tried not to step into puddles of blood, but there were two smudges on the bottoms of her sneakers. She ran to the kitchen, used a dab of bleach to wipe the rubber soles clean.

She turned on the shower, and when the water was warm, she got in and began to scrub herself clean, wishing she could scrub away everything bad in her life and in the world. Lena Harris had been raped. The men who had assaulted her hadn't deserved to walk free, but neither had they deserved to die. She wondered if Lena would live. She hoped so. There was too much death as it was.

Once Sawyer had towel-dried her hair, dressed in sweatpants and a T-shirt, and started a load of dirty clothes, she made a pot of strong coffee.

The information on the piece of paper found in the cereal box made it easy for Sawyer to log in to the group. The female vigilantes had been dubbed the Black Wigs by the media, but they called themselves The Crew and they all had nicknames. She started from the beginning, which took her at least a year back in time. She skimmed through month after month of conversations as the group plotted and planned.

It wasn't difficult to figure out who was whom. One of the members of The Crew went by the nickname Bug and had taken off, abandoning the group after Myles Davenport's death. Could Bug be Tracy Rutherford?

Malice was Harper. Apparently Malice had entered the warehouse on Power Inn Road and seen that Otto Radley had broken free from his restraints and was sneaking up on Psycho. Malice had picked up a rifle near the door and shot him dead. They all agreed that Malice had saved Psycho's life.

There was another crew member who called herself Lily. Sawyer had no idea who Lily might be. Lily had been drugged by Brad Vicente, but it was Cleo who had worn a blonde wig and met Brad at the Blue Fox. Things had gone wrong from the start. The plan had been to get Brad to her car, give him a sedative, and take him to the warehouse. But with the help of Ian Farley, Brad had gotten the upper hand. If not for the other crew members, who knows what might have happened to Cleo.

Sawyer got up and filled her mug. When she returned to the laptop, she noticed someone had commented.

Psycho and Lily had both logged on. Sawyer's heart began to race.

LILY: Cleo, what's going on? You're all over the news. They're saying you were killed by Felix Iverson.

PSYCHO: Where are you?

When Sawyer typed a response, it automatically inserted Cleo's name as the person responding.

CLEO: I'm not Cleo.

LILY: Who is this?

CLEO: A friend. Your secrets are safe with me. Remove the hard drive from your computer and destroy it. Now! I will be doing the same for Cleo.

CHAPTER FORTY-FIVE

Sleep had abandoned Sawyer. The pot of coffee she'd consumed hadn't helped. When she was done reading through The Crew's messages, she had used instructions from a video she found on the internet to figure out how to remove the hard drive and destroy it with a hammer.

But the computer was the least of her worries.

For most of the night she lay in bed, restless, unsure of what to do next. Harper was Malice. And Malice had helped form The Crew, a group of five women who had met on the dark web over a year ago.

Sawyer grabbed her phone from the nightstand, disheartened to see that there was still no text or return call from Harper. She needed to call Nate and find out if he'd heard from his wife.

Where could Harper be?

She looked at the time. It was still early. Not yet six a.m. She would wait until her niece and nephew were at school, then call Nate. She slid her legs over the mattress, got dressed, brushed her teeth. At eight o'clock she called Lexi and told her she'd be late. At nine a.m. sharp, she picked up the phone again.

"Hi, Nate. It's me, Sawyer. Are the kids at school?"

"I just got back from dropping them off."

"Is Harper home?"

"No."

"Did she call?"

"She sent me a text last night, letting me know that she's okay. That's all I know."

Sawyer exhaled. "I'm coming over. We need to talk."

"I'll be here."

Fifteen minutes later, Sawyer pulled up to the curb outside Harper's house, just as she had done so many times before. So much had changed since she'd found her sisters ten years ago. They had all been through so much. But the one thing that stood out, year after year, was that Harper had always been there for her. She was her rock.

Sawyer grabbed her backpack, got out of the car, and made her way to the house. Nate was waiting for her at the door.

Aria lived in the detached garage apartment. She must have seen Sawyer pull up, because she joined them. Aria went on and on about the cuts and bruises on Sawyer's body and face. She then asked where Harper was and demanded to know what was going on.

"Let's go inside," Sawyer said to Nate and Aria. "We have a lot to talk about."

They gathered in their usual spot in the kitchen. Aria and Sawyer sat on stools at the counter and watched Nate set about making fresh coffee and gathering mugs while Sawyer told them everything, starting with her first visit with Lena Harris and how Nate had followed Harper to Power Inn Road. She told them about her drive to that same warehouse and how the place had been swarming with technicians and cut off to her and the public with crime tape. And finally, Sawyer talked about the connection between Eddie Carter, Don Fulton, and Felix Iverson. The three men had been accused of raping Lena Harris at a fraternity party. In the end, they had walked free.

Nate and Aria were quiet as she talked. Nate slid a mug of fresh coffee to her, and Sawyer took a sip before she told them the last part, the worst part.

"The trailer was covered in blood. Felix Iverson was dead, a hunting knife protruding from his chest. And next to him was Lena Harris, cut wide open with a machete as far as I could tell. Hanging on by a thread, Lena had already called 9-1-1. She told me that if I wanted to save Harper, I needed to go to her apartment, use the key hidden in a planter to get inside, find her laptop, and destroy any evidence."

Aria gasped. "Please don't tell me you went to the apartment and stole her computer?"

"I didn't steal it. She told me to take it."

Aria rubbed her hands over her face. "This can't be happening."

"What did you find on the computer?" Nate asked.

Sawyer met his gaze. Nate wanted to know how his wife was involved in all this. He understood why she'd had no choice but to go to Lena Harris's apartment.

"Harper helped form the Black Wigs," Sawyer said. "Only they call themselves The Crew. They all have nicknames. Harper goes by Malice."

"No way," Aria said. "This is crazy."

Sawyer kept her gaze on Nate. "I'm sorry. It's true. Apparently, she shot and killed Otto Radley after he escaped and was sneaking up on one of the other crew members. From everything I've read, Harper never meant to harm any of the men they went after."

Aria paled. She looked as if she might be sick.

Nate remained composed.

"The Crew buried him near the abandoned warehouse where they also found Eddie Carter's body. I'm sure Detective Perez and his men have located the grave by now."

"Where's Lena's computer?" Nate asked.

"I destroyed it."

“This is so fucked up,” Aria said. “If she’s part of the Black Wigs—or The Crew—or whatever, then she must have shit hidden around here somewhere.”

Nate was already headed for the bedroom.

Sawyer and Aria jumped up and followed him.

Without another word spoken, all three of them began searching through the closet and dresser drawers, under the bed, and in the bathroom.

“Got it!” Aria said from the bathroom attached to their master bedroom.

Nate and Sawyer headed that way.

Aria was sitting on the tile floor with an open box in her lap. Inside were a black wig and a black mask.

The stunned silence was broken when Harper walked into the room.

Chapter Forty-Six

"What are you doing?" Harper asked when she found Nate and her sisters going through her things.

Aria pushed herself to her feet and held out the wig, letting it dangle from two fingers. "I think a better question is, what is this?"

Harper walked into the bathroom and snatched away the wig. Heat flushed through her body. She wanted to be angry with all of them, tell them to get out and mind their own business, but before the thought could take root, her shoulders slumped. They knew the truth. It was over.

"Where have you been?" Nate asked before she could find her voice.

Harper looked at him. His eyes were filled with sadness and disappointment and maybe dread for what was yet to come. "I spent last night at a hotel, trying to gather my wits, hoping to find the courage to tell you everything."

She and Nate had been together long enough for her to see the doubt in his eyes. He wasn't sure if he could believe her.

Aria crossed her arms. "Prove it."

Harper knew she didn't have to answer to her sister, but she reached into the purse still strapped to her shoulder, pulled out her receipt, and handed it to Nate. "Call the hotel if you don't believe me."

He did just that. When he hung up, he nodded and said, "She's telling the truth."

When Harper finally had a chance to look at Sawyer, who was sitting on the edge of the bed, her jaw dropped. "What happened to you?"

"I was being followed by a woman named Lena Harris. Also known as Cleo."

Harper's insides flipped over. "She did that to you?"

Sawyer nodded. "I was lucky to get out alive. She said she wanted to kill me."

Aria grunted. "You put all of our lives in danger. How could you?"

Harper shook her head. Aria had never liked conflict, but she was upset and she wanted answers. "I didn't mean for any of this to happen. I swear."

"Cleo is dead," Sawyer said.

Harper had seen the news, watched as two bodies were taken from Felix Iverson's trailer. The description the anchorman had given fit Cleo. "I thought so."

"Why did you return to the warehouse in the middle of the night?" Sawyer asked.

The master bath was an extension of the bedroom, and out of the corner of her eye, Harper caught her reflection in the mirror. Her eyes were red and bloodshot, her face puffy from crying. She grabbed a tissue from the bathroom countertop and blew her nose before she answered Sawyer's question. "After Cleo's husband took the kids and left, she lost her mind. The Crew never planned to hurt anyone. We just wanted to teach the men who had harmed us a lesson, show each of them what it feels like to have no control. What it feels like to be trapped and powerless." She shook her head. "Cleo was the last member of the crew to choose her targets, and she wanted to go after Eddie Carter first." Harper swallowed. "The honest-to-God truth is that I went to the warehouse to let Eddie Carter go. But he and Cleo were already gone."

Poor Nate looked haunted, Harper thought, as if he'd been living too long in the shadows of the dark unknown.

Harper wished she could make her husband see that she'd never meant to hurt him. In her mind, it all had started out so innocently. She hated to see him hurting. "I love you, Nate. I love all of you. You have to understand that when I first met these women on the internet, it was so amazing to have other women who understood what I had been through. We had all been in the same dark place at some point in our lives. We shared so much pain and suffering, and at first, talking about it was enough."

"You could have talked to us," Sawyer said.

Harper shook her head. "No. I never would have done that. I spent my entire life trying to protect you two. I never would have dreamed of putting such a burden on either of you." But she understood in that moment that, in the end, she had done exactly that.

"If I could turn back time and do things differently, I would," Harper said. "But I can't." She wiped her eyes and then straightened so that she was standing tall, even though she wanted to collapse. "I need to go to the police and tell them everything."

"No," Aria said.

Harper frowned.

"You've paid your dues," Aria stated firmly, as if there would be no further discussion about going to the police. "Your entire life has been a shit show of abuse. If you file a report, you'll be arrested for aiding and abetting, and Sawyer could go to jail for being an accessory after the fact."

Aria's hands were rolled into fists at her sides. She let out a low growl as if she couldn't hold in her frustrations any longer. "After all we've been through, what sort of justice would that be? You would not have harmed Otto Radley, a man who never should have been released, if he hadn't been going to kill your friend. You had no other choice." She put a palm to her chest. "I know that for a fact because any one of us would have done the same thing."

Nate had been quiet while everyone else talked, but he cleared his throat and said to everyone in the room, "I fell in love with Harper the minute I laid eyes on her."

Harper's eyes filled with fresh tears.

"I knew she was in pain," Nate said, "but I didn't know why. When she told me what was happening to her and her sisters in River Rock, we started making plans to get all three of you out of that house and away from that town. Since that time, I have stayed in the background, content to let the three of you figure out where you stand with one another." He paused for a second or two. "Your time is up. It's my turn to speak and to let you all know that from here on out, we're going to handle things my way."

Harper, Aria, and Sawyer all opened their mouths at once, but Nate shut them down. "I'm going to have my say, and then you two"—he gestured from Aria to Sawyer—"are going to leave us alone."

He walked over to Harper and took her hand in his. "In all these years we've been together, I've never once told you what to do."

Harper nodded.

"But I'm telling you now, and I expect you to listen and listen good. Let it go. Can you do that? Relax. Right now. And let it go. Stop trying to fix everything. Stop trying to change me and the kids. We're fine just the way we are. And so are you, which is why you need to let the past go. What happened to you was tragic. Killing a man to save your friend must be eating away at you, and I'm sure you'll never ever forget it. Nobody expects you to. But it's over. All of it. Nothing good can come out of you trying to take control and change things, because no matter what you do, it won't change the past. The tighter you cling to memories of your father and what he did to you, the longer you hold on to the darkness. The more you resist, the longer you'll suffer. Let it go, Harper. Not for me or your children or every woman out there who has been wronged, but for you. Give yourself a fighting chance and let it go."

Aria walked over and joined the huddle. Sawyer did too.

Harper knew that Nate was right. It was time to let it all go and start over. This was her family. Somehow, some way, she and her sisters had seen the worst of humanity. All three of them had been raised by monsters, neglected and abused, and yet they were stronger for it. She would never let any one of them down again.

It was just past noon when Sawyer left Harper and Nate's house. She could hear Aria's footfalls close behind as she made her way to her car parked at the curb.

"Do you think Harper will be able to let it go?" Aria asked.

Sawyer opened the door to her car and said, "I think she'll listen to Nate, but none of us will ever forget what happened in River Rock, let alone Harper's involvement with The Crew."

"I do wish she could have talked to us."

Sawyer nodded in agreement. "Nate was right when he told her she needed to find a way to let it all go. In the end, every one of us needs to find a way to forgive ourselves for the choices we've made and then do our best to keep on going."

"True."

"What about you?" Sawyer asked. "Are you going to be okay?"

"I'm good. I'm also stronger than you think."

Sawyer smiled. "I've always known you were tough."

"Do you think the police will see through Lena Harris's confession?"

"No telling," Sawyer said. "The entire Sacramento Police Department is overworked as it is, so I guess it depends on who's working the case."

"They released Bruce Ward's wife, Sandra," Aria said.

"That's a relief."

"You don't really think that Lena Harris killed Nick Calderon and Bruce Ward, do you?"

"No," Sawyer said before another thought came to her. "I didn't want to say anything about the Copycat Killer in front of Nate earlier, but I was wondering whether or not you were able to visit Stanley Higgins."

Aria made a face. "I did and it was horrible. Have you ever been to a taxidermist?"

"No."

"Well, I think I would have been fine if I hadn't seen what he had in his back room. Preserved animals with human faces made from wax."

"What?"

"Not kidding you."

"What did Stanley Higgins look like?"

"Five foot nine, heavyset, slow walker, slow talker, monotone, quiet voice, and creepy smile."

"How heavy would you guess?"

"Over two hundred and twenty pounds, at least. Are you going to give his name to the police?"

"I have more work to do."

"Okay, well, I'm going to go to the shelter, but let me know if you need me."

Aria gave Sawyer a quick hug before she left.

As Aria walked away, Sawyer thought about the man she'd chased on the railroad tracks.

He was lean and he was fast.

If she eliminated Stanley Higgins as a suspect, the only one left on her list of possible copycat killers was Jimmy Crocket. Emily Stiller had told her that Jimmy Crocket worked downtown.

Sawyer needed to go home and gather a few things before she drove back to town. Although she was hungry and every part of her ached, she knew she wouldn't be able to rest until she checked him out.

Chapter Forty-Seven

Back home, Sawyer made quick work of reading through her notes until she found what she was looking for. According to Emily Stiller, Jimmy Crocket worked at Midtown Design Studio.

She grabbed her bag and headed out. The studio was located on Sixteenth Street. Sawyer found a parking spot on the street. The office was small. Three people sat at various desks, two to the right, one to the left. All women. All busy.

The one sitting to the left with a wild tangle of silver hair looked up. "Can I help you?"

"I'm looking for Jimmy Crocket. I was told he works here."

One of the other women sitting to the right pulled off her eyeglasses and said, "We only have one man who works here, and his name is Corey Moran."

"Corey Moran works here?"

"That's right. Do you know him?"

"I know of him," Sawyer said, her mind swirling with speculation and ending up in a black hole since no logical connection formed.

"He's been working here longer than any of us. If he's not here, he's at home."

"He's good at what he does," the silver-haired woman said, "which is why he can work wherever he chooses."

Sawyer felt completely off her game. Wanting to make sure they were talking about the same person, she pulled out her phone and showed the woman the picture Aria had taken. "Is this Corey Moran?"

The woman leaned closer for a better look. "Yep. That's him, but it's awful blurry." She picked up a framed picture on her desk and handed it to Sawyer. "Here's a better picture of the gang. That was before he grew his hair out."

Sawyer felt sick to her stomach. She was pretty sure that was the face of the man she'd seen leaving the trailer park. How could that be? Nothing made any sense. She handed back the picture. "Is he expected in today?"

The silver-haired lady shrugged. "He comes and goes. I haven't seen him in weeks."

"I saw him two days ago," one of the others said. "Do you want to leave a message for him?"

"No, that's okay. Thank you."

The minute Sawyer stepped outside, she moved away from the studio windows looking out to the street and leaned her back against a brick wall. She didn't like the funny feeling swirling inside her.

Think, Sawyer, think. Start from the beginning. They met at the shelter when Corey Moran brought in a dog.

A lost dog.

Nick Calderon had a dog.

She needed to go to the shelter and talk to Aria right away.

Sawyer walked into the shelter and rushed over to the counter where Tiffany was doing paperwork.

"Is Aria here?" Sawyer asked.

Tiffany looked up and her eyes went wide. "Whoa! What happened to you?"

"It's a long story." Sawyer looked around. "Is Aria walking the dogs?"

"No, she went to lunch with that handsome new boyfriend of hers."

Sawyer did her best to remain calm. "Any idea where they went?"

"No. Sorry."

Sawyer's heart was racing. "Speaking of her new boyfriend. He brought in a dog, is that right?"

"Yes. His name is Duke. Funny you should mention Duke, because we just found him a forever home."

"Does every dog that comes in get checked to see if it has a microchip?"

"Yes. Of course."

"Did Duke have one?"

"I can check right now." Tiffany skimmed the papers in front of her. She looked up and frowned. "Looks like Duke got missed. It happens. In fact, I remember that being one of our busier days." She opened a drawer and grabbed an object that looked to Sawyer like a magnifying glass.

Sawyer followed Tiffany down the aisle lined with cages. Each cage had a tiny chalkboard strapped to it. Tiffany stopped at the cage with the name Duke written on the board.

Sawyer watched Tiffany put the scanner at the dog's head and slowly scan side to side all the way to the tail. She made several passes. It wasn't until she scanned the dog's neck that Tiffany said, "Oh, my goodness." She quickly locked the cage, and Sawyer followed her back to the counter.

"What did you find?"

"Give me just a moment," she said. "Duke has been chipped, and now I need to look the number up on the registry." It wasn't long before she had the owner's name: Linda Calderon.

Sawyer ran out the door without saying goodbye. Once she was in her car, she was shaking so badly she had to count to ten to calm herself.

She called Aria again, but there was no answer. She sent a text asking her to call, told her it was an emergency.

And then she called Lexi.

"Where are you?" Lexi asked. "I thought you would be here by now. We have a lot to discuss."

"I need a favor," Sawyer said. "I'll explain later, but I need your help."

"Sure. What is it?"

"I don't have my laptop with me, but I need to know if a person named Jimmy Crocket had his name legally changed."

"Give me a second."

Sawyer could hear papers rustling and then fingers clacking away on the keyboard. Seconds felt like hours as she imagined Corey Moran taking her sister home with him. The thought of Aria being taken to his basement or tied up in some sketchy bedroom made her feel sick to her stomach.

"Jimmy Crocket is now Corey Moran. Do you need anything else?"

"An address. I need his address."

"Are you okay?"

"I just need an address," Sawyer told her.

"Okay. Okay."

Minutes later, Sawyer was on the road, headed for a town house located a few miles away.

Corey Moran was the same man she'd chased after when she'd gone to see Aston Newell at the auto shop—his light-brown hair blowing back behind him.

She'd seen him again at the trailer park. He'd looked right at her.

If he'd hurt Aria, she'd never be able to forgive herself for not putting two and two together soon enough.

The town house was located on T Street between Ninth and Tenth. She parked as close to the place as she could, then shut off the engine, readied her pepper spray, and ran a half block to his place. She rushed up the stairs to the patio and knocked on the door to the right. "Aria! Are you in there?"

Corey Moran opened the door, and she shoved her way past him.

"What the hell—"

She whipped around, her teeth gritted as she aimed the canister of pepper spray at his face. "Where's my sister?"

He raised his hands in self-defense. "Your sister?"

"Aria. Where is she?"

"Oh," he said. "Aria and I had lunch at the Burger Patch on K Street. When we parted ways, she told me she was going home."

"I know what you did," she said, not realizing how stupid she'd been to confront a possible killer until that very moment. She took a step backward, her hand shaking.

"I don't know what you're talking about," he said.

"That dog you brought to the shelter, the shelter where you met my sister, had a microchip."

"I see."

Palmer always said she reacted before thinking. He was right. She considered pushing past him and rushing out the door, but what if he was lying and Aria was inside? She turned and ran to the back of the house, calling Aria's name.

"She's not here," he said, following as far as the kitchen. "I would never hurt your sister."

Sawyer was in the bathroom, her chest tight and her nerves frayed as she yanked the plastic curtain hanging over the bathtub to the side.

Nothing. Her emotions were running high, and she felt on the brink of crying with relief. She checked the bedroom closet next. Nothing there.

Aria wasn't here. *Please be safe at home,* Sawyer thought as she returned to the main room. "I talked to Nancy Lay," Sawyer told him, glad to see he hadn't moved. "She told me how you were bullied." She walked past him as she talked.

He followed her into the main room.

"You burned down the Children's Home of Sacramento, didn't you?" she asked.

"I did."

Surprised by his admission, she stopped to look him over.

His gaze met hers.

He didn't look like a killer, but since when did a killer look like a killer? How many women had walked off with Ted Bundy? The BTK Strangler had installed security alarms. People had opened their doors and let him right inside.

But still, there was something about Corey Moran that made her believe he was telling the truth. Her phone vibrated. She pulled it out of her pocket and saw a text from Aria: *Call me when you get a chance. I met with Corey again and I need to talk to someone. My heart is broken.*

Her sister was alive. Brokenhearted, but alive. Corey Moran had not harmed her sister. He'd gone after the men who had abused him, just as the Black Wigs had done.

She slipped her phone back into her pocket. She was about to ask him straight out if he had killed Nick Calderon and Bruce Ward, but then thought better of it. She knew the answer. But what she didn't know was what she would do with the information if he answered her truthfully. She also wondered about Felix Iverson. Who really killed him? But again, did she want to know the answer?

"Bringing the dog to the shelter was your downfall," she finally said.

"Maybe. But then I wouldn't have met Aria."

"So everything you did was about revenge?"

"Something like that."

"Why now?" she asked, but had a feeling she already knew. The Black Wigs had started a movement. That hadn't been their intention, but that was exactly what had happened. Lexi's niece, The Slayers, females everywhere were tired of being assaulted and then watching the perpetrators walk free. Corey Moran had been no different. An opportunity had presented itself to him, and he'd jumped at the chance to finally get even.

"They needed to be punished for what they did," he said.

"It was the Black Wigs, wasn't it? They went after the people who had harmed them, which drove you to do the same."

"*Inspired* me, would be a better word." He looked sad, but also resolute in his actions. "If only I had met your sister last month or the month before."

She couldn't stop staring at him. He had a boyish face and friendly eyes. Sadness fell over her at the thought of everything that had happened. "That would have changed things?"

"It would have changed everything."

Sawyer noticed a suitcase off to the side. "Going somewhere?"

He nodded.

"So what did you say to my sister?"

"I told her I was leaving town and wouldn't be back."

Sawyer said nothing.

He exhaled. "She deserves better."

"Yes," Sawyer said, "she does."

His phone buzzed. "Looks like my ride is here."

Through the front window, Sawyer saw a car with an Uber sticker pull up outside. She looked at him. They both knew it was up to her to make the next move. "You better get going," she said.

He nodded, then grabbed his suitcase and headed out. Sawyer watched him climb into the car. She waited until the vehicle drove off and disappeared before she stepped outside and walked back to her car. It wasn't her job to call the police. How many times had Detective Perez told her to mind her own business? More times than she could count.

So that's exactly what she would do—mind her own business.

Chapter Forty-Eight

Two days later, at exactly five o'clock, Sawyer finished writing the article about Lena Harris and how her inability to get justice had likely pushed her over the edge.

Overall, Sawyer talked about vengeance and society and how people who have been humiliated or harmed sometimes looked for ways to restore their self-worth. One way to do that was, of course, to punish the offending party, but any gratification would most likely be short lived. Another way to deal with rejection or bullying, for example, was to use compassion and forgiveness, which wasn't always easy. She talked about how two-thirds of attackers in school shootings had been bullied. Bottom line: a child who bullies needs the same support and compassion as the person who is being bullied before a culture change could happen.

She ended her story with a quote attributed to Gandhi: "An eye for an eye makes the whole world blind."

Next, she wrote her letter of resignation, printed it off, and carried it with her as she made her way down the hallway toward Lexi's office.

She was ready to move on.

Aria's idea to open Forever Sunshine, a place where old dogs could live out their lives in peace, had prompted Sawyer to think about her own goals and dreams. She already knew she wanted to help solve crimes, not write about them, so she'd decided to use her share of the inheritance to start her own investigative agency.

From a distance, she could see that something was going on just outside Sean Palmer's office. As she drew closer, she saw storage boxes piled high.

"You're just in time," Lexi said when she spotted her.

There were plastic champagne flutes and a couple of bottles of champagne on Palmer's desk. Lexi filled one of the glasses to the halfway mark, then handed it to Sawyer. "Are you okay? You look like someone who might have just written a Pulitzer Prize–winning story."

Sawyer smiled. "I guess you never know. I just finished my piece and emailed it to you."

"Perfect." She clinked her glass against Sawyer's. "Did you hear the news?"

Sawyer shook her head.

"Sean Palmer has officially retired, and I was just informed that I'll be taking his place."

Sawyer congratulated her. "I'm happy for you, Lexi. You deserve the promotion."

"Did you just fall and hit your head? What's going on?"

"You're good at what you do, and I've enjoyed working with you."

"But?"

Sawyer handed her the letter. "I was coming to talk to you to see who I should give my letter of resignation to. Looks like you've answered my question."

Lexi pulled out the letter, read it, and set it on her desk. "I cannot pretend to be happy about this. Are you sure this is what you want?"

"I'm sure."

Lexi's brow furrowed. "You know what's strange?" she asked.

"What?"

"Lena Harris confessed to killing all those men on her own, and yet Ian Farley told us there was more than one woman wearing a wig when he went to Brad Vicente's house."

"I reported what we learned to Detective Perez, but he wasn't interested. Maybe there really is no justice."

Lexi frowned. "Why would Ian Farley lie?"

Sawyer shrugged. "Maybe he was looking for attention."

"Speak of the devil," Lexi said under her breath.

A booming voice came from behind Sawyer. "I hear congratulations are in order."

Sawyer recognized Detective Perez's voice at once.

Lexi smiled and raised her glass. "What are you doing here?"

"I told Palmer I would grab some of these boxes you packed up and deliver them to his home."

Sawyer turned toward the detective and said hello.

"Looks like our local hero couldn't solve this one," he said to Sawyer. "What a shame."

Sawyer shrugged. "You win some, you lose some." She looked at Lexi. "Congratulations again. We'll talk later." She set her glass on the desk, waited for Detective Perez to move aside, then headed back the way she'd come. Instead of going to her cubicle, she walked straight to Derek's office, glad to see him there. She stepped inside, shut and locked the door behind her, and closed the blinds covering his only window.

"I tried calling you last night," Derek said, "but you didn't pick up."

"I know," she said. "I'm sorry. I was working on my Pulitzer Prize–winning story, but you'll be happy to know that it's finished. I'm here to make it up to you."

He stood, walked around his desk, and took a closer look at the marks running down her jaw and neck. "Looks like you're healing nicely. Does it hurt?"

"I'm not here to talk." She pulled off his tie and began unbuttoning his shirt, kissing his chest as she did so.

"Now? Really?"

"Now," she said.

She held his gaze as she kicked off her shoes, then unzipped her pants and stepped out of them. After she pulled off her shirt, she stood bare naked before him, bruises and all.

He stepped close, leaned over, and covered her lips with his own. Every single time he kissed her, it was better than the last.

He pulled her against him, his hands on her buttocks as she struggled to remove his belt. His pants fell to his knees. Breathing hard, he pulled away. For a hot second she worried she'd been too aggressive, but she was wrong.

He took a step backward, turned, and used one arm to swipe his desk clean. In-box, stapler, and a small stack of papers fell to the ground. He then kicked off his pants, turned back to her, and picked her up so that her legs straddled his waist.

Never in a million years would Sawyer have thought she would fall in love with a man. But she had. Proving that anything was possible.

EPILOGUE

Three weeks later . . .

Today Sawyer's therapist, Jane Thomas, wore an eye-popping blue polka-dot shirt and bright-pink scarf over black leggings. "It's good to see you again," Jane said. "I wasn't sure you would be coming back."

"I thought I was good to go, but I realized I need this. I need you."

Jane smiled, then said, "The last time we met, we talked about your recurring nightmares and the story you were working on."

"How do you remember all that without taking notes?"

"I read a lot and I play Sudoku."

Sawyer couldn't quite tell if Jane was pulling her leg.

"Any improvements as far as nightmares go?" Jane asked.

"I haven't had a nightmare since I saw you last."

"Good," Jane said. "You're no longer conflicted?"

"I don't think I am. For whatever reason, I've always felt as if I were alone. Not just in living my day-to-day life, but in everything . . . the neglect, abuse, and sexual assault that I was forced to endure. That might seem strange, considering I had two sisters who were also abused, but even so, we all sort of took our pain and suffering inward and dealt with it differently." She paused to think. "It seems to me that maybe the Black Wigs and all the copycats that emerged made me see that we're all in this together." She opened her arms. "Not just me and my sisters, but everyone who has been touched by neglect or abuse." She took in a deep breath. "I'm no longer the person I used to be. After all I've been through, all the ups and downs, I'm finally ready to move forward."

Sawyer could see that Jane was using her best strength. She was listening, and for the first time Sawyer didn't wonder why she had come. She knew why, and she just kept right on talking. "I think the nightmares had more to do with my fourteen-year-old self than the grown woman I've become. I realize now that I am one of the lucky ones. I have support. I have my sisters, my brother-in-law, my niece and nephew. I have you," Sawyer said.

Jane gave a subtle nod.

"I also have Derek, the boyfriend I told you about. You might be happy to know that we had sex. I won't go into details—TMI and all that." Sawyer smiled broadly. "There's a good possibility that Derek Coleman might really be 'the one.' And that's not all. My sister Aria, an anti–people person if ever there was one, is dating a guy whom Derek's sister introduced her to. He's a civil rights lawyer, which I think is pretty cool. The best part is he loves animals and has two dogs of his own."

"I can see that you care a lot about your sister."

"I do. I care about both of my sisters." Sawyer drew in a long breath as she thought about Corey Moran. She'd never told Aria about her chat with Corey, what he had done, and how much he'd cared about her.

"Are you okay?"

"I'm fine," Sawyer said. "I was just thinking about my sisters. It took me a long time to understand Harper, my oldest sister, but I've come to realize that she's always been there for me and always will be. There isn't anything I wouldn't do for my sisters."

Sawyer continued on and talked about everything under the sun. She told Jane all about meeting Derek's family and how Derek had lied about his dad not being a hugger. His entire family liked to hug, but the worst offender was definitely his dad.

"I almost forgot to tell you," Sawyer said. "I quit my job."

"Now that is a surprise."

"I'm going to start my own private investigation agency, but before I can go off on my own, I have to work with a PI and get in my five thousand hours."

"I'm sure you'll find someone eager to take you on."

Sawyer felt the urge to get up and walk over to Jane and give her a big squeeze, but decided against it. Jane was a professional, and a therapist was not supposed to be your friend.

The hour flew by, and when she was done, Sawyer thanked Jane for being such a good listener.

"It's what I do. And you're welcome."

Sawyer stood and got as far as the door before she turned around and said, "By the way, I also meant to tell you that you were right."

Jane raised both eyebrows. "About what?"

"I'm not weak and broken, after all."

Jane smiled.

"When I was too young to know better, I often asked myself, 'Why me?' But I don't look at my suffering like that any longer. My pain and trauma made me who I am today. With the help of people like you, people who listened to me without judgment, who helped me dig through all the layers of misery, I have grown stronger than ever."

Sawyer took a deep, satisfying breath as she realized how much had changed. Her life had meaning and purpose, and she felt happy to be alive.

ACKNOWLEDGMENTS

Many thanks to all the amazing people who work so hard to take the eighty thousand words I hand in and add clarity and logic, and help to make the words pop and sing and entertain. That's no easy feat.

Those people include Liz Pearsons, Charlotte Herscher, Amy Tannenbaum, Sarah Shaw, Laura Barrett and her meticulous team of proofreaders and copyeditors, Joe Ragan, Cathy Katz, and Morgan and Brittany Ragan. I'd also like to give a shout-out to my hype man, Deuce Mason, whose enthusiasm for *Don't Make a Sound* made release day extra special.

Thank you. Thank you. Thank you.

About the Author

Photo © 2014 Morgan Ragan

T.R. Ragan is the *New York Times*, *Wall Street Journal*, and *USA Today* bestselling author of the first two books in the Sawyer Brooks series, *Don't Make a Sound* and *Out of Her Mind*; the Faith McMann trilogy (*Furious*, *Outrage*, and *Wrath*); the Lizzy Gardner series (*Abducted*, *Dead Weight*, *A Dark Mind*, *Obsessed*, *Almost Dead*, and *Evil Never Dies*); and the Jessie Cole novels (*Her Last Day*, *Deadly Recall*, *Deranged*, and *Buried Deep*). In addition to thrillers, she writes medieval time-travel tales, contemporary romance, and romantic suspense as Theresa Ragan. She has sold more than three million books since her debut novel appeared in 2011. An avid traveler, her wanderings have led her to China, Thailand, and Nepal. Theresa and her husband, Joe, have four children and live in Sacramento, California. To learn more, visit www.theresaragan.com.